Marie-Antoinette's Present

Marie-Alix Ravel

Cover design by Marie-Alix Ravel

On the left, Vigée Lebrun, Louise Élisabeth (1755-1842) *Marie-Antoinette, Queen of France, with a rose* (detail) 1783. Châteaux de Versailles et de Trianon, Versailles, France © Réunion des Musées Nationaux / Art Resource, NY

On the right, *Meditation* © Marie-Alix Ravel

In the center, *Marie-Antoinette's Monogram* © Marie-Alix Ravel

You may order this book directly from:

www.marieantoinettespresent.com

Original title: Le Présent de Marie-Antoinette

Translation by Estelle Antonini

Corrections by Sue Otto

www.mariealixravel.com

ISBN 978-2-9812143-4-8 Marie-Antoinette's Present

Legal Deposit — Bibliothèque et Archives nationales du Québec, 2012

Legal Deposit — Bibliothèque et Archives du Canada, 2012

To my daughter, Estelle,
Who made me discover the key of the universe.

'In time, the understanding of reincarnation and its mechanics will reinvent the world'.

Walter Semkiw

Preface

On a Novel Based in Emerging Science

Could the soul of Queen Marie-Antoinette, brutally separated from her body by its decapitation in October 1793, have been reborn as a baby girl in the sixties? If you believe in reincarnation, you may consider it possible. Otherwise, you are likely to be skeptical. Whether you are a believer or skeptic, this compelling narrative by author Marie-Alix Ravel will cause you to question some of your current beliefs about the nature of reality.

The book is not science fiction partially based in reality. It is reality cloaked in fiction, based in the emerging science of reincarnation. Pseudonyms and some fake details have been used to protect the identities of the protagonist and her family and friends.

The most important is that Kiera does not want to make claims to her past identity — while well documented and theoretically sound — as they have not yet been accepted by enough scientists. However, the individuals investigated by the project take very seriously their role in helping science evaluate the widespread belief in reincarnation.

For these reasons, Marie-Alix Ravel has carefully disguised some of the facts, but not their substance, to protect the identity of Kiera Hermine, her family, and their friends. Otherwise, the narrative (written in the first person of the central character for the purpose of a novel) is a biography of an extraordinary adventure. Weaving the bare facts of scientific research into this novel, the author creates a life story that reveals the most important secrets associated with the life of Marie-Antoinette.

And it reads like an intriguing mystery that probes some of the deepest mysteries of human life in the universe.

As a hypnotherapist and an intuitive reincarnation researcher, Marie-Alix Ravel learned of Kiera Hermine's life story in the course of her psychological counseling and spiritual therapy practice in Los Angeles, California. She attempted to verify Kiera's claims when possible. Based on her natural intuition honed by years of helping her clients, Marie-Alix Ravel systematically studied the clues Kiera had accumulated from her dreams, inexplicable coincidences, psychics, and channeled information.

Her prodigious amount of research and evaluation convinced Marie-Alix Ravel that it made a strong case for the possibility of Kiera being the reincarnation of Marie-Antoinette. After reading of my book 'The Soul Genome', Marie-Alix Ravel asked me if she could use our scientific protocols to assess the evidence she had accumulated and any new data that was required. Impressed by the scope of her research and its meticulous documentation, I agreed to help Ms Ravel evaluate the validity and reliability of Kiera's case as it had been developed over the course of almost two decades.

The Reincarnation Experiment was organized in 2005 to test the reincarnation hypothesis through empirical evidence that could be verified for both lifetimes. Its underlying theory posited that, if reincarnation is real, science can identify the effects of the same soul acting in two or more lifetimes. Its reincarnation model was based on four decades of research by American psychiatrist Ian Stevenson at the University of Virginia prior to his death in 2007 and a meta-analysis of scores of other strong, independently-researched cases.

Stevenson's approximately 2500 cases from around the world and our meta-analysis suggested that physical features, specific memories, cognitive styles, interpersonal traits, emotional profiles, and talents carry forward from one lifetime to another. In order to verify and document these similarities our project designed procedures to measure and validate all these areas of evidence and determine if their coincidence in two lifetimes could be attributed to chance or something more solid and real. The use of these factors to measure the strength of alleged reincarnation cases was evaluated in a pilot test — reported in the book 'The Soul Genome'.

The same methodology was used to assess the evidence already accumulated by Marie-Alix Ravel. Finding her work to be credible, we collected the additional psychophysical data required by our research methodology. We started with biometrics to compare the genotypes of both Marie-Antoinette and Kiera Hermine.

Finding that they were biometrically similar enough to have been in the same family, we had to test whether Kiera was a biological descendant of Marie-Antoinette. (This requires use of mtDNA which is passed only from mother to child.) Using such DNA samples from Kiera and maternal relatives of Queen Marie-Antoinette, a qualified laboratory determined the mitochondrial sequences were different. Thus, the similarities we found cannot be attributed to family relationships. Could the reason be a past-life legacy carried forward from Marie-Antoinette to Kiera?

In the second stage we evaluated historical and psychological materials on both personalities in order to ascertain if both lifetimes could have been expressed by the same personality. Finally, we used quantitative measures to assess just how likely the similarities between Marie-Antoinette and Kiera were attributable to chance or fraud.

When our investigation was complete, I was persuaded that if reincarnation is real, and the soul of Marie-Antoinette has reincarnated in this era, she is most likely in the body of an anonymous young woman we now know as Kiera Hermine. The evidence is so powerful that any reasonable person would conclude that something like the theory of reincarnation is the most likely explanation to account for the story you are about to read.

Nightmares of a wheel rolling over cobblestones, feet climbing steps and feeling the blood in her mouth just before waking up troubled Kiera's childhood. At age twenty-three, told that her newborn might be mongoloid, Kiera's nightmare returned. Disturbed by psychological turmoil, Kiera received help from a psychic who suggested a connection between her nightmares and Marie-Antoinette's death by guillotine. Visiting

Versailles again, Kiera experienced a flood of memories from earlier in Marie-Antoinette's reign.

Continuing with hypnotherapy, Kiera began to understand the vicissitudes of her relationships in light of a possible past life involving centuries-old personality patterns and relationships. Her historical research confirmed many of her memories, but that knowledge made her life even more complicated. Author Marie-Alix Ravel has woven Kiera's unusual life into a story of the soul.

As scientists we cannot yet say that we have absolute proof of reincarnation, but, on the other hand, we cannot say that we have a better explanation for the many verified facts taken from the lives of Marie-Antoinette and Kiera Hermine.

While 'Marie-Antoinette's Present' is a compelling story in its own right, I suggest it be read thinking "If this is true, could I be the reincarnation of someone who lived 200 years ago?"

Marie-Alix Ravel as an Associate in the Reincarnation Experiment has assisted in developing evidence and serving as an evaluator in many other cases. As a therapist, researcher and the author of 'Marie-Antoinette's Present', Marie-Alix Ravel has been intimately involved in the evolution of Kiera's reincarnation case.

Paul Von Ward

Paul Von Ward, author of 'The Soul Genome: Science and Reincarnation' and other books based in a 21st-century paradigm of natural science, coordinates 'The International Reincarnation Experiment' that you can find on the website:

www.reincarnationexperiment.org.

PART 1

Chapter 1

Birth

— There's a good chance your child has Down syndrome!

This sentence falls like a death blow and cuts my breath. I close my eyes and manage to take in a breath of fresh air. I feel like I'm going to die. My husband touches my hand in an effort to calm me. I do not want to open my eyes. I do not want to look at him. I am so ashamed. I am only twenty three and life did not train me to see reality like this. I am touched deep down all the way to my stomach that, only yesterday, was holding my child; I am touched all the way down my soul which for the past couple months could not contain its joy about the birth of this long-awaited little girl. There was need only for a couple words and not less than thirty seconds for my life to become a veritable hell on earth. My childhood nightmare comes back to me. It is been awhile since I have had it. "An old wheel on the cobblestone. Nothing seems to be making it move. Some feet walking up wooden stairs. A crowd screaming obscenities. A cold, crisp feeling on the back of my neck. An ear-splitting noise. A repulsive metal taste fills my mouth. I can't breathe. Silence. Emptiness. Darkness. The fear of death. Death… An old wheel on the cobblestone."

— Excuse me? Asks Philippe, in dismay as he sees the doctor putting down his daughter in her crib and walking away.

— I'm very sorry! Answers the doctor without even looking back. We have to do some tests after she leaves the hospital to figure out what is going on. I'll give instructions to the nurses, continues the doctor while walking out the room.

— Wait up! You can't just throw something this tremendous and leave without an explication! Shouts Philippe fiercely.

I feel completely lost. I close my eyes. I do not know which reality calls to me: my childhood nightmare that keeps on coming back or this final verdict that makes me want to die right there right now. I am falling in an endless well. I finally manage to open my eyes to keep from drowning in my thoughts.

The doctor explains to us that our daughter has ears that are lower than average; her eyes are almond shaped; the shape of her cranium is one of a child with Down syndrome.

— The test we have to do is called a Caryotype. We will basically take a sample of her blood to see how many chromosomes she has to determine if your daughter is normal or not, continues the doctor, like an automaton reciting a lesson well learned.

— That means there is a chance she could be normal! Says Philippe rapidly.

— Yes, but I would not want to give you false hopes. I'm very sorry, repeats the doctor. He then quickly leaves the room, looking as if he was trying to flee from an upcoming storm.

I close my eyes again. I cannot bear it anymore. I want to run away. I want to die. I hear the door closing and the doctor's footsteps already down the hallway. I can finally let go of the suffering that's eating me up inside. I want to scream my pain but I can't wake Sophie up. I let my tears run down my face in silence. Philippe has not moved. I would like to die now to end this incessant nightmare: A wheel on the cobblestone. An old wheel. This wheel is not attached to anything. Only a pin seems to be pushing it. A few stairs. A repulsive metal taste fills my mouth. The emptiness. Death. I am lost.

I want to leave this cursed place and bring my child far away from this absurd reality that alters even the most beautiful event – one of life– into a horrible one –of death. At the same time, I have the feeling I am paying for the unreasonable act I committed nine months earlier…

Philippe tries to clear up my confusion, in vain. He eventually leaves the room, totally helpless. I find myself alone with Sophie. I look at her crib and stand up painfully, as if I had suddenly become an old woman, instantly. I look at Sophie for a long time, before taking her in my arms. My love for her overwhelms me and I realize I want to protect her — no matter what.

I am leaving the apartment to get the mail and to go grocery shopping. I am holding Sophie in my arms and am simply genuinely happy. I even forget the fact that we have been longing for the results for more than a month. As I open the mailbox, I instantly spot the letter adorned with the laboratory stamp where we drew Sophie's blood when we left the clinic. I suddenly feel weak and my heart is beating faster and faster. I do not dare open it just yet. I look at Sophie with a weak smile. I reason myself and weigh the envelope to reassure me. My hands are shaking. I look at Sophie and a flash of lucidity grasps me as I see Sophie smile in her sleep. This gives my enough courage to finally tear open the envelope.

I unfold the letter while closing my eyes. When I finally open them, I read that she has the right number of chromosomes to be a normal child. I am so relieved that I hug my daughter with passion and cover her with kisses. She wakes up for a moment, smiles at me and goes right back to sleep.

I am grateful for the experience I just went through: this test makes me stronger and more confident in myself. I feel a new faith in life and all that has happened rising within me; I am determined to adjust my life accordingly.

Chapter 2

Anxiousness

A wheel on the cobblestone. An old wheel. This wheel isn't attached to anything. Only a pin seems to be pushing it. A few stairs. A cold crisp feeling on the back of my neck. A repulsive metal taste fills my mouth. Emptiness. Silence. Death. I am afraid of death. I scream. I feel shaken and wake up.

— Shushhh… It's just a nightmare, says Philippe gently while stroking my hair.

— It is not just a nightmare: it's always the same nightmare. I can't take it anymore… I want to sleep… I need to sleep… I say as tears roll down my face.

— Calm down, baby…

— I can't sleep anymore, since the nightmare started again.

— Started again???

— Since Sophie's birth, I've had the same nightmare as when I was a child and I was always so scared to go to bed.

— And what does that nightmare tell you? Asks Philippe, worried.

— I see a wheel on the cobblestone. It's an old wheel. It's weird because this wheel isn't attached to anything and only a pin seems to be pushing it. I walk up a few stairs. There is noise surrounding me, people screaming loudly. Then I have a cold crisp feeling on the back of my neck. You see, here, I say while lifting my hair up and showing him the back of my neck. After this, I can't breathe anymore and a repulsive metal taste fills my mouth. Then it's the emptiness, the darkness, the silence, and I always wake up with this intense fear of death.

— Did something must have happened when you were little, for you to have these kinds of nightmares?

— I fell down the stairs and I cut open my forehead..

— Do you think your nightmares started around that time?

— I have never put things together this way, but it's possible.

Lost in my thoughts, I am walking around the big fountain of the château de Versailles. A man gives me a kiss in the crease of my neck, without warning. I jump, startled.

— You shouldn't ever dot that, I say as I turn around, angry. I hate it when you come up from behind me, I continue, still shocked.

— I thought it was romantic! Says Thomas as he tries to take me in his arms so I can forgive him.

I push him off.

— What's the matter? He asks me, surprised while backing off.

— We need to stop seeing each other, Thomas. I cannot stand this situation anymore. I feel guilty about everything and it drives me nuts. I have terrible nightmares and I am exhausted.

— But I love you, Kiera…

— I don't love you anymore, Thomas, I say looking down.

— Oh yes? What happened?

— I am fed up with this situation!

— What made you change your mind so drastically? I always told you I wanted to live with you and Sophie…

— You don't see that I am paying for everything that we have done. Hell, Thomas, I cannot sleep at night. Are you not listening to me? I want us to stop everything completely, I can't do it anymore, I say quickly as I run away towards the grove.

Tears keep dripping down my face and I arrive, out of breath, in the grove called the Ballroom because of the lavish parties once held here, out of breath. My nightmare comes back: an old wheel on the cobblestone… I open my eyes to stop it but the frightful images continue to flash before my eyes. Feet walking up wooden stairs. I want to get up and escape this nightmare, but my body stays numb. I cannot do anything but stay here and bear with it. I feel so much anger growing inside me. I cannot stand this metal taste in my mouth anymore, this taste of death. I try to breathe in, but my mouth will not open up. I close my eyes. I am in a huge black tunnel that is taking up speed. I cannot seem to stop it. I fall in a deep well and try to dig into the wall with my nails to stop the fall, with no success. An immense feeling of suffering invades me. It is so strong that, for an instant, I feel as if it could reduce me to pieces. I am now two years old. I fall down the stairs and blood covers my face. My dad throws himself on me and holds me tight in his arms. I see a tunnel that is full of light, but my dad is speaking to me and I cannot manage to go toward this light that is attracting me like a magnet. I cannot hear what he is saying to me. I am floating and loving this sensation. I arrive in a big white building and a man in white lowers me to a table. I am in the tunnel and I would like to stay in it now. I can see my body from above and the doctors trying to revive me. I look at them with a lot of love. I try to listen to what they are saying but cannot seem to hear anything. It is as if my body was pulling away from my soul, or my soul pulling away from my body. Everything is turning silent. I have the feeling that I am not two years old anymore but way older. I am seven years old and my parents put in a disc. My brother starts singing and I cover my ears to block the noise. I want to go back to the white tunnel's silence, but I cannot do it. This music, on the contrary, brings me into a dark endless tunnel that leads to an even more endless well and I keep on falling. I am looking through a very large window. I am very unhappy. Someone comes to tell me that I have to leave. I cover my ears, once more. I do not want to leave. I am now older and younger at the same time. It is as if time didn't exist anymore and I find myself in a car with my father. He is very angry at me. I cannot hear everything he is saying but the word "whore" comes back a lot. We get to the house and my father orders me to my bedroom immediately. A fight erupts in between my mother and my father. I stop and sit down on the stairs to listen.

— You need to stop getting after her like this, all the time, my mother says, furiously.

— I am so afraid that something might happen to her...

— You are doing everything for that to happen, by acting like this. She is going to leave and make a mistake if you continue.

They both stay quiet. My father, less unpleasantly, ends up saying:

— I am so afraid she is going to get raped. I don't know why. It's stronger than me.

— So, what would you do???

— I would kill the guy, my father answers back, angrily.

— It wouldn't do us much good, with you in jail…

I do not want to listen anymore. I walk up the last stairs, being careful not to let the floor boards creek under my feet. I go to sleep fully clothed. I bury my head underneath my pillow just so as not to hear the screams anymore. The nightmare comes back: A wheel on the cobblestone. An old wheel. This wheel isn't attached to anything. Only a pin seems to be pushing it. A few stairs. A cold crisp feeling on the back of my neck. A repulsive metal taste fills my mouth. The emptiness. The silence. Death. I am afraid of death.

I jump when I feel a hand resting on my shoulder. I open my eyes. The day is falling and it is starting to get dark. I do not know where I am anymore.

— The château is closing, says the woman.

I drop my bag in the entrance and walk towards the living room. Philippe is standing in front of the fireplace, rocking Sophie who is crying in his arms.

— Where were you? He asks me in a very dry tone.

— Philippe, I told you. I was at the doctor's.

— I called the doctor, and you didn't have an appointment. And, what's more, the telephone rang and rang, and when I answered, whoever it was, hug up. What's going on?

Panicked, I take Sophie in my arms and place her comfortably on my breast.

— Do you have a lover, or what?

— What are you talking about?

— Cut the chase and tell me what's going on, Kiera.

— Please, let me finish breastfeeding Sophie quietly.

Philippe leaves the room and I try to think of something to say but nothing comes to my mind. I put Sophie to bed. Philippe is waiting for me behind the door, furious.

— I want an answer!

— I had an affair, but it's over, I end up saying.

— I don't understand. What are you saying? Philippe asks, devastated.

— We just broke up.

— And you are telling me this like that?

— I am sorry, Philippe, I say, crying.

— And you think that all you have to do to be forgiven is to be sorry? You don't seem to realize what you are doing to me.

I do not say anything.

— When did it start, with this guy?

— Two years, I think.

Philippe looks at me, suddenly skeptical. I cannot hold his gaze and lower my eyes, ashamed.

— Who's the father, then?

— How can you ask me such an insulting question, Philippe? This is ridiculous!

— I want to know and I will not stop until you answer me. Who is the father, Kiera?

— You!

— How are you so sure???

I do not know what to answer. Philippe stares at me intensely, as if attempting to read my soul: I feel he is determined to know the truth. I cannot keep myself from trying one more time.

— Sophie is yours, I assure you, I end up saying.

— You are lying. I can see it in your eyes.

I can see that I cannot escape.

— Sophie is his.

— I knew it! He shouts as he throws the lamp to the wall.

Philippe slams the door and I hear him breaking everything in the bedroom. Then, a big silence invades the apartment. I do not move and wait. Worried, I go into the bedroom to find everything turned upside down. Philippe is crying on the bed. It is the first time I have ever witnessed Philippe crying. I sit on the edge of the bed without a word. He lifts his head and looks at me in a totally different manner now, as if he just lost it. His features have changed and I do not recognize him anymore. I am afraid of what is going to happen. I start to get up but he grabs my arm so I sit back down, panicked.

— You can't say that he is the father. You would be Machiavellian to know it: we have always slept together, if I can remind you!

I do not know what to answer. I do not dare move. Philippe lets go off my arm, stands up and leaves the room, slamming the door. I blame myself for everything. I would like to run away from all this suffering that is going on inside me, but am afraid that Philippe will not let me come back and that I will not be able to see my daughter again. I want to take a bath to calm myself down, but am scared of Philippe trying to talk about the situation in more detail while I am exhausted. All I want to do is go to sleep to stop my mind from thinking, but I am afraid of these nightmares that keep coming back. I stay there and lay down in my bed, my eyes staring at the ceiling. Time does not exist anymore. An old wheel on the cobblestone…

The door opens up quietly. Philippe comes in and sits down next to me. I do not move.

— I am sure that Sophie is my daughter, Kiera. I just went to see her and she smiled at me in her sleep, he says. She knows it, as well as she knew that she did not have down syndrome, remember? You are the one who told me that.

I don't know what to answer. What if he was right? He takes me in his arms. I still cannot move.

— I love you, Kiera, and I love Sophie, more than anything in the world. Nothing, and no one, will be able to change this, says Philippe as he covers me with kisses.

I open my arms as we start kissing passionately. Philippe lies down next to me and we make love in tears. I feel relieved I told the truth, even if I am not sure anymore of what this truth really is.

Chapter 3

Voyage

As I am in the kitchen fixing dinner, Philippe approaches to me with a big smile on his face.

— Guess what?

— I don't know, I say, looking at him surprised.

— What would make you the happiest? He asks, teasing.

— Writing and painting, you know that!

— What would allow for you to do all this?

— I don't know… What?

— We are moving to Montreal, Philippe tells me, excited.

— Are you joking? I ask, incredulous.

— Trust me, we only need to fill a couple formalities and we are leaving. I was offered the position of director of an important veterinarian clinic in Montreal. You won't have to work anymore and you will be able to go back to your studies in Fine Arts, as you always wanted.

— How come you didn't tell me about this earlier?

— I wanted to surprise you. You've never felt as though you belonged in France and you wanted to live in America. I know that Quebec is not California, as you always dreamed of, but it comes close. It's going to be a new life, a marvelous adventure for the three of us.

Leaving for Quebec is a great change for us. We start off staying in a hotel, buying ourselves time to find a nice apartment in the city of Montreal. Philippe works and I watch Sophie during the day and we all meet at night to visit the city and talk about the apartments I have found during the day. After a couple visits, we settle our choice on my dream apartment: immense windows facing the sun all day long, huge rooms, and moldings everywhere, a splendid fireplace, old antique wooden floors, a beautiful kitchen and two modern bathrooms in a luxurious building in downtown Montreal. We move in immediately. We buy a mattress and eat on the floor as we wait for our furniture to come from France.

I rapidly find a nice daycare for Sophie close to our home and leave her there two days per week. I enroll in a Beaux-Arts program at Concordia University and start my session in fall, after having fully enjoyed the Canadian summer with my daughter. I feel blessed with my new life.

After the Indian summer and its heart-warming colors, winter arrives in full force with its white sparkly coat. In the meanwhile, the emptiness and anxiousness that I was feeling inside while living in France, are slowly coming back to the surface and starting to take a toll on my early first months' enthusiasm. My studies and writing cannot even seem to stop them.

I cannot explain this deep sadness that I am experiencing now, again and on a regular basis. I have and can do whatever I want, but I am not happy. It is stronger than me: the euphoria of earlier times now gives space to profound confusion. I am sick of myself and my emotions, of these nightmares that have been coming back lately. I feel worthless and useless, although I love the life I have made for myself, my husband, my little girl; I live in the country I want to live in, in my dream apartment, with a very privileged status and great financial conditions; I am studying what I have always wanted to study; Philippe is the sweetest and always craves to please me; Sophie, on top of already being beautiful and smart, is the incarnation of joy and graces me with her smiles. Even though I have everything I could ever want, I am still simply not happy. Despite the appearance of a prosperous, blossoming woman, I see myself as destitute, searching for my soul.

This state of mind could have lasted all my life, have I not met the man that would allow my life to plunge in a totally different dimension: the one in which the lives we touch seem to belong to another time, this time out of the land of time where everything gets tangled and untangled at all times.

Chapter 4

Meeting

It has now been a little while since I have been waiting to meet an interior decorator who could help me decorate our new apartment. One morning, after dropping Sophie at her daycare center, I discover a little shop on the street, close to my place and I decide to go take a look inside.

— Good morning, I would like to see a decorator, please.

— Yes, sure. Here is Olivier Fertari, answers the hostess as she presents a man standing next to the desk.

— Call me Olivier, he says as he extends his hand with a beautiful smile.

— Alright. Kiera, I say as I shake his.

— Let's go to my office, he says showing me the way. Do you have any pictures of your apartment?

— Yes, I say as I hand him some pictures.

Olivier looks at the pictures thoroughly.

— Here what I would do: your fireplace is very beautiful and I would enhance it with bright colors on the walls. What do you think of this nice burgundy red? He asks me as he shows me some samples.

— I like this one better, I say pointing at the nearest one.

— Well then. So let's use "Venice Red Passion" that would work very well with this green apple "Night Asparagus". What do you think?

— This green is my favorite color.

— Do you paint Kiera?

— Yes, how do you know? I ask, surprised.

— Your apartment is decorated with lots of good taste. But actually I was going to ask you if you paint walls.

— Oh, I say, blushing.

— Excuse me; I didn't want to embarrass you. I just wanted to tell you that you could do it yourself and that it would cost you less than to use our services, even if I am not charging you for this consultation. I like to help foreigners that come to live here. You're French, aren't you?

— Oui.

— I love France! What brought you to Montreal?

I tell him and we talk with each other for a good hour, not worrying about time passing by: we cannot seem to break apart. Born to Swedish parents, and even though he was born in Montreal, Olivier is really attracted by anything that relates to Europe. As we are talking, I see that I could not stop myself from getting closer to Olivier. When I realize this, I seek to know if my attraction is reciprocal. I move away from him slowly. Little by little, imperceptibly, he finds himself two steps away from me. Confused, I do not know what to do. I feel trapped and have the sudden urge to run away. I pretext having to go get Sophie, letting him know I have to leave right at this moment. I am in front of the door and we are both standing there, like two lost souls. We do not know how to leave one another. We feel something profound and intense uniting us, without really being able to define it. I would like to be able to give on to this sensation, but I am afraid of what I could do and I know that I need to leave right now.

— I would very much like for us to have lunch together, one day, Olivier, I hear myself say, surprised.

— With pleasure, Kiera, says Olivier as he puts his hand on the door to keep me from leaving. Tomorrow at one o'clock, at the Palatino restaurant on Sherbrooke, how does that sound?

— Great! I say, turning towards the door in order to leave as fast as possible.

Olivier takes his hand off the handle and opens the door for me with a big smile on his face. I leave the office without looking back. Outside, I take in a great breath of fresh air. I feel so happy and unhappy at the same time. Happy to have met Olivier and to know that I would be seeing him again the next day. Unhappy to know that my life will never be the same if I go to this rendezvous. I know I can still stop the current of things but am also very conscious that it is already too late; I am in love and this love is consuming my body and soul as a whole.

I find myself at Sophie's daycare, without really knowing how I got there. We go buy some paint, and head home. I put Sophie in bed for her nap. I get the paint and brushes out and start painting the walls, after having protected the floors. I am so absorbed in the painting of the walls that I do not see time flying by. In the meanwhile, Sophie wakes up and I put her to the task with me. She is having as much fun as I am and we finally finish just in time when we hear the lock open in the entrance. I whisper for Sophie to be quiet and show her the table for us to hide under. I take her in my arms and let her know to be still. Philippe's reaction comes immediately.

— Wow. Kiera, what an intense red! And this green; it's something! It's beautiful.

We get out from our hiding spot and Sophie runs into her father's arms. I don't have time to grab her before she puts paint all over the place.

— It's okay, Philippe says, kissing his daughter who just got paint all over his hair. Kiera, you who usually likes discrete colors, you surprise me, my dear!

— You like it? I ask proudly.

— To tell you the truth, I am not really sure. But I think I will get used to it.

— Oh, I am so sorry. I thought you would like it. We can always change it, you know.

— I live with an artist and I have to assume the consequences, says Philippe with a kiss.

— It's that terrible?

— You like it! That's all that matters, my dear… I'm sure I will like it, at one point. It will only take me a little bit more time, that's all. What about you, Sophie, you like it?

Sophie waves her head up and down.

— Why don't both of you get in a warm bath while I clean up everything and make some dinner for us? Says Philippe, giving me Sophie and looking at the walls at the same time. I like it a lot, my love. Can you see the magical effect you have on me?

— I'm glad! I say taking a last step towards the bathroom.

When I get to the restaurant, Olivier is already there, reading a newspaper. He welcomes me with one of his nicest smiles and gets up to kiss me on both cheeks.

— I recognized these colors! He says, as he looks me up and down and grabs me a chair. They fit you perfectly.

— Thank you. I followed your advice and it's beautiful!

— What, you have already painted the walls? You are fast, he says as he sits down, looking at me straight in the eyes.

— I was inspired, that's all.

Silence falls upon us.

— Tell me more about you, Olivier ends up saying. I want to know everything.

— There's not much to be said about that actually. I traveled a lot because my father worked in the importation/exportation business. Otherwise, I was a more or less solitary and melancholy child. I don't really carry any memories. I loved to leave France, because it never felt right for me to be out there. I thought of it as very heavy even if I didn't really know why. Although, when I got here, I automatically knew that this was my country, as I told you yesterday.

— It's incredible…

We are inexhaustible. The more we talk, the more we have this impression of having known each other for ever and finally reuniting after a long separation.

I feel like I am floating, like I could do something crazy, anything for that matter. I do not get tired of being around Olivier and need to realize that I have never been in love with someone as I am now. This makes me conscious of a new dimension of my life, the one I knew existed, the one I have yet to explore. I have the feeling that my body is dissolving, that my soul is trying to fuse with Olivier's. I have the feeling of having found the man I have always been looking for, to have found my lost half and, with him, to finally feel complete and whole. I am just simply happy to be close to Olivier and to know he exists. Nothing else matters now.

Olivier ends up talking about himself and his situation, and despite it, the magical link that is operating between us continues to flow.

— I have an ex-wife and one kid and am currently living with a woman I am unhappy with. If I was happy, I would've never accepted to have lunch with you!

— As you already know, I have a little girl. I thus also have the daddy that comes with it...

— It's pretty clear it's not going to be easy for both of us, but the attraction I have for you is stronger than anything. I really want to try it out and see where this could take us. I need to know if you are the woman I have always been looking.

— Me too, Olivier, I want to know if you are the man I have always been looking for, I answer, surprised to be giving myself away so easily.

We look at each other without a word. Words aren't necessary anymore. We have told one another everything that needed to be said. Olivier gets up without looking away from my eyes, and takes my hand, inviting me to get up with him. I think I am going to faint, as strong as this contact is between us. We leave the restaurant hand in hand, still in perfect silence.

We walk down the street, completely mesmerized by each other. I am aware of every single movement; our steps, perfectly in sync, our hips barely touching under all our clothing, our hands, enlaced. Noises and outdoor smells are amplified. Olivier and I are one. One with the other in the street, one and the other with the universe.

We arrive at Olivier's car. I do not want to leave him. I would rather have him kiss me, as time comes to a halt while our lips meet. Olivier opens the door for me. My arm brushes against his and this contact heightens the intense attraction that is occurring between us and I cannot keep myself from putting my arms around his neck and kissing him softly on the lips. He grabs my waist, pulls me closer to him and kisses me back with as much passion as the red of my wall. Everything vanishes around us. I almost have this feeling of kissing a man for the first time. He gently pushes me towards the car and runs to the other side to come meet me and continue this kiss. I glide my hand through his hair, which is soft and full. I do not want to leave this man, whom I barely knew yesterday, but whom I feel my soul has been wanting to meet again for so long. I want to make up for lost time by enjoying this stolen moment to the fullest.

Olivier drops me off in front of my building, not without a last kiss and the promise of a phone call.

I get back home, completely amazed by what I have just gone through. I have the impression of living a dream. Never in my life have I felt such an intense and profound happiness. The phone rings. It is Olivier.

— I just wanted to tell you that I already miss you.

— I miss you too.

— I cannot wait to see you again... I will call you back soon.

— Thank you for your call, Olivier. It's really touching.

Olivier calls me back numerous times that day and each of our conversations is a true delight. As life does not only do things halfway; the morning after my lunch date with Olivier, Philippe reminds me that he is leaving for New York the next day to give a conference. I had completely forgotten. The night of Philippe's departure, I invite Olivier for dinner, after having put Sophie to bed.

The door bells rings and I run to the entrance. I cannot wait to squeeze him in my arms. Surprisingly, he casually kisses me on both cheeks. I decide to play his game, not crossing the amicable barrier that he just imposed. We sit down on the couch, facing the famous 'Venice Red Passion'. I grab two glasses and fill them with wine.

— It's really beautiful, Kiera. I feel so comfortable in your house… says Olivier as he gently puts his arms around me. Then tightening his grip, he kisses me passionately. Nothing exists anymore besides him, and me.

I love this long, never ending embrace. I have the feeling that his soul is joining mine in pleasure, as Olivier starts taking off my clothes. We find ourselves naked, surrounded by the warmth of the fireplace and the comfort of the plush new carpet. We do not control anything, anymore. The fusion of our enlaced bodies is the only thing that is important to us. A feeling of fulfillment invades me. I do not know where I am anymore and I could not care less. I want to stay in this place where time does not exist and where love is all that matters.

We fall asleep at dawn, facing the dead fire. Olivier wakes up in a jolt, a little bit later.

— I need to be going, honey, he whispers to my ear.

— Alright, I answer, still half asleep.

— Stay put, don't wake up, he says as he gets his clothes back on.

I go back to sleep, as if I just dreamt something and never really woke up.

The next morning, very early, the doorbell rings. Still a little bit asleep, I roll over the covers, get up and slowly open the door. It is Olivier, with a beautiful bouquet of flowers. He takes my hand and brings me back to the fireplace. We make love, even more passionately than the day before.

— I fell asleep, you were here. I wake up, and you are still here. It feels as if you never left; as if we really spent this whole night together, I say amazed.

— I love you, Kiera. I really cannot live without you anymore.

— Me too, Olivier, I answer softly as I put my lips against his.

For the rest of the week, Olivier and I cannot stop seeing each other and our relationship takes an unexpected direction, as we get to realize the extent of our love for each other.

The last day before Philippe comes back home, Olivier, moved by my tears, tells me about the strategy he has been considering for us to live together.

— Let me settle myself with my girlfriend, Kiera. It won't be easy with her and I need time. We might have to see each other less often during the next couple of weeks, but trust me, please.

— I don't know if I will be able to not see you as much anymore, I exclaim, helpless.

— It's only for a little bit. As soon as I can, I will break up with her, get an apartment for the both of us and your daughter and you will come live with me. It's worth the wait, isn't it?

— You are right, I say, cuddling up in his arms as I try to impregnate myself with the scent of his skin as much as I can. I cannot wait to be with you, always.

— Me too, honey. Don't worry. You will see. Everything will go as planned. We just need to be patient and cautious.

In the arrival hall of the airport, I wait for Philippe, Sophie in my arms. I wonder how I am going to react. When I see Philippe getting out of customs, so happy to see us, I send Sophie ahead of me in a vain attempt to get a few more seconds for myself to calm down. Philippe grabs his daughter up and covers her with kisses as she squeezes his neck tightly. I try to smile as they arrive in front of me.

— Are you crying? He worries.

— No, I was just pretty emotional at the sight of Sophie clinging onto your neck, I answer, surprised by my own audacity.

— Is this lie true?

— I assure you…

— I really missed you guys, Philippe says as he grabs me closer.

— We missed you too.

Sophie captures all her father's attention on the way back home, which relieves me immensely, as I try my hardest to keep my tears to myself. I drive in silence, looking at Sophie and her father playing together, with the beautiful new doll he has brought back for her from New York. When we get home, Philippe puts Sophie in bed, as I sit down on the living room couch, staring at the 'Venice Red Passion' wall, nostalgic. Philippe comes to join me and hands me a nice little velvet box.

— It's beautiful, I say, as I discover a magnificent sapphire ring.

Philippe takes it from me and delicately puts it on my finger.

— Happy anniversary, my love.

— Oh, my God, I say, confused. I completely forgot. I am so sorry. I have nothing for you…

— It's alright, don't worry about it. Your presence is the most wonderful gift to me. I missed you so much, he says, hugging me. What about we go to bed, he continues as he grabs my hand.

I follow him without resisting on the outside; but on the inside I am completely tense. I wonder what kind of excuse I will be able to come up with to avoid the intimate moment Philippe desires. Philippe tells me to wait for him because he wants to take a shower. I take advantage of the situation to get to bed and fake sleeping. I am faking so well that I actually end up falling asleep, and do not feel Philippe coming in bed a little bit later.

In the following days, Philippe feels that there is something wrong with me. Every time he tries to get closer to me, I find an excuse to get away. I realize that I cannot stand even the slightest physical contact with him, as I have the impression of cheating on Olivier. I know very well that I will not be able to play this game much longer. I talk about it to Olivier and he asks me to be patient, since he is trying to get everything together.

Weeks go by, and the tension grows. I don't know what I am going to do. Philippe tries to bring up the question with me, but I avoid it, as I avoid any physical contact with him. He adopts a suspicious and aggressive attitude towards me, as he clearly sees that I am hiding something from him. I feel trapped between Olivier, who does not want me to talk, and Philippe who is only asking for me to open up. I do not dare imagine the events that will follow and am already tired just thinking about it. I would like for everything to be over, although nothing has even started yet.

One weekend, Philippe, Sophie and I leave for the cottage we have rented in the Laurentians for the season. Tension is at its highest point between us while we are in the car, driving to destination. Only Sophie seems to be able to ease the atmosphere. The trip feels endless and I cannot wait to get there. As we start getting settled in the cottage, Philippe puts Sophie in front of the TV and takes me to the kitchen.

— I can't continue like this. I can't stand it anymore. There is another man, isn't it?

— No, I promise, I answer, trying to hide my discomfort.

— I have already been through this, you should know, and you are acting exactly as you were two years ago.

— There is nothing, I assure you... I'm just tired...

— Can you tell me why you are so tired? You don't work, you study what you like and Sophie is at her daycare most of the time. I would really like to know what is making you so tired in those conditions.

I stay silent and turn my back to him, so he doesn't witness the panic that is slowly taking hold of me. Philippe takes my arm and turns me around so as to force me to face him.

— You can't ignore me like this Kiera. It's inhuman. Tell me what is going on.

I realize how much I am hurting him by acting as I am. I cannot do this anymore. I cannot continue to live this double life I have made for myself for the past few weeks. I am exhausted by all these accumulated anxieties since I have met Olivier. If I could, I would run away. Philippe insists.

— Well, yes. There's indeed another man and I want a divorce because I love him, I toss out without looking at him.

— Again? Aren't you sick of this Kiera? Of always destroying everything around you?

— I am so sorry.

— I refuse to divorce, answers Philippe. If you think that you can decide everything and that I will accept anything; you are highly mistaken!

— You cannot do this, I answer, walking away.

— Watch me. This is the second time you've done this to me. I accepted it the first time and you came back to me. I can still do it a second time. You'll end up coming back to me, at one point.

— This time it's different, Philippe.

— Oh yes?! And what's so different?

— I really love this man.

— It will go away, like it went away with the other one, although you still told me that you had a child with him. You are not pregnant, at least?

— No.

— I never know with you; you are so unpredictable! Says Philippe, leaving the room.

The rest of the weekend is a real disaster: Philippe and I do not utter a word to each other. On the other hand, we manage to act as if nothing was wrong in front of Sophie. I feel time will never end and I cannot wait to go back to Montreal, to talk to Olivier.

When we get back home, Philippe puts Sophie in bed and locks himself in the bathroom. I take advantage of this to call Olivier and let him know about what happened. To my great surprise, he is furious at me.

— I told you not to tell him anything, Kiera! You ruined everything.

— I didn't have a choice, he was harassing me.

— Kiera, we are hurting too many people around us. All you can do now is to forget about me.

— But I cannot forget you, I love you, Olivier, I answer, crying.

— I am begging you, Kiera, Olivier continues on a dry note. Do not make things worse than they already are. My girlfriend is already having doubts. I am trying to tell her that I want a separation because it isn't going well between us but she doesn't want to believe it. It's all really hurting her. I tried, I assure you, but I cannot be happy if I make people unhappy around me. Let's stop everything before we destroy anything more.

Olivier hangs up. I cannot believe that my relationship with Olivier has just ended like this. The suffering that inhabits me is so strong and poignant that I lose all sense of reality. I cry without being able to stop myself. I would like to die this instant in order not to feel this unbearable pain that slowly fills up my soul and body. I don't know what to do with myself. Philippe is standing in front of me now, not really grasping what is going on. I distance myself from him, afraid I might get violent.

— I think we have to talk, he says, following me.

— I don't have anything to tell you. You ruined everything, I answer without looking at him.

— What do you mean, I ruined everything?! You are the one who is cheating on me, I'll remind you! He says, angry now.

— Look, you're going to be happy; I am not cheating on you anymore, I say as the tears keep coming. It's over between Olivier and me, because of you. And it's over with you too. I need to find myself. I can't stand my life here.

Livid, Philippe sits on a chair and puts his head in his hands. I cannot believe what I just told him: I am letting Olivier destroy me on the inside as well on the outside. I feel totally disoriented, destabilized, lost. I don't see anything else in front of me. Only a wheel on the cobblestone. An old wheel. This wheel is not attached to anything. Only a pin seems to be pushing it. A few stairs. A cold crisp feeling on the back of my neck. A repulsive metal taste fills my mouth. Emptiness. Silence. Death.

The moonlight enters the apartment and I feel mesmerized. I get up. I think of suicide: I have the impression that this suffering that is stabbing my soul is too intense for me to deal with. I imagine myself going through the glass window two voices start debating in my head: 'it's obvious that I am going to hurt myself, because of the glass breaking under my weight. And it will surely hurt even more when I hit the ground.' As all these thoughts go through my head, I cannot help but laugh at my own craziness. Philippe stares at me, disconcerted, and leaves the room. I feel like I am going crazy. Or is it simply a dim light that just brightened up the end of this dark tunnel I have been in?

Filled with new-found hope, I leave the room to go in Sophie's and gently take her from her bed. I avoid waking her up, and cover her up with her blanket. I head towards the entrance, Sophie still cuddled in my arms. I open the door, when Philippe calls to me and closes the door in front of me, using his body as a shield to keep me from leaving.

— What on earth are you doing, Kiera? He asks me, truly angry now.

— I am leaving you, can't you see? I thought I just told you so, I say with an ironic touch, that won't allow any riposte.

— Let's take some time, please, says Philippe, trying to calm me down so we don't wake Sophie up. You don't know what you are doing anymore.

— For the first time in my life, I know perfectly well what I am doing, actually.

— We have been through so much, together. We have worked out so many ordeals, you and me. You can't just leave like this.

— You accepted the ordeals, I did not. Now, I have to leave. Or else, I have the impression that I will never get out of this dark hole I have fallen into, I say, reopening the door.

— You can do whatever you want, but leave Sophie here, Philippe answers back, closing the door again.

— I need to keep Sophie. She is the only thing that I have left. If you keep her, I will die from it.

Sophie, who just woke up, starts to cry and Philippe takes a step back, so as not to traumatize her. I take this opportunity and open the door, getting out with Sophie still in my arms, without a look at Philippe, or a look back on my life, which, I feel, is now already part of my past.

Outside, I run to one of my university's friend's house who lives not so far away from us. Selma opens her door at the first knock and lets me in without a word, or questions, when she sees the makeup running down my face. She takes Sophie in her arms and tells me to calm down as she puts her to bed.

Only a couple minutes were enough for my life to crumble without me being able to go back to fix it. I can now only advance forward on the new road I have chosen for myself unconsciously. I don't have anything anymore, no husband, no lover, no place to live; only twenty dollars in my pocket, my credit card and my passport in hand. Selma comes back and sets the sofa for me in the living room, after I told her everything that just happened.

— Don't make a decision just yet, Kiera. Olivier doesn't deserve you to waste your life for him, you need to realize this. You have a daughter, and you need to think about her. She needs her father. Have a rest and we will talk about it tomorrow.

I lay down, but I can't fall asleep. I have the feeling I am going to die if I do not leave; my life is somewhere else, although I do not know where, yet. I had everything and I chose to lose it all, but I have a feeling that I will gain something that is even more precious than a comfortable home; I will gain myself and this is the most wonderful gift I can give to myself. At peace with this revelation, I fall asleep, serene.

The next day, I let Selma know about my decision and she does not even bother trying to make me change my mind. Later, I head to a travel agency and pay for two one-way tickets for Paris, for Sophie and myself, for the next day. Everything is going really fast; maybe even too fast. Although I know that I have made the right decision, I am still worried and anxious.

Philippe, on his side, is not making things better. As soon as he hears that I am leaving, he starts calling me all the time to make me change my mind. The more he tries to convince me, the more my old obsessions come back to me with no interruptions. A wheel on the cobblestone. An old wheel. This wheel isn't attached to anything. Only a pin seems to be pushing it. A few stairs. A cold crisp feeling on the back of my neck. A repulsive metal taste fills my mouth. Emptiness. Silence. Death.

Chapter 5

Comeback

In France, Sophie and I find asylum at my parent's house, for a certain time. I feel so weak. I have lost a lot of weight because of all the conflicts that have been occupying me, these past few weeks. And, despite myself, I am missing Olivier terribly.

I spend the next two weeks in a profound depression, crying all the time and not being able to eat, or sleep. I have the impression of having jumped from one prison to another, without realizing it. As I thought I could start a new life in France, I find myself back into my parent's coach house and this takes all initiative out of me.

Fortunately, one morning, without really knowing how, I find the energy to go running under the rain. I run without slowing down for a good hour. It is difficult, but it gives me the determination I was waiting for to move on to something else. When I get home, I work on my resume and send it to people my parents know.

The job I find doesn't really meet my expectations, but it has the advantage of being close to my parents' house. This allows me to get my financial independence back and to get my mind occupied. I work in the editorial department of a local journal and am well paid.

Thanks to the new job, I can soon reorganize my life and Sophie's. I find a lovely apartment close to a park ; my parents lend me some furniture, frames and some dishes in order to get installed correctly and I buy a couple of indoor plants to make it even more welcoming.

The first night in my new apartment, I am completely exhausted by the reoccurring nightmares. The next day, I hold on to what I have left: my routine. I bring my daughter to school, early in the morning, head to work and reunite with my daughter at the babysitter's house later in the afternoon. I give Sophie a bath, play with her and make dinner for both of us. I do the dishes while Sophie brushes her teeth, then I take her to bed and read her a bedtime story until she falls asleep. I get myself to bed and fall asleep, drained. I wake up the next morning, still weary, to start my day all over again, until I go to bed even more tired than the previous day, but ready for the next one. This routine, which used to depress me, becomes the mechanism that allows me to hold on and get on with my life. My nightmares are being less repetitive.

Even though I am putting lots of energy to get myself out of my past and get on with my life, I still do not understand the ups and downs of what I have been, and am, going through. Although I believe that this episode of my life is very important for me to finally define myself, I feel that I need answers to my existentialist questions; Why did I make Sophie in this manner? Why did I have to separate from my husband, while he gave me everything I desired? Why did my relationship with Olivier stop as fast as it started, if we loved each other as much as we did? Why do I keep having the same anxiousness, the same nightmares? WHY?

PART II

Chapter 1

Revelations

One night, I am invited by a coworker, Véronique, to a diner with a few other people, most of whom I do not know. On my arrival, I am warmly welcomed by Véronique and her guests. Introductions are made. I talk lightly and with a detached manner with everyone. I concentrate more while at the table when it is question of reincarnation and karma. It is a subject I have always been interested in, but never really lingered on. I am surprised by everyone's experience with the subject and listen to each story with a lot of consideration.

— My throat has hurt me for as far as I can remember. My mother always gave me antibiotics and medication but nothing seemed to be working. As an adult, I went to see a few specialists, without success. One day, one of my girl friends suggested that I go see a person who does past-life regressions. Having nothing to lose, I made an appointment. I will admit that I was a little scared of what I was going to discover. In the first meeting, I did not see anything, but at the second one, I understood everything. I never regretted going there. I saw that I had been hung for a petty theft. I experienced all of it again: the hanging, my thoughts at the moment of my death. It was incredible. Like a movie happening before my eyes, while I was feeling everything at the same time. Very strange. But, you will know that my throat never bothered me again after that.

— I am sure it was psychosomatic, says Amelia, coldly.

— It doesn't matter! Responds Benoit. The important part is that I was cured.

— You are right, acknowledges Amelia.

— Anyway, reincarnation has never been proven scientifically, says another person.

— That's not true, replies Véronique. There are thousands of cases that have been referenced: people having memories of past lives that have been verified and validated by Ian Stevenson of the University of Virginia. For example, there was the case of a little girl who couldn't stop talking about her husband and their kids. She asked for them incessantly. She could give their names, describe them physically, and talk about their habits, their village and even more. Her parents did not believe her until a priest had the good idea to verify the facts. They got the husband in question to come and visit them. The child instantly recognized him and asked him if he had held the promise he gave her on her death bed; that he would never remarry. Sheepish, he did not know what to answer: he never entrusted anyone with this promise and never held it either.

— Let's suppose that this theory is right. How would you explain that there are as many people as there are on this earth in our era? Asks Amelia, skeptical.

— There are many theories, answers Véronique. I will give you two of them that I relate to the most and you cam take it as you please. The first is that one single soul could reincarnate itself multiple times in different bodies at the same time. We are coming to the end of the millennium and there are some very interesting changes regarding the soul's evolution. Because there's an urgent need for souls to evolve, a same soul can then choose to reincarnate itself into numerous bodies at once to live the same experience under different angles. It is even possible that a same soul would choose to live the same event, for example in the case of a rape, as the executioner as well as the victim, for a better understanding of the situation. It allows the soul to evolve faster, because both lives are lived simultaneously instead of one after the other.

— This sounds absurd! Go tell that to an abused woman, you will see what she has to answer to you, answers Patrick angrily.

— Don't say that. Maybe there's some truth in this, even if it's not easy to accept, says Sarah, a very sweet woman. I am going to tell you something. I was raped four years ago. I finally came to terms with it, reluctantly, because I did not have a choice anymore, or else I would have let myself die. This theory makes me wonder. It allows me, I think, to make peace definitively with myself and my executioner.

Everyone stares at Sarah respectfully in silence.

— So what? You see, there's no need to make a mountain out of it. That is past, adds Sarah. What is the second theory? she asks Véronique.

— The second theory is that souls from other plans than the earth would have wanted to incarnate themselves in this end of the millennium era to experiment the karma that is linked to the earth.

— What is karma? asks Sarah.

— That is the law of cause and effect: everything you do to others, either good or bad, comes back to you so you can experience others' emotions and compassion for them. That helps you evolve on your own path so you can free your soul from the grip of reincarnation.

It is late. Two in the morning approximately. The night is slowly ending. Even though I am very interested by the subject, I cannot wait to go to bed. A few people left at the same time Amelia did. There's only Véronique left, one of her friends, Carmella, and myself. I help clean up the house before leaving. Carmella, whom I barely know, but am aware is a psychic, starts telling me, without warning, what she is seeing around me.

— I see you in a tumbrel. You are going to be beheaded. You are cold. I see also where you lived before all this. A prodigious château. A smaller one too, and a little farm. You are very wealthy and look for simplicity at the same time. You were living in another country when you were a child and you were very happy. I see you, you are charming and smiling. Then all degenerated and because there were a lot of people that were jealous of you and that used you to put in place a change they had wanted for a while then. Your life totally transformed during the French Revolution and you lost everything, even your children. Oh, my God!

— What? asks Véronique, anxiously.

— She was Marie-Antoinette, says Carmella, completely chocked.

— You are kidding, says Véronique, even more surprised.

Stupefied, I start crying uncontrollably. All of what this woman has said, rings in my head like something totally plausible and accessible. It triggers in me this old memory that had been buried deep, deep in my soul since my childhood, and for centuries. A wheel on the cobblestone…

— It is strange, I have the impression that all of what you are telling me is true. I have an incredible felling of déjà-vu. When I was a kid, I would always have this same nightmare that I could not understand or explain, but that would disturb me to the fullest and this as far as I can remember. This nightmare disappeared for a while but now comes back every time I go through rough patches since the birth of my daughter. I feel that there is a link between this nightmare and what you are telling me, even if I don't really know why.

— Your daughter was there at the time. She must have reactivated your memory. If you tell me this nightmare, I may be able to help you understand it.

— It is a wheel on the cobblestone, I start. An old wheel. This wheel isn't attached to anything. Only a pin seems to be pushing it. The cold. The lethargy. A few wooden stairs. A cold crisp feeling on the back of my neck. A repulsive metal taste fills my mouth. I cannot breathe anymore. Emptiness. Silence. Darkness. Death. I am lost. I always wake up in tears with an intensifying fear of death. When I had this nightmare as a child, I felt lonely and at the same time was astonished to find myself in the little girl's body when I'd wake up. I wouldn't ever want to go to bed because I was so afraid of death all the time.

— Every night you relived each and every of your anguishes of that era's death. Actually, you were being beheaded every night.

We all stay quiet.

— I always wondered why I hurt my husband so much, I ask, still shocked by everything I just learned.

— He was there and he opened to the door leading to the guillotine, in a way.

— What does that mean?

— I don't know. I guess I don't have access to that information. You will know when time comes. If you want, tomorrow I will take you to Marie-Antoinette's hamlet at Versailles. You will see if the place calls to you and maybe will you find answers to your questions.

— That is a good idea, I say faintly.

— Let's all go to bed, I am exhausted, says Véronique. You sleep here, Kiera? I'll give you my bedroom and Carmella and I will sleep in the living room.

— That is out of the question, I am going home, I say standing up to leave.

— I saw your face. I will not let you drive after all that you have just been through.

— Well, then I will sleep in the living room.

— If you think I am going to let Marie-Antoinette sleep in the living room, laughs Véronique, you are out of your mind. I now beg you to accept my humble bedroom in my very modest residence, your Highness, she continues while kneeing before me.

— This will do, I say as I give her my hand to receive her kiss.

As an answer, Véronique throws me a pillow and we all burst out laughing.

In the bedroom, it feels nice to be on my own, even if I quickly realize that I am not well at all, in contrast with the image I was trying to give a little earlier. I cannot stop crying. I have the repulsive taste of metal in my mouth. I am afraid of the darkness, the silence, the death.

I think about Olivier, whom I miss terribly, even if he did not act properly with me. Why did he act like this? A soothing force takes a hold of me and I quit resisting to what is happening. I suddenly find myself very calm and begin to see the wonderful present Carmella just gave me: the gift of my current life by the comprehension of my past death. Thanks to tonight's gift, I find hope and go right to sleep.

The croissants' marvelous odor, mixed with one of coffee, wakes me up gently. I take time to stretch and rethink about last night's events. I wonder what I will discover at Marie-Antoinette's hamlet. I don't really have the impression of having been Marie-Antoinette, considering her notoriety, even if what Carmella told me is familiar. I meet Véronique and Carmella in the kitchen.

The atmosphere is heart-warming and in good spirits. I enjoy a croissant that I delicately dip in my hot chocolate. I feel rather reserved this morning and I do not really feel like talking, which my friends feel and respect. I just need to get back in contact with life, very gently. I savor each bite of my croissant, as if it was the first time I ever tasted one, as if it was the last time. I have the impression of being in a world out of this time that has been protecting me of something that I still know nothing about. Véronique and Carmella are talking to the side about the planning of the day and even if their voices are only background noises, they reassure me.

In the car, I am in a different state. To find a place that I know nothing about, but that I am supposed to recognize is a strange experience for me. I have trouble setting my mind on anything around me. The trip seems like a drag without really being long. It is as if I was here without really being present. What will I feel? What will I see? Is it possible that the place does not affect me in any way?

— We are here, shouts Carmella while stopping the car, far enough from the hamlet.

I find the walk leading to my past as a good transition. The place is magnificent. I suddenly feel transported to some other time. I have to close my eyes, because the images unravel too fast before my eyes. I see the house where Marie-Antoinette would find herself with friends, the dairy, the cows, the fields. I see her walking. I see her with her friends. I open my eyes because I have the feeling I am going to faint. I am then attracted by a path that leads me to the Trianon. I feel like I now the road by heart. What is weird is that, even though I am irresistibly attracted by the Trianon, there is an opposite force that keeps me from getting there. I am confused and stop. Emotions then flow through me and I have to put my back against a tree to keep myself from falling: sorrow, fear... love. This last emotion surprises me. I close my eyes and the images come back to me. I do not know where the present or where my past is anymore. Everything seems mixed up together. I hesitate. I walk toward the pavilion that once upon a time Marie-Antoinette cared for so much, because it was her harbor of peace, because it was hidden away from the stares, the slanders and the scandals. I see Marie-Antoinette, but at the same time see myself through her. It is a very weird sensation. I do not know who is who but have a strong feeling that we are one and one person only. I then see myself covered with a hooded cape of a dark color, hiding a sumptuous dress with brocaded pearls. I hold a lantern in my hand. I leave the Trianon and walk toward a charming little pavilion. I leave to meet my lover at night, the man I loved at first sight, the man who had been there during the worst moment of my life, the man that I had to leave at the moment of my tragic death, the man that I met again in this current life. My God, this man, it's Olivier. I recognize him as I see him waiting for me. The same facial features, the same haughty bearing, the same smile, the same class. I'm bewildered and the scenery disappears.

I come back to earth in an instant. I have to sit down against a tree in order not to fall and to regain contact with reality. My friends, who were watching me from afar, reach me, worried. I tell them everything I just experienced.

— In what way does it matter to me to know all of this? I ask disoriented. Olivier isn't with me and that makes me suffer so much…

— We meet our soul mates from one life to another to conclude unfinished business and help one another, tells me Carmella. Things reproduce themselves until we are finally able to recover from these emotions that are attached to us, until we are completely detached from the result.

— Even if he ruined everything, I still love him and I hate myself for this.

— Marie-Antoinette and Hans Axel de Fersen had a beautiful love story, but this story gave great prejudice to Marie-Antoinette. Maybe you need to break a connection that is not good for you!

I don't know what to say. I would like to forget him, but at the same time, I can't do it, even if it hurts me a lot.

— I know a very good hypnotherapist who could help you, continues Carmella. His name is Dr. Justin Malayane. Marie-Antoinette's life was traumatizing and if you are in contact with this information, it means that you need to cure it and maybe transform this experience into a bigger and better one!

— Do you think this will allow us to be back together again, if I do it?

— I have no clue. Would you be able to forgive him for what he has done? That is the question you should ask yourself.

— It's true that I have no idea about that!

— So until then, let time and circumstances do their work. For now, Olivier is not part of your life anyways and that gives you time to take care of yourself. The most important part is not that you find him and get back together with him, it is that you get back together with your soul.

Chapter 2

Regressions

I arrive to the Dr. Malayane's office, a little anxious. As I sit down in the waiting room, the sun's rays pass through the stained glass and through bits of greens and purples and create a mesmerizing aurora borealis on the wall. I am completely hypnotized by the phenomenon and jump when Dr. Malayane comes to meet me.

— Hi Kiera. I see that you also are mesmerized, says the Dr. I never get tired of it. Actually, it is a test to know if you are hypnotizable and if I let you in my office or not.

— Really? I ask naively.

— I am just kidding! he says as he bursts into laughter and opens the door for me. Welcome to my world.

I am in awe at the place. Orange and red transparent veils cover the yellow walls and prodigious buddhas lay here and there, giving the room a very particular Tibetan atmosphere that makes the place magical. Dr. Malayane goes ahead of me to push the veils on the side so I can walk through. In the middle of the room, pillows are laid in a circle and candles flicker away. The doctor smiles at my amazement.

— Do you like it? That is good. That proves that you kept your childhood spirits. Lay down here and explain to me what brought you here.

— I met a man in Montreal and even if it is over and I am mad at him, he continues to haunt my thoughts. I saw Carmella who told me that it was connected to my past life. That is why I am here. To let go of this link that binds me to him.

— Very good. At least, you know what you want.

I blush and stay silent.

— If you met Carmella and are now here, I imagine that she gave you your past life.

— I would not dare telling you. You would not believe me, I say as I put my head down.

— If you do not say it here, where else would you want to mention it?

We keep quiet and he waits for me to talk. Sensing that I am not going to say anything, he continues:

— Do not worry. I have heard so many things in this office that I will accept anything. Also, if it can reassure you, Carmella has never been wrong in her prognostics, until now!

— Did she ever send historical figures your way???

— Not that I know of... but you have nothing of a historical figure that I can see. On the contrary, you seem very real to me, the Dr. says while laughing.

I laugh with him.

— So, are you going to tell me who you were???

I hesitate and blurt out:

— She said that I was Marie-Antoinette, I say in one breath.

— See? It was not that difficult to say and you are still alive, right?! If you inhale again, of course.

— I just feel like all this is a little too crazy, that's all, I say, inhaling with a smile.

— She had to be reincarnated somewhere, this Marie-Antoinette. Don't you think? And why would it not be you?

— That is true... I did not see it that way.

— That is why you are here: to see things differently. Does your throat cause you any problems?

— I had my tonsils removed, right after the birth of my daughter. I had a constant strep throat during my pregnancy.

— So your daughter must have had reactivated your past life! Do you have any memories that could lead in the ways of this past life?

— A nightmare I have had since I was a kid (where I could not breathe, actually): an old wheel on the cobblestone that isn't attached to anything. Only a pin seems to be pushing it. Wooden stairs. A cold crisp feeling on the back of my neck. A repulsive metal taste filling my mouth. I can't breathe. Emptiness. Silence. Darkness and a terrible fear of death.

— That is an interesting nightmare. You have the real ingredients of death. The metal taste is the taste that the blood leaves when it floods the brain. Then this can very well be associated with the guillotine, and your operation also seems to confirm this aspect from this possible past life. When you tell me that only a pin seems to be pushing this old wheel, it refers to the era's atmosphere: there was nothing in Marie-Antoinette's case that deserved the death penalty. Interesting! Was there an incident in your life that could have led to this nightmare? Asks Dr. Malayane while taking notes.

— When I was a kid I cut open my forehead after falling down a staircase. My nightmare is my first memory, it seems.

— Very good. There must be a connection between these two. Did you bleed a lot when this happened?

— I do not recall actual memories but my dad always told me that there was blood everywhere. Oh, hold on, I remember visions I had a few years back. Yes, there was blood everywhere.

— That's the connection… the blood in your past life… the blood in your present life. Do you have any other memories?

— I often see a very large window through which I admire some gardens. I am miserable and someone tells me we have to leave.

— Interesting… Anything else?

— Not really… oh, yes, when I went to Marie-Antoinette's hamlet, I saw some things.

— Like what?

— I saw that I would meet my lover at night in a little pavilion.

— Do you know this man in your current life?

— Yes, he's the man I told you about.

— Perfect! Have you studied Marie-Antoinette's history in school?

— Of course. I remember that she was decapitated during the French Revolution but I cannot remember why.

— Did you feel close to that era?

— No, I hate the revolution. Although I loved the dresses from this period. As a child, I often thought my dress was too big to go through doors. I imagined myself having to turn on my side to make it pass.

— Interesting!

— Also, when I was a kid, my brother often played songs of the French Revolution. My mother took me to see the Conciergerie when I was a little and I remember Marie-Antoinette's cell very well. We went to Versailles a couple of times and I loved it.

— So you are pretty aware and keen of this environment!

— I also have had this strong feeling forever: I have the impression of not being born in the right period.

— Very interesting. It is often a feeling that people that are truly in contact with their past life have. At least, we already have a lot of information to be able to start the hypnosis... Have you ever done such a thing before?

— No.

— Very well. I am going to explain to you what we are going to do. I am going to put you in a state of hypnotic sleep and you will be able to see things that you have forgotten. After seeing these things you will feel much better. For this to happen, you just need to follow the instructions I am going to tell you. Are you okay with this?

— Yes.

The doctor grabs a crystal at the end of a chain that had been in a sculpted pretty little box near him and begins to balance it from left to right before my eyes.

— You are going to keep your eyes open for a moment, Kiera, and you will look at this crystal in front of you. I just want you to follow the movement with your eyes.

I follow the crystal with my eyes.

— You feel your eyelids becoming heavier and heavier and you cannot keep them from closing, the doctor continues. They now close themselves very gently. That is good, says the doctor as he sees me closing my eyes.

Dr. Malayane keeps quiet for a moment.

— You will open your eyes again for a couple minutes.

I open my eyes slowly with lots of difficulty.

— I want you to be aware of your left hand. I want you to place it far away from your face.

I take my hand approximately twenty centimeters away from my face and wait for directions.

— Now, you can close your eyes. Let your hand get closer to your face all this while looking at your hand. It is getting closer and closer to your face. For each respiration you take, your hand needs to be getting closer to you face. It is getting closer and closer.

My hand approaches my face slowly, jolting with each move forward.

— That is good. Your hand continues to get closer to your face while your body sinks deeper in the chair. Your left hand becomes heavier and heavier with each breath. Now that your hand is getting so close to your face it could touch it... at the moment your hand touches your face, you will enter hypnotic sleep.

When my hand touches my face, the doctor snaps his fingers and announces: "Deep sleep".

— You can put your hand down now. Every time I will suggest the words "deep sleep", for the hypnosis objective and with your permission, you will enter a state of hypnosis very rapidly, calmly, and profoundly and your physical body will let go completely.

The doctor snaps his fingers while saying "deep sleep" again.

— I will now count from five to zero. At every number mentioned, your mind and body will allow you to enter the hypnotic sleep more and more deeply all the way to zero. I am starting to count Five... we are going down now... deeper and deeper in the hypnotic state... Four, you are physically relieved... Three in a completely calm state... Two you are now mentally relaxed... 1 you are deeply going down in zero deep sleep, finishes the doctor as he snaps his fingers.

Dr. Malayane pauses for a couple seconds and goes on.

— We are going to visualize a large white tunnel that you are now entering in total trust. I would like you to walk through this tunnel. Are you okay with that?

— Yes, I answer, feverish.

— You are walking in this tunnel while I am counting from five to zero. Five... Four... Three... Continue to walk toward the light at the end of the tunnel... Two... One... Zero and deep sleep, says the doctor while snapping his fingers.

My body lightly jolts forward and I can feel my face displaying a timid smile followed by a deep sadness.

— I would like you to look at your feet and at your hands, Kiera, and I would like for you to tell me what you are seeing, continues the doctor.

— I am wearing very chic little shoes, but they are old and used, I answer. I have on a long black simple dress that is all worn out. I am very cold.

— Look around you and tell me what you see...

— I am leaving a huge room and policemen are with me. I am crossing a hallway... It's strange; I feel at peace and am resigned at once. I cannot wait to get this over with, but I do not know what "this" is yet. I feel very weak physically but I do not want to show it.

— Very well. What is your name? Asks the doctor while snapping his fingers.

— Anto… Antoine… I manage to articulate.

— And how old are you? Asks Dr. Malayane as he snaps his fingers again.

— Thirty seven. I will turn thirty eight on the 2nd of November.

— And what day is it? Asks the doctor while snapping his finger one more time.

— The 16th of October 1793… My God… This is it, I know, I am going to die… the impressive room… it was my judgment room.

— Tell me what happens now.

— I am in a little dark humid room.

The room's setting vanishes, all this while Dr. Malayane and I are still sitting in the middle of the room. Little by little, a new setting appears and I find myself floating right into Antoine's body, wearing a black dress and a black cap. I am very cold. I tighten my scarf around my shoulders but the cold has already penetrated my bones and I cannot warm myself up. I am writing a long letter to Elisabeth, my sister-in-law, with the help of the candlelight. "I have just been sentenced, not to a shameful death, like the one of criminals, but to reunite with your brother. As innocent as he was, I hope to show the same resistance in my last moments. I am as calm as can be when you have nothing for which to reproach yourself. I have profound regrets about abandoning my poor children. You know I only lived for them." I take a break because my heart is closing up on itself and the tears are pricking my eyes. I want to stay strong because I want to finish this letter before they come to get me. I continue my letter. "I sincerely ask to be forgiven by everyone I knew." I cannot see what I am writing anymore. "I forgive all my enemies for all the pain they imposed me." "God, how awful it is to leave them forever." "Goodbye, goodbye, from now on I will only take care of my spiritual duties." I finish my letter and have a long moment of despair. I am afraid I will not find the strength to confront all of the people's hatred. I turn over the letter and go lay down on my bed. I stay there, my head and my heart as empty as can be, for I do not know how long. Time does not exist anymore: in a few hours, it will all be over. I am surprised by the detached feeling that is taking a hold of me. I think about my children. I miss them terribly and I feel I am a horrible person for abandoning them this way. The door opens. I do not move. Rosalie comes in with a bowl of warm soup. She insists I eat a little, which I do more to please her than for my own sake. She asks the guard to turn around, which he refuses and I am obliged to take off my clothes and put the new ones on in front of him, while Rosalie does the best she can to hide me. I have already lived through the worst humiliations possible so one more does not change much for me. My shirt is filled with blood and I do not want to leave it here. I hide it behind the stove, hoping Rosalie will come back for it. I will not show them any private aspect of me. I concentrate on my children to avoid thinking about the horrible vision of the guillotine in order not to faint.

While I am praying, men enter my cell. I get up, painfully. One man reads me my sentence. I do not react. The executioner, a tall man, arrives soon after. I cringe. He walks toward me to tie my hands behind my back. I protest, shocked and say that my husband did not have his hands tied to go to death, in vain. I stop resisting and I hold back my tears. The man gets a pair of scissors from behind his back and cuts my hair off with one chop. I look at the strands falling to the floor, thinking how my head will soon follow. I am afraid, but make an effort not to show any emotion. The abbot, who is trying by all means to give me the absolution, comes back for more. I refuse it again, as I refused it earlier, since he gave oath to the Republic, and I believe in the catholic and apostolic church. I accept his demand to accompany me to the guillotine. We walk towards the exit, closely followed by the guards.

Outside, I am blinded by the light. It has been a long time since I have seen the daylight. I adjust my vision as I open and close my eyes a couple of times. In a cloud of dust, I see the tumbrel waiting for me.

I have a deep moment of panic, but I catch myself immediately. We open the gate, and the people greet me with a stony silence. The guards get closer to me to protect me. I keep my back straight. I try not to look at the people and focus on an invisible point between my eyes. The horses rear up. I am mortified by the hatred of all these people whom I do not know. I finally get into the tumbrel and the abbot sits next to me. My back is to the drive. Even this insult, reserved for the biggest criminals, does not affect me. The crowd, angry, becomes louder and louder as we move forward, very slowly. The journey seems endless. I look back at the journey from Varennes to Paris, and regret that time, when I was still with my children and my husband.

I feel alone, so alone. I want to scream, but I remain silent, alone with my grief. I cannot stand all these insulting looks, all these threatening screams, all these hateful insults on the way to my execution. I'm cold. I would like to cry, but I cannot. I want to prove that all of this does not affect me, even if it is not true. Suddenly, I look back to the Catholic priest who is waiting for me at one of the windows to give me the last rites. I had forgotten about him. I hope that, lost in my thoughts, I did not miss him. I mark and number the buildings. Relieved, I see that he is giving me the sign of the cross at the top of the window, when I pass by. I feel freed of a great weight; I can now die in peace.

The cart stops, at last, on the place de la Révolution where I will be executed right in front of the Tuileries. All of a sudden, I feel very ill. I think about my life at the Tuileries with my children and my husband. I am afraid I am not going to be able to make it. I do not want to leave my children alone in this pitiless revolution. I am afraid of what they will do to them. They still need me. The executioner helps me to get out of the tumbrel. I climb the few steps leading to the scaffold. The executioner whispers to me to be brave. I am surprised by his concern. This gives me the strength to keep on going. Unintentionally, I step on his foot. I apologize, confused.

Suddenly, it seems to me that I can see my father waiting for me. I close my eyes and reopen them: my father is still there, in the light, looking at me with a warm smile. I sigh with relief. The executioner's assistants put me on the board. I let them do so. They then lower the plank with me now above it horizontally. I see the basket on the floor and, once again, think about my children. I say in one breath 'Farewell my children. I now join your father '. I hear a loud noise. I feel the cold at the back of my neck and a horrible metallic taste flooding my mouth. I cannot breathe. Silence. Darkness. Death. My father is here with me, but I move towards one of the executioner's assistants who is showing my head to the crowd, as some people start shouting 'Long live the Republic'. They then put my body in a basket, with my head between my legs. My father reaches out for me to come to him. I cannot. I remain prostrated over my body.

The scenery suddenly vanishes and I hear the far away voice of Dr. Malayan.

— You will now return to consciousness, the doctor says softly. I'll count to five. Zero... One... Two... Three... Four... Five... Open your eyes. Your eyes are now fully open.

I open my eyes softly. Tears run slowly down my cheeks.

— How do you feel? asks Dr. Malayan.

— I don't know...

— That's normal... Take your time.

We remain silent for a long time.

— I feel very sad and relieved at the same time, I say weakly.

— Take time to relax today, to assimilate all that you have just received.

— It's amazing, all this. It looks like this confirms my nightmare completely. Everything explains itself so well now. Thank you, Dr. Malayan, I say, looking at him, full of gratitude.

— It's a pleasure. I will see you Monday evening to see how you feel.

— How much do I owe you, Doctor? I ask the doctor as I'm getting up.

— Nothing. It is a pleasure to work with you, answers Doctor Malayan with a large smile lighting up his face as he accompanies me to the door. I'm as curious as you are to know more.

— I can't accept, I say, opening my wallet.

— Of course you can! I was always fascinated by the story of Marie-Antoinette and I feel that our sessions together will bring me satisfaction as much as they will for you.

— Thank you so much, Doctor.

I leave the Dr. Malayan's office still completely in shock from everything I've just discovered. I do not know what to think or what to hold on to myself. Everything looks so real when I think about what I had to relive in the hypnosis, especially the cold sensation when the blade of the guillotine touched my neck and the taste of the blood that overflowed my mouth. At the same time a part of me refuses to believe it. I take a deep breath of fresh air as I head outside and walk towards the Luxembourg Gardens.

It is nice outside and I feel better. I walk around the water basin, then go lie on the grass, despite the sign prohibiting walking on the grass'. Nothing matters anymore. I close my eyes to fully enjoy this new feeling inside me: a vast consciousness of life and a deep serenity. I'm floating and external noises seem amplified: the fountain flowing, birds singing, wind in the trees, the grass under my body. I am one with nature and I have the feeling of floating.

— Do you know that it is not allowed to lie on the grass? Didn't you see the sign? Asks a male voice.

I jump and open my eyes, afraid. A man is bending over me smiling. I sit up facing him and I am confused because I see no uniform or badge on his clothing.

— My name is Samuel, says the man.

— Do you know that it is forbidden to talk to a stranger?

— I could not help it. Sorry if I scared you. Can I invite you to have a coffee with me to be forgiven, Miss Rebel?

— Kiera.

— Pleased to meet you, Kiera. So are you up for this coffee?

— Why not? Provided it is taken next to a sign that forbids us to do so, I say to find a countenance.

— You are more brave than I ever imagined. I love it, says Samuel holding out his hand to help me get up.

At the height of Samuel now, I am surprised to see a very tall and slim man. His brown hair, which falls onto his shoulders, gives him the air of a dandy that makes him look great. His green eyes are penetrating and force me to look down when I meet them. Samuel feels my confusion, but as a gentleman, dare not make any comment.

— I know a little café nearby that makes delicious coffee. Do you like art? he asks while walking.

— A lot, but I must admit that I do not like coffee, actually.

— I am not surprised. As a good rebel, this could not have been otherwise, Samuel says with a smile. A tea will do. I know the perfect place to enjoy this forbidden tea: we're lucky, it happens to be the same café.

We stop at the café and head to the Museum in the Luxembourg Gardens. We hide our herbal teas under our jackets and we sit in front of a painting to enjoy this famous tea, taking care not to drink too openly.

I really enjoy being in this place in the presence of Samuel. I have a very strong feeling of déja-vu, because Samuel and I make fun of everything, like teenagers, as if we have always known each other. What I feel for Samuel is less strong than for Olivier, but it is much more balanced to me. Everything is spontaneous between us and it is so natural that we later find ourselves at a restaurant on the river boats.

Samuel is a Business consultant. This work fits him like a glove, because when I listen him to talk I feel that he knows what he wants. He works from home and travels to businesses too. He emphasizes the quality of life, just like me. He likes sports and enjoys traveling, just like me again. But what I love most of Samuel is his sensitivity and gentleness. This mesmerizes me. As time passes, we find that we have a lot in common, like art and decoration.

— I would love to see you again, dares Samuel, when he drops me off at home, much later in the evening.

— Me too, I say sincerely.

— Here's my phone number. Call me when you're ready and I'll make dinner for you.

— My pleasure.

Samuel kisses me on both cheeks and I suddenly think with nostalgia of Olivier. I make an incredible effort to stay strong, without really succeeding. I then try to hide my confusion by trying to find my keys in my bag. I turn towards the door when I find them. After closing the door, I start to cry. I am suddenly scared to attach myself to another man than Olivier. I go into my studio and I take my wax and pigments. I let my fingers slide on the canvas, while closing my eyes. I see Samuel and Olivier. I want to go to Samuel but I am afraid of losing Olivier. I forget myself in my painting and do not see time passing. I stop painting in the early hours of the morning, when I am satisfied with the result: on a blue turquoise background, a man and a woman look at each other with love without worrying about the world around them. The painting does not tell me if the man is Samuel or Olivier, but it does not matter, I am too tired to dwell on this detail.

I wake up in the morning with the return of my daughter, after she has spent an evening with one of her friends. As it is

Sunday and the weather is fine, we go for a walk and picnic in the Luxembourg Gardens. Sophie asks me to rent a small boat that she sails on the water basin with a lot of fun. She even does a race with a boy and wins. I watch her with pleasure while thinking, to my surprise, about Samuel. I imagine him coming toward us, while running, and inviting us to have a small ice cream at the booth in the park. Sophie takes me out of my reverie to tell me she wants to eat an ice cream. We are licking our ice cream while walking, when I see Samuel jogging on the other side of the path. Surprised by the synchronicity, I pretend not to have seen him. He comes to me in the most natural way.

— What a surprise, he says, stopping next to us.

— Yes, I say, smiling. Let me introduce you to my daughter Sophie ... Sophie, I want to introduce you to Samuel, I say quickly not to show my emotion.

Samuel knees down to Sophie.

— Tell me if this ice cream is good.

— Oh yes! And before, we were boating and I won.

— Congratulations, Sophie. Tell me, Kiera, would you like to have lunch tomorrow?

— I would love to. I work near Saint Michel. What about meeting at Rue de la Huchette?

— Very good idea ... Does the Greek restaurant on the corner of St. Michel work for you?

— Okay. I can be there at 1pm.

— Perfect for me.

— It was nice meeting you Sophie, Samuel says, holding out his hand. See you tomorrow, Kiera, he says while going back to his jogging.

— Who is he, mom? asks Sophie.

— A friend ...

— Do you like him?

— Yes ...

— Me too!

The next day when I arrive at the restaurant, I try not to have expectations, but I must confess that I am very anxious to see Samuel. I promise myself not to think of Olivier, whatever happens and not to spoil the moment again. Samuel arrives behind me as I arrive at the door.

— Really, it looks like we have the same timing, he says in my ear.

— You could say so, I say cautiously.

— I'm sorry, I did not want to scare you.

— I have trouble with people who come up behind me and whisper in my ear, I say, while trying to stay calm.

— I will remember... Sorry again.

The waiter accompanies us to our table which is located downstairs. We go down a long stone staircase. I hit my head on the arch, unintentionally. The pain is so intense that I faint in Samuel's arms which catch me in time. The surroundings disappear. My head starts to turn very quickly and I end up in the body of Antoine that is a large room, sleeping. Someone just knocks on the door sharply. It is dark. I get up and dress quickly before opening the door. Commissioners come to tell me I am transferred to the Conciergerie. I know very well what that means: people who are imprisoned there will die at the guillotine soon. I do not react to this news, or to the search they impose on me. I am used to it. I hug my daughter telling her to be brave. I hug my sister Elisabeth, while whispering to take care of my children. I leave the room without looking back, surrounded by the gendarmes. We go down a stone staircase and I knock my head on a beam that is a little too low at the bottom of the stairs.

— Have you been hurt? asks a guard with empathy.

— Oh no, I answer calmly. Nothing now can hurt me anymore.

The surroundings disappear and I find myself in the arms of Samuel looking at me panicked.

— Kiera, Kiera?

— What happened? I ask, still in shock.

— You fainted. How do you feel?

— Fine. Don't worry, I say, rubbing my forehead.

— Are you hurt? the waiter asks, worried.

— Oh no, I say calmly. Nothing can ... I suddenly stop realizing that I am repeating the phrase that I have said during my transfer to the Conciergerie.

— Let's sit, Samuel says, giving me his hand very naturally.

We sit down and I return to normal very quickly, thanks to Samuel's jokes.

— In any case, you should have told me you wanted to be in my arms instead of doing this theatrical production.

— You know I like to live dangerously, I say, smiling.

— It is never boring to be around you.

Samuel asks me many questions about Sophie and my life in Montreal. Unfortunately, the clock is ticking and I have to return to work. Samuel invites me to have dinner at his place the day after. I accept without hesitation. He accompanies me to the entrance of the building where I work.

— Don't you want to faint right now, so I can take you in my arms? Samuel says, laughing.

— It is not necessary, I say, while giving him a hug.

Samuel takes the opportunity to give me a passionate kiss. I kiss him back the same way. We look at each other with a smile. I am late, but happy as I have not been in a long time. I run to my office. Along the way, I meet Véronique.

— I bet he kissed you ... she says when she sees me.

— I can't hide anything to you.

— I want to know everything. I just installed your client in your office with a coffee. We have five minutes!

In the evening, I arrive at the doctor Malayan's office. The door is open and I enter. Dr. Malayan is waiting for me in his chair with a big smile.

— Hello Kiera, he says. How are you today?

— I've just had a strange experience today, I say while sitting down. I hit my head and fainted. I then had memories of my past life who have returned spontaneously. Is this normal?

— Yes. You just opened a door on your conscience with our session, and a small thing can reset the process. Often the same event can bring back the memory of a past life like this.

— That's exactly right: I bumped into the beam of a staircase and that's what happened in my other life!

— Have you seen something else around that event in your previous life?

— Before I hit my head, I had to leave my daughter and my sister in law because the gendarmes had to transfer me to the Conciergerie.

— This is the result of what you saw last time. Please lay down and let's begin. Take a deep breath and close your eyes.

I lay down, take a big breath and close my eyes

— Very well, says Dr. Malayan. As you have already had one session before, it will be easier now to get into a deep state of hypnosis. You will see a tunnel of light. I'll count from five to zero. Five... four... three... two... one... zero... deep sleep. Now tell me what you see.

The surroundings disappear, giving way to the same small, dark and sinister cell as last time. In one corner of the room is a camp bed with two mattresses and a little further, a screen that hides the facilities. Closer, on an old wooden table, lies a woman who seems lifeless. Despite my apprehension, I cannot stop my soul from integrating the body of Antoine instantly. I feel like I am dead and yet it hurts between my legs and I feel warm blood running down my thighs. My dress is pushed up to the edge of my buttocks. A man lowers my skirt and my dress with disdain, as if he wanted to hide the evidence of a crime that he is not really proud of anymore. He adjusts his pants and heads toward the front of the room. The other two men who are with him adjust their genitals, laughing heartily. I dare not to move on the table, because I feel dirty and, in this unspeakable act, I lost what was left to me into my life until now: my dignity. I would rather die than hear what they are saying.

— She was good, says the first with a vulgar smile.

— You bet, agrees the second. Can you tell that we just screwed the last queen of France, he continues proudly?

The third one tells them to lower their tone of voice and not to speak harshly.

— Don't tell anyone. You would be guillotined immediately.

The two other ones laugh uproariously.

— We would rather be rewarded! says the first one.

— Especially as everyone says she is a whore, adds the other one.

— If you talk of what just happened, you will see what I am capable of, continues the third one very angry. Do you hear me?

The two other ones stop immediately.

— What's happening? asks the first one surprised. I remind you that was your idea.

— It was a very bad idea, says the third one full of remorse. We touched something sacred.

— You are completely out of your mind, interrupts the first one. You see that she is made the same as other women. I do not need to draw you a picture.

The third one does not know what to say. He knocks the first one down and leaves the room. The second stops the first one who wants to continue the fight.

— Stop, says the second one, handing him a bottle of alcohol he had in his pocket. You know him. This is not the time to tease him. He is so angry that he would kill you without even realizing it.

The first one takes the bottle, opens it and empties it in one gulp. The second one lets him do it; he sits at a small table and prepares his cards.

To the horror and violence of what just happened, follows the silence interrupted by the noise of the cards slapping on the table. I have no strength to move anymore. I look into the void of darkness. Tears run down my cheeks gently. Finally, I get up and go painfully in the dark on my bench, taking care not to make any noise. I do not want to pay attention in fear of their reaction. It is very dark. Only a very small window leaves a small ray of moonlight seeping into the cell and allows me to advance in the dark. I fall down on the bed and roll over. I cannot stop crying and repeating, 'Why me, why me? ".

I hear someone put the key into the lock and turned. The two guards stand up. I stop breathing. The door opens into an unbearable grinding. The sounds seem amplified when I would like to hear nothing. Rosalie enters with a bowl of soup in one hand and a candle in the other one. She stops in terror when she sees the blood on my clothes and my bed. She rushes to my side, pushing the guards.

— What have they done, Madame? My God, how did they dare? Rosalie says, trying to straighten my dress. Do not worry, Madame. I will return with water and towels to clean all that.

Rosalie tries to touch me to reassure me before leaving, but I reject her, scared. She leaves the room with a reproving look at the guards, who drunk do not even notice it. She returns a moment later. She walks very slowly to me, am looking for any movement.

— It's me, Rosalie, she says, stepping forward. Don't be afraid, Madame. I'll just clean all the blood and change your clothes.

I do not resist. Rosalie looks after me with great gentleness and patience. When she is finished, she puts the cover back on me and I fall asleep immediately. Rosalie picks up the laundry and cleans all the blood on the ground and on the table. The first guard has sobered up and comes to her silently. Rosalie did not hear him and startles when she feels his hand on her buttocks. She pushes him away violently.

— What? Did not you have enough with Madame? Rosalie says, outraged. How did you dare? She is the Queen of France!

— She was! Now, she is a citizen like you and me. And be careful if you still say that she was Queen of France. You're taking a big risk big, you know, says the guard while trying to continue to caress her.

— I forbid you to touch me, says Rosalie by pushing firmly away.

— Why do you worry like that, Rosalie? I can tell you that she liked it, he replies, stroking her shoulder. And I'm sure you'd like that too.

— Do not you play this with me or you'll regret it, she says, pushing him violently this time and heading for the door.

— Never talk to anyone about all this! Do you hear me? Asks the guard suddenly aware of the situation. If you say or do anything, we will kill you.

— You can kill me, I do not care, Rosalie replies, eyeing him.

— What would you say if we deal with your family then? He says, taunting her.

Rosalie lowers her head and leaves the room without answering. The key is turned in the door. The guard looks at me, touching his parts with a vulgar look and sits down to play cards with his sidekick.

I wake up in the night and do not dare to move when I remember the horror of what happened. I stay there with no sense of time and space. I see my father suddenly materialize before me.

— Dad, is it you? I say weakly. What are you doing here?

— I have come to help you go beyond what just happened, my father says gently.

— Why did I have to live it, Dad? I ask suddenly subdued and detached.

— All that was needed to burn your karma, Antoine, but especially to open yourself to a new awareness, the consciousness of the soul. You had, alas, to experience this trauma so your soul can see me and take you to your destiny.

— Will I die soon, Dad?

— Yes and I will help you prepare it as best I can. We're running out of time before this will happen.

— They'll guillotine me, is that it?

— Yes, says my father with great affection.

— But if I must die, Dad, how do I still have a destiny?

— There is no death, Antoine. It's just a transition to something else. Knowing this, you will develop a consciousness that will help you achieve your mission in your next life.

— What mission?

— You will discover it when you remember this life in your next life.

I hear a distant voice.

— ... will now count to five. Zero... one... two... three... four... five. You are now wide awake, Kiera.

I open my eyes, still asleep. I remain silent for a while.

— What a wonderful meeting I just had with my father! I feel so much at peace now.

— That was beautiful to hear you... Do you know him in this life?

— No, I don't think so, although, I would love to meet him. He really helped me to accept the rape, you know. That was so awful. I would have preferred never to experience that again.

— You've seen that so you can heal.

— I know. That's what my father told me. I am not saved, you must admit: the guillotine, that rape! There is nothing really nothing worse that can happen to a woman ... except the death of her children, I say sadly.

— Remember your past is not enough to detach from it completely. It must be understood by bringing it back to the present. You have been relieved to see your death, at the first session, because you had nightmares when you were a child, connected to it. There was a logic that liberated you, that gave meaning to an event that did not seem to have one: your nightmare. The rape, if that still touches you in spite of your great experience with your father, must be related to something of your present life it is trying to explain. Do you have an idea?

— I have no memory of being raped in this life.

— This may be something else. Do you know someone you know who could have been raped?

— Not really...

— Do you remember any event around a rape, then?

— Yes, I say, surprised. I remember that I heard my father saying that if I were a victim of a rape, he would kill the guy who did it. My mother replied that he would not help because he would then have to go to jail. And my father said he did not care...

— That's it! You have two fathers in two different lives that are worried about you concerning a rape...

— What does that mean? Was he my father then?

— What do you think?

— I don't feel it. Was he was one of the rapists?

— No. I think he could have learned of it and could not protect you in his previous life, just like your father at that time. It was his way to repair what he could not do in his past life and prove to you he loves you in this life.

At these words, I feel my shoulders lightened from a heavy burden. I feel very grateful to my present father.

— There are many ways to show one's love, Kiera, whispers the doctor Malayan. Being in touch with our past lives allows recognize it in all its forms.

In the street, I feel light and serene. I always thought my father was indifferent to me, and now I learn that he was closer to the needs of my soul than anyone. 'Barnave Barnave Barnave'. This name keeps coming into my mind. What a funny name that the name of Barnave. I must have invented it.

The next evening, I arrive at Samuel's, very late. I had to stay at the office for a client and there was traffic after that. To be forgiven, I stop at a grocery store near Samuel's and buy a bottle of champagne and a bouquet of tropical flowers, my favorite ones. I run to his house and ring the bell while readjusting my hair. Samuel is in his usual good mood. I hand him the bottle and the bouquet, while being careful that he does not see me.

— This is a very masculine way to be forgiven, he says, taking the bottle and the bouquet. You will never cease to amaze me.

— Am I forgiven?

— You won. Come in, he says, while opening the door wide.

I come in very slowly, intimidated by the soft light of the candles and the lovely background music.

— Come in, I won't eat you. Would you like a drink?

— I would love it…

I follow Samuel, amazed by the sophistication of the place where he lives.

— My turn to be surprised! You have very good taste for a man, I say with a smile.

— Thanks, he says, handing me a glass of champagne. I'm glad you like it. So you think that decoration is the prerogative of women?

— So you think that bringing champagne and flowers is the prerogative of men?

— Bravo. You win a point. I love it. It seems that the roles are reversed in our story.

— Oh ... because we have a story?! I laugh.

— A tea, a restaurant and a dinner at my place. Yes, I call it a story. And what about you? What do you call that?

— An adventure ... uh, I mean, the beginning of a great adventure ...

— Phew ... you just barely get out of it. What about coming back to the traditional roles! I think it will be easier for both of us, Samuel says, pushing in my chair.

— Good idea, I answer while sitting down.

— On the menu: a salad with endives, walnuts and apples. Chicken with mustard on a bed of rice and as a dessert, chocolate cake. Is that all right? He asks, while bringing me the first course.

— You could not have chosen better! Tell me, Samuel, where did you get the taste for antiques? I ask, looking at the layout of the table. My father was in the import and export of antique furniture and I always loved going with him to the flea market. Everything you have in your place reminds me of him.

— Really?! My mother took me too to the flea market every Sunday. I will also often go to auctions and that's where I buy most of my furniture. If you're interested, I could take you with me next time.

— I'd love to.

— I wonder if this is not where we met, says Samuel suddenly becoming more serious. I know this is going to seem cliché, but I feel I have always known you since the first time I saw you lying on the grass.

— Really?

— Don't you?

— I do not know, I answer, embarrassed. But I must admit that it's true that I feel very good with you!

Samuel gets up to clear the table. While taking my plate, he touches me and I feel electrified. I close my eyes to better savor the moment and get a very delicious kiss which I reply to gently. Samuel departs quietly with a smile and puts the dishes in the dishwasher. He returns with the next course, which is a delight. Samuel really knows how to behave with me: he is soft, gentle and jovial, everything that I love.

At the end of the meal, Samuel brings the dessert and we sit in the living room. I dare not move. He feels it, puts his hand on my forehead and gently caresses me. I close my eyes to better appreciate the moment. When I am completely relaxed, he kisses me very gently. I am his, I am granted. He takes my hand and walks me to his room. I surrender to his caresses without any resistance and we make love in the same softness. We fall asleep in the arms of one another.

Morning wake up is as good as the night. Samuel takes care of me and brings me breakfast in bed. The plate is beautifully presented and the contents are delicious: freshly squeezed orange juice, toast with maple syrup and fruit, everything complemented by the famous candles of Samuel. We make love again after this delicious meal. I then get into the shower before leaving for work, where I arrive late. Samuel calls me during the day to invite me to go to the opera on the following Saturday night. I accept the invitation with alacrity. I keep on thinking of him and that makes me feel very good to see that I am still able to fall in love again.

I arrive at the Dr Malayan's office.

— My God, says Dr. Malayan, you are radiant, Kiera.

— Thanks, I say, blushing.

— Is it hypnosis or ... love? he asks, giving me a wink.

— Both, I guess!

— It seems that love comes at the right moment, anyway!

— Exactly. Just after I set my relationship with my father ... In fact, I received a name for my father: Barnave. This name keeps ringing in my head when I think of him, but I have no idea who he might be.

— You will have to check and see if it is connected in one way or another to the life of Marie-Antoinette. This could give you confirmation or not of this past life. Now let's see what will happen in today's session.

I lie down and close my eyes without further delay.

— You will visualize a tunnel of light. I go from five to zero. Five ... four ... three ... two ... one ... zero ... deep sleep. You will now return to the time of your death, says Dr. Malayan with a snap.

The setting disappears and I find myself drawn into the mind of Antoine. The executioner shows my head to the crowd screaming "Long live the Republic '. They put my body in a basket, my head between my legs and I follow it, as it is transported in a cart to the cemetery. My body is thrown into a common grave and coated with quick lime. I stand there. The time is gone.

My father is with me, but I do not see him. He tries to take me to the light, but I cannot move. My mind is blank. I am lost. I stand there which seems an eternity, then, without knowing when or how or why, I find myself with my son in his cell. The place is dirty, damp and smelly. My son is curled up on a bench. He is in a semi-conscious state. I sit on his bed. To my surprise, he wakes up and sees me. He just says 'Mama, I'm sorry' crying. I stand beside him and stroke his hair. He goes back to sleep, a smile on his lips.

I stay with him and I remember: when he was taken away from me before I was separated from my daughter; how I collapsed after his departure and spent all my time waiting for the moments when I could see him through a slit in the wall when he was playing in the courtyard; when they dared to tell me at my trial that my son accused me of incest and I did not respond to such an offense. I remember asking myself what they could have done to him in order to extract such charges and remaining silent, walled in my pain, when one of the jurors insisted to know my answer. I remember having replied, indignant. 'If I did not answer is that nature itself refuses to answer such a charge against a mother. I appeal to all those who may be here!"

My son moves in his sleep. I am relieved to have found him and be with him. I thought that death would separate me forever from my children and I am pleased to see that, in the opposite, it gives them back to me.

I think of Charlotte, my darling daughter. This only thought takes me to her instantly. I find myself in the room where I left her. Curiously, Charlotte, who is currently reading, looks up at me. Her look goes through me and a tender smile lights up her sweet face. I approach her and whisper that I love her and will always be there for her. Charlotte, who had started to read again, stops, as if she has heard my words and whispers to herself: 'I love you, Mama'. That touches me deep in my heart to feel that we are still connected in this way.

I think of Charles and come back to him immediately. I feel now that he will die soon and stay close to him to accompany him. The time is gone. He breathes his last breath in my arms and together we join my father who is patiently waiting for us in the light.

The surroundings are disappearing. Dr. Malayan is finishing counting, four .. five ... eyes wide open. I open my eyes.

— How good that was to see my children and my father, I say, soothed.

— Do you recognize them in your present life? asks Dr. Malayan with great empathy.

— Certainly. Charlotte is my daughter Sophie. What is amazing is that we wanted to call her Charlotte in this life. But, during a spirit session we learned I was pregnant — which was impossible to know, because I had just been fertilized apparently — and that I would have a daughter who would be called Sophie.

— And what about your son? Do you have any idea.

— I think he was a child I had with my husband and I lost in a miscarriage. I recognize his energy. I have no idea where he may be today.

I cannot talk because I feel overwhelmed with emotion.

— Do you really think I was Marie-Antoinette? Honestly!

— You have access to her memory in any case. The problem is that we study history at school and it is possible that you have stored this information in your subconscious.

— We studied History but not her personal story and what I discovered is very personal.

— I agree with you and if your personal memory is accessible, it may be because it is personal to you too!

— What do you recommend?

— Do some research on Marie-Antoinette's life! Read all the books you can read. If you were Marie-Antoinette, you may have access to information that you have not studied at school and that you will not find in books ... For example, I've never heard of the rape of Marie-Antoinette. As of today, we still do not know if the son of Marie-Antoinette, Charles, as you call him who was also known as Louis XVII, died in the prison of the temple. There is a controversy about this, as there are some people who claimed to be Louis XVII and that he would have survived his imprisonment. And, you have just discovered that he is dead in his prison! This could be evidence in itself.

— Why do I have access to all this?

— Normally you can access past lives for healing and change. In your case, because this past-life concerns Marie-Antoinette, I imagine that there might be a greater purpose, but I must admit that I have no idea at the moment.

— Do you think I had to recover from the loss of my children?

— It's clear ... But I feel there is something bigger. I'm here to help you find out if you need to.

— Thank you, Doctor Malayan.

— My pleasure, Kiera. Do your research and call me when you are ready to go further or when you feel the need of it.

— Why don't I still see anything on my husband, or Olivier?

— Because you have to deal with major trauma prior having access to this information, as your death, the loss of your children, the rape. I am sure you will know when it is time. That looks like the new man you have met is there to help you in some way.

— It's true that everything moves more quickly since he entered my live.

With this understanding, I feel a great release inside of me as well as a great determination, to know more. I also feel excited to come home and see my daughter. After paying the babysitter, I rush into her room to lie down next to Sophie. I tell her how much I love her, with a whole new understanding: that of the knowledge of your lives after death. Sophie hears me in her sleep, opens her eyes with a smile, puts her arms around my neck and goes back to sleep immediately. I fall asleep looking at her sleeping, happy to have found her again.

The next day, Sophie wakes me up by playing with my hair.

— I like it when you come and sleep with me, Mom.

— Me too, honey. Do you want to ride a pony today?

— Oh yeah, Sophie responds by jumping on the bed.

As I look at Sophie on the pony, I feel a new presence in my relationship with her. Knowing that she was my daughter in my past life, and perhaps in other ones, make me appreciate her even more.

— Mom, Mom, did you see? says Sophie, after the trot.

— Bravo, honey. We will leave soon. Caroline awaits you to sleep over. Did you forget?

— Oh yes. I want to go now, says Sophie by leading her horse off of the track.

I leave Sophie at her friend's and return home to get ready. I jump in the shower and I put on a navy blue satin strapless gown. I put a cashmere shawl over my shoulders, a faux set of diamonds that looks very real with matching ring and earrings. I put my long blond hair up in a bun and a simple line of eyeliner around my eyes to accentuate my blue eyes. A pale beige lipstick and I am done. I look at myself in the mirror, satisfied. Someone knocks at the door. I grab my bag and open the door. Samuel is hiding behind a beautiful bouquet of red roses and a bottle of champagne.

— Thanks, I say, giving him a kiss. Do you have something to be forgiven? I ask with a wink.

— Yes. To find you fabulous, he says, hugging me and kissing me. I want you now.

— I don't think so, I reply as I slowly release myself from his arms. I have to go put those beautiful flowers in water, I continue on my way to the kitchen. He follows me, stroking my buttocks.

— Come on, darling. Don't you think the table looks beautiful?

I put the flowers in water and look at the table, suddenly worried. The images of the rape come back to me suddenly. I try to chase them away. 'Arrête-toi, Arrêtoi, Artoi, Arrête-toi, Arrêtoi, Artoi (stop, stop, stop)' continue to repeat in my mind. I put my hand on the table to avoid falling.

— What's going on? Samuel asks, suddenly worried. Did I say something I shouldn't have?

— No, no. I'll be fine. I would like to go, if you don't mind, I say as I walk toward the door.

— I think you're forgetting something, Kiera.

— What?

— Your shoes. You were leaving barefoot.

— Oh, I say running to my room.

I come back with a pair of black high heels that I put on at the door.

— Is everything there, you think? I ask giving him a kiss, to hide my embarrassment.

— Yes and even more: you are beautiful. I'm sorry I behaved so badly, Kiera.

— It's forgotten, I say, closing the door.

— So how's our little Sophie? asks Samuel to change the subject when we get in the car.

— Fine. She rode a pony today and she loved it. She is good at it, you should see her.

— She is really an adorable little girl. The portrait of her mother!

— You flatter me, honey, I say, smiling.

We climb the steps of the opera together. Samuel gives the tickets at the entrance and we follow the usher who leads us to a private box.

— You are amazing, Samuel. It's wonderful, I say as I lean toward him to give him a kiss.

— A woman like you deserves the best, Samuel says, kissing my hand while looking at me with passion.

I am speechless, my eyes lost in his. The opera begins. I recognize the music of Puccini that I particularly love. I turn to Samuel, kiss him on the cheek and thank him. He looks at me with a smile. I am touched to the depths of my soul, I do not know why. I feel like an incredible déja-vu. Despite the immeasurable happiness that lives inside my entire being, I do not understand why the words "Arrête-toi, Arrêtoi, Artois' (stop) constantly repeat in my mind. I force myself to concentrate on the opera, but I feel torn inside: I want to let myself go in this wonderful relationship with Samuel and enjoy this beautiful opera and still I get the message to stop. I really do not understand what is happening. I am lost. My nightmare returns. An old wheel on the cobblestone. This wheel is attached to nothing. I want to stop the images. I make an incredible effort to focus even more on the opera, in vain. I do not know what to do.

— What is going on? Samuel wonders, certainly sensitive to my change of energy.

— Nothing, I'm fine, I answer with a faint smile.

We finally arrive at intermission.

— Olivier, I do not know what is happening to me, I say very emotional. I must go home.

— I'll take you.

— No, no, I'll take a taxi.

— I will take you home, insists Samuel, taking my hand.

We remain silent in the car. I appreciate that Samuel does not ask me for an explanation, because I do not have any to provide him. In front of my house, I give him a quick kiss.

— I'm sorry, I say getting out of the car.

Samuel does not say anything and waits for me to enter my building before leaving. I fall to the floor and lower my head to my knees and cry. I do not understand what is happening. A man across the hall asks me if I am ok. I answer yes and get up when he leaves. I climb the stairs with difficulty to get to my apartment. I open the door and I fall on my couch, completely confused. I sob without knowing why. I turn on the TV and I turn it off immediately because the noise is unbearable. I am completely panicked inside. I get up and go to the kitchen to escape what is happening inside myself. I see Samuel's flowers and throw them in the sink. I head to the bathroom. I run the shower, undress and stand under the hot water. I stand there for what seems an eternity to me. When the water begins to cool down, I get out and put my on bathrobe, then I lie on my bed. I fall asleep immediately when my head touches the pillow. My nightmare has been repeating all night, but I could not do anything to prevent it: A wheel on the cobblestone. An old wheel. This wheel is attached to nothing. Only a pin seems to push it. Some wooden steps. Feeling cold in the back of the neck. A terrible metallic taste in my mouth. Nothing. Silence. Death. Darkness and a terrible fear of death.

I finally wake up the next morning completely lost and dejected. I do not know what to do. Like a robot, I dial the Doctor Malayan's phone number. To my surprise, he answers.

— I feel like as though I am in two realities simultaneously, I say right away. I don't feel well. I don't know what to do with myself.

— I'll be at my office in less than half an hour.

Chapter 3

Connections

I put on my jeans and a tee-shirt and jump in my car. It is Sunday: Paris is deserted and I get to the doctor Malayan's office on time. I enter his office, relieved and lie down on the armchair without a word.

— Tell me what's going on and start with the beginning.

— I do not even know where the beginning is.

— Close your eyes and take five deep breaths.

— It started when Samuel tried to have sex with me on my kitchen table, I say after five deep breaths. I saw the rape and I panicked. Then there was the opera and it was wonderful. But I kept hearing strange words in my head and that made me leave the opera at intermission.

— What were those words?

— Stop, arrêtoi, artoi, again and again. I do not understand. I love Samuel and the voice tells me to stop.

— Sometimes, what we perceive has a different meaning than what we believe.

— Anyway, I cut him off, I think it will end the relationship, because I must have looked really crazy! I must admit that I scared myself.

— There must be a reference to your past life, continues Dr. Malayan. I have started to read books about Marie-Antoinette. Why don't we look at it together?

— There is no need for me to be hypnotized? I ask, surprised.

— It's Sunday... let's take time to read and do the research we talked about during our last session. There is a book by Stefan Zweig, which is particularly rich in information, Dr Malayan continues, while taking the book in question on his desk. We will go in an orderly manner. We must look for something related to the rape of Marie-Antoinette, the conditions of the detention of her son, his death. Ah, there is also Barnave. So we will start at the end of Marie-Antoinette's life. I will read aloud and you stop me when it's meaningful to you. And Dr. Malayan states: 'The last voyage. At five o'clock in the morning, when Marie-Antoinette was writing '... I cry listening to him.

— Is it too difficult? Do you want me to stop?

— No, no.

— 'She does not see Marie-Antoinette and frightened, she realizes that she is lying on her bed fully clothed […] But the girl is desperate to bring her a soup she made especially for her, Marie-Antoinette finally accepted […] When, at ten o'clock, the executioner Samson, a young man of gigantic size, enters to cut her hair, she quietly lets him tie her hands behind her back without the least resistance […] miserable cart moving slowly on the cobblestone. It takes its time […] Refusing assistance, Marie-Antoinette ascends the stairs.' This seems to correspond to your regression. What do you think?

— I'm beginning to wonder if I did not just read what I told you.

— It's a possibility. That is why we are checking. I'll go through the passage about her son, Charles. The incest scene is well-known and I will not read it again. Although, I want to check what the words that Marie-Antoinette used at trial are, to describe the atrocity of the thing says Dr. Malayan flipping through the book. Ah that's it. 'The president is obliged, despite himself, to question Marie-Antoinette. She proudly looks up suddenly — 'Here, the accused appeared deeply moved' — and responds aloud with an indescribable contempt 'If I did not answer, it is because nature refuses to answer such a charge against a mother. I appeal to all the mothers who may be here '. Dr. Malayan compares these words with those of my regression and says satisfied, that the two match.

— I could have read it!

— Sure. I'll continue, says Dr. Malayan, flipping the pages one by one. Oh, I just found something interesting. 'Long ago she suffered the worst: nothing can be worse than her life in her last months. What lies ahead looks easier: there is only death. She almost rushes to it. She is so eager to get out of this terrible turn populated by memories — perhaps her eyes are dimmed with tears – that she does not think to duck her head and hits her forehead on a beam. Commissioners run to her worried and ask if she got hurt. 'Oh no,' she answered quietly, "nothing can hurt me now'. It quite looks like what you've seen again and you still think you've read it, I'm sure!

— Maybe I say with a weak smile...

— Wait! I have something better. I just found Fersen ...

— Tell me, I want to know!

Dr. Malayan states: 'Since by letter, it is impossible to explain fully, Fersen decides to go to Marie-Antoinette, to rush to Paris, where he is outlawed and where a certain death waits for him if he shows up. "

— I knew that Olivier was capable of such an act. If Olivier was Fersen, I cannot understand why he's acting like he does today.

The doctor Malayan continues: 'Fersen enters: after eight months of cruel separation, unspeakable events – an entire world has transformed — the lover finds the beloved, Fersen is for the last time with Marie-Antoinette. "

I count on my fingers feverishly.

— My God, I say excitedly, it has been eight months since I have seen Olivier. I'm sure that's why I am receiving 'Stop' about Samuel ...

— Kiera, do not jump to conclusions immediately. Let me read on and you decide for yourself.

'Fersen', continues to read Dr. Malayan 'has not been received this evening by the two majesties, as he made the King of Sweden believe, but only by Marie-Antoinette, and – there is no doubt — he spent the night in the apartments of Queen .' [...]

'For anyone who feels with his heart and his senses, who believes in the power of the blood as an eternal law, it is certain, that even if Fersen had not long been the lover of Marie-Antoinette, he would have become so on this last and fatal night, achieved at the cost of the most beautiful human courage. "

— They have been lovers for a long time, obviously!

— How do you know?

— When Carmella took me to the Queen's hamlet, I saw Marie-Antoinette join Fersen in a small pavilion. It was dark and I felt like I was there. I saw everything.

— I remember you have told me this that is true.

— It's weird, because I feel that I must return to Montreal. I have my new visa, you know!

— Before making such a decision, take this book and read it. Go to the library and do further research. This is a decision worth considering, though.

— Fersen risked his life for her, I might as well risk a move.

— It's up to you. Read this book and return to tell me when you are ready.

— Thanks, I say, hugging the doctor Malayan. I feel reborn.

— I did nothing, that was always yours. I just helped you make a good use of it.

I leave the doctor Malayan's office, feeling over the moon. I have to get Sophie at the Luxembourg Gardens in two hours. I decide to go there right away. I find a free chair near a pool and immerse myself in the book that the doctor Malayan has just given me. I read all the passages related to Fersen. I learn that Fersen and Marie-Antoinette met when they were young and that they were often separated by Fersen's travels. Their meetings were always filled with much joy and love. There is no evidence they were lovers, but it is certain that Marie-Antoinette was really in love with him. He helped her escape with her family during the flight to Varennes, but the plans failed and Marie-Antoinette and her family had to return to Paris. Fersen tried to do everything to save her, in vain. He was very affected by her death and died nineteen years later, the same day as the escape to Varennes, in the same way he would have wanted to die for her then: trampled by the crowd. I have tears in my eyes when I read this. Lost in my thoughts, I startled when I hear the voice of Samuel.

— Well! I see that you have become more reasonable. A chair instead of grass. What happens to you, my rebel?

— It's Sunday and there are guards everywhere!

— I tried to call you to hear from you, but you didn't answer.

— I went to see one of my friends and I'm reading until Sophie arrives.

— Do you feel better?

— Yes, thank you. I wanted to apologize for last night. I'm really sorry.

— It doesn't matter. It happens to everyone. I have a question that obsesses me, though: Who is Olivier?

— How do you know that name?

— You called me Olivier last night.

— My God, I'm sorry, I say confused.

— Don't worry, I'll get over it. I just need to know.

— He's a man I deeply loved, I finally say.

— It's rather flattering, then. Do you still love him?

— I don't think so I say in a tone that I feel is very far from being convincing.

— Ok. That was just what I needed to know. I have to go, says Samuel, resuming his jogging.

I feel bad. I want to run after him, but I think of Olivier and all I have just read. I hear Sophie crying 'Mummy, Mummy' while running towards me. I open my arms and she jumps onto me so hard that we fall from the chair laughing.

— So how was your night at Caroline's, honey?

— You'll never guess. We went to bed at 1 am!

— Wow?! And what did you do so late? Did you go out dancing?

— Nope. I am too young, you know that. We watched the Little Mermaid and Cinderella.

— How lucky, I say, walking toward Caroline and her mother.

I run a bath for my daughter, while listening to my messages. I have two messages from Samuel. He wonders how I am doing. I have one message that makes me almost drop the phone in the bath when I recognize the voice.

— I want to apologize, Kiera, for the way I behaved, says Olivier. I keep thinking of you and I miss you so much. Life is not the same without you. Not breathing the same air as you is a real torture for me. I can not live without you. Call me, please. I love you.

I replay the message dozens of times to the point where I forget Sophie's bath which nearly overflowed. I stop it in time and call Sophie who arrives naked and runs into the bathroom splashing everywhere. I sit on the toilet and watch her play. I hear Olivier's words in my head again and again and I can not get enough of it. I can not believe that he contacted me at the same time I read our past story. I am looking for the phrase that Olivier told me over the phone in the book on Marie-Antoinette, because I suddenly realized that I think I read it in Zweig's book. It is amazing. Olivier said in his message: 'Not breathing the same air as you is a real torture for me', and now I read what Fersen wrote to his sister Sophie, 'I am accusing myself of the air I breathe. I pause and suddenly realize that Fersen's sister is called Sophie and my daughter is called Sophie. What a coincidence. Does that mean that Olivier is the man of my life, as Fersen was the one in the life of Marie-Antoinette? Or does that mean that we should let life separate us as happened in the past? I do not know what to think. I remember my meeting today with Samuel. It is obvious that I love him too. And then what? Why do I hear all the time

'Stop, Arrêtoi, Artois'. I do not understand. If I call Olivier, maybe I would understand more. I realize that it is too late to do so because we have a six hour time difference with Montreal. I am forced to wait until tomorrow.

— I am cold, mum, says Sophie standing up in the bathtub.

I take a towel and rub her to warm her up and Sophie puts on her pajamas. We prepare the meal together and have dinner on the small coffee table. I read her a story, She brushes her teeth when I am finished.

— I miss Daddy says Sophie in tears, when she gets into her bed. When will you get back together?

— We won't get back together, honey. You know that Dad has a new girlfriend now, I say, taking her into my arms.

— Yes, but I want him to be your girlfriend... his girlfriend is not really nice to me and she always says bad things about you.

— I know, honey, and I don't understand why since I don't even really know her... you have to sleep now, honey.

— Could you stay with me?

— Of course, I answer while lying down next to her.

— Touch my hair so I can fall asleep, please, Mom.

I caress her hair. She closes her eyes and falls quickly asleep with a smile on her face. I leave the room and go in the fridge to find the chocolate ice cream I eat in the living room, while still continuing to gather as much information as I can about Fersen. I fall asleep on the sofa. I am awakened in the night by the phone. I manage to grab the receiver before the answering machine switches on.

— I am so happy to talk to you. I was afraid you wouldn't call me back, says Olivier.

— I was going to do it but I was waiting the right time to do so, I say still half asleep.

— My flight is in an hour and I will be at Paris Charles de Gaulle at noon. Would you pick me up?

— Of course.

— I gotta go. I can't wait to see you.

He hangs up. I am amazed by what I just heard. I cannot sleep anymore and I prepare a bowl of cereal. I think about everything that has happened since Saturday evening. What a wonderful story. Two days ago, I went to the opera with Samuel thinking I was about to enter a stable relationship with him. Now, in a few hours, I will be with Olivier at the airport to begin a relationship that is more than uncertain. All this is quite disturbing, and I admit not really knowing how to behave. I take a shower to clear my head up and stay a long time in front of my closet before finding the right dress. I choose a pale blue-green suit and a white T-shirt. I put my make-up on with shades of beige and leave my long curly hair loose. I wake up Sophie, to take her to school. She gets ready and the phone rings again. It's Samuel.

— I can't stop thinking of you, Kiera. I would like to spend more time with you and get to know you more. I feel that there is an important part of you that I don't know.

— I would love to Samuel, but I'm pretty busy right now.

— Is this a polite way of saying you're not interested?

— No, Samuel, it is a polite way to tell you that I have to deal with setbacks.

— Is this setback called Olivier, by chance? asks Samuel.

Surprised of Samuel's intuition, I decide to play the honesty card.

— Yes. He's arriving from Montreal to see me. He called me last night to let me know. Nothing planned, as you can see.

— Does that mean I will lose you?

— I think it just means I need to understand certain things to move forward. To tell you the truth, I met Olivier when I was married and it was love at first sight between us. We had to separate to be together. I did, but not him.

— Why do you need to see him, then?

— To clarify some contradictory things that I still do not understand, as I told you. Olivier is arriving at a key moment when I began to forget him because of you.

— He must have felt that and that's why he's coming. He is rather sure of you, this guy, anyway. He snaps his fingers and you come back, despite everything he did to you, despite everything good that comes to you.

I do not know what to say. I know Samuel is putting his finger on something important that I do not want to hear.

— Samuel, I have to go. I'll be late for Sophie's school. I'm sorry. I promise to call you later to keep you posted.

I hang up and leave the apartment in a hurry with Sophie. I drop her just in time and rush to my work. I think back to my conversation with Samuel. Talking to him that frankly made me feel good and much closer to him. I still do not understand why I have the words 'Stop-Arrêtoi, Artoi' in my head when I think of him and that bothers me a lot.

Once at my job I directly go to my boss' office. I ask him if I can take the afternoon off. He tells me that I have a lot of overtime coming and gives me the week off. I thank him and leave his office, very happy to go and see Véronique.

— So, how's it going with the handsome Fersen?

— It's not that simple ... I want to go ahead in the relationship with Samuel but my mind tells me 'Stop-Arrêtoi' all the time when I think of him. In addition, Olivier is coming to see me.

— You're kidding! How come? Véronique asks, incredulously.

— I don't know ... it's a funny coincidence. Yesterday, I checked with Dr. Malayan elements in the life of Marie-Antoinette I had seen in a past-life regression. They corresponded a lot, I must admit. Then we came across information about Fersen, who is Olivier, as you know. I was very upset and I wanted to call him. And now he calls me to tell me he is arriving in Paris at noon today.

— You did not tell him he behaved like a real jerk, the last time you spoke to him, did you?

— Yes. At the same time, I miss him a lot.

— It looks like you do not know to choose the right guy! Véronique says, ironic.

— It was to undo the ties with Olivier that I went to see Dr. Malayan, I remind you. But it seems that life has shown me something else. In addition, Olivier is returning to me the same day I am working on the relationship between Marie-Antoinette and Fersen. It is rather strong as a synchronicity, do not you think?

— It's true. Beware, however, because as Carmella told you, this relationship with Fersen has affected Marie-Antoinette a lot. And I can say that your relationship with Olivier has done the same thing to you so far. I would not like the same thing happens to you again in this present life and breaks down the life you've just rebuilt. We should call Carmella, just to see what she has to tell you, says Véronique while taking the phone.

Véronique tells Carmella everything I just said. She asks to talk to me and advise me to pay attention: according to her, I will be tested and I have to listen to my intuition instead of my passion. Samuel is a good person for me and he will certainly not stay with me it there is anything happening with Olivier. I tell her about what I hear in my head: 'Stop, Arrêtoi, Artoi'. She says that it is there to force me to learn to listen to my intuitions: the same information can be interpreted in different ways, depending on where one is and it is important that I am aware of that.

— But do you know what that means, these words in my head?

— I think you must stop, refocus and know what you really want: that is my interpretation though and I don't want to influence you. This step is critical to you. You have a gift and you have to develop it to go further in your mission. This stage of your life is there to take you there. Follow your intuition.

— How can I do it when everything is so contradictory?

— Listen to your heart, observe the events around you and make your decisions only when you're at peace with yourself: that is the key!

— And how do I know if I make the right choice?

— You'll always make the right choice for you because it is the choice you need to make when you make it. It is exactly what you need at that time. If you choose to go with Olivier, it is because you have something to live and finish with him. If you choose Samuel it is something else that you will live. Know what you want and observe the circumstances around you to see if they confirm that what you want is good for you. In this life, you have to learn to see people the way they are and to recognize if they are good to you. Marie-Antoinette was raised in wealth and that was hard for her to be able to do it.

— Okay...

— You have to be aware that your life is not in danger because of your choice as it was in Marie-Antoinette's time.

— Thanks Carmella.

— One last thing that comes to my mind and that can help you: feel Samuel and Olivier deep in yourself, in your emotions, your feelings. It's your memory with them in your past life that will allow you to identify the right person for you in your present life. Do research, read books on the life of Marie-Antoinette and you will know what is still good for you and what is not anymore.

— Don't worry. you will be fine, says Véronique, after I hang up with Carmella.

— You know it's strange, I imagined all sorts of scenarios to see Olivier and now it's there, I'm not sure you want to see it. He has been so horrible to me. Samuel is right: he calls me that and I immediately go back to him. Don't you think I must be crazy?

— You're not crazy. Just passionate. That's why you should be careful. Call me and tell me how it goes.

— Okay. In fact, I came to ask you to take Sophie with you, if you can. That way I can stay as long as necessary with Olivier and see what is there for us. If you can't, don't worry.

— Of course I can. What time do I need to pick her up?

— 4:30 p.m. Here's the address and the authorization for you to pick her up. Here is her bag with her belongings and the keys in case she needs something at home. I have already told her that you would come to pick her up at school.

— You thought of everything. Leave. I'll look after her so well that she won't want to go home.

I leave the office and go down to get my car. I am surprised to suddenly feel impatient to see Olivier. I arrive on the freeway and find myself stuck in a traffic jam. I feel that I will never arrive on time at the airport. After two hours in slow motion, I arrive just as the plane is landing. I wait for the announcement of Olivier's plane in the arrival hall, while looking at the books to calm down. I come across a book about Marie-Antoinette by Antonia Fraser. I buy it immediately. I sit down and start to read it right away. Lost in my book, I forget about Olivier and I am surprised to feel his presence in front of me. I look up and see him looking at me with a big smile. Without a word, he takes my hand for me to get up. He hugs me and kisses me passionately. Completely bewitched, I kiss him back with the same passion. He takes my hand and we head to my car.

— I am so happy to see you. I missed you so much, says Olivier.

I vacillate between love and fear and I do not know what to say. I am surprised to think of Samuel, while Olivier is busy making conversation.

— I have a hotel next to the Place de la Concorde.

— How long will you stay?

— Four days!

— Why four days, Olivier?

— Because I miss you and I couldn't live without you anymore.

— This is not the answer I was expecting. Why did you call me back, Olivier? I do not understand.

— What about taking advantage of our four days together instead!

— And then what? You're going back to Montreal and we start all over again as before? I'm not that kind of woman, Olivier!

— I came to see if our relationship is solid. If it is, I'll go back to Montreal and I leave Nora. This has been very bad between us lately and it's now or never for me to leave her.

— What did you tell her to be able to come here?

— I needed a change of air.

— I see!

— Have you decided to ruin everything, have not you?

— You did ruin everything!

— Ok. I'm listening. Tell me everything you have in your heart.

— What heart? You've destroyed my heart, Olivier. You have rejected me and I do not know if I love you, actually.

— I can tell you. I know it by the kiss you gave me at the airport. I apologize for everything I have done to you and want us to forget the past. We have four days, just for us. This could change everything for both of us. It's worth trying anyway.

I am torn. Olivier is right: I still love him. And because I know our past life, I do love him more. But I am afraid of the consequences of the choices I have to make. Am I ready?

We arrive at the Crillon Hôtel and Olivier asks me to stop the car.

— You ask yourself too many questions, honey, says Olivier while opening the door. Take this moment and everything will fall into place for the best, I promise.

I leave the car and allow myself be mesmerized by the beauty and luxury of the place. I follow Olivier without any resistance anymore. I am amazed by the hotel and feel totally in my element. I forget all my doubts and decide to live the experience that is offered to me completely. We arrive in the room. He orders champagne, runs a bath, puts bath gel into it and light candles. I am at the height of romance and I am ecstatic. We enter the bathtub with glasses of champagne. We toast to our love and drink while we kiss. We talk, we laugh: we find each other again. We step out of the bath and make love on the beautiful canopy bed in the room. Olivier has certainly left nothing to chance to win me back and that works beautifully. We remain in the room all evening, all day and all night the next day and again all day and all night the day after. We are never tired of each other and cannot stop making love: we only take breaks to eat, talk and sleep. Our souls are in perfect harmony and we enjoy every amazing second that passes. The outside world no longer exists. I know Sophie safe with Véronique and can peacefully devote myself to the happiness of being with the man I have loved for centuries.

I start to feel the first signs of separation on the day before Olivier's departure and we decide to go for a walk not to think about it. We leave the hotel and find ourselves in front of the obelisk at the Place de la Concorde: my heart sinks. I see the guillotine and stop. Olivier pulls me by the hand and we walk into the Tuileries gardens. Everything reminds me of the last moments of my past life. The Tuileries is the last place where Marie-Antoinette saw Fersen. Is it a sign? I feel sick. I just want to go back to the hotel and I lead Olivier in that direction.

— Why don't you change your return date, honey? I don't think I could survive your departure once again.

— I love you so much, Kiera and I just spent the best three days of my life with you. I have something better to offer you. I want to go back to Montreal as soon as possible so that you can come to live with me as quickly as possible.

— Olivier, you couldn't say anything that would make me happier than that, I say while jumping in his arms.

— Give me just enough time to resolve my situation with Nora and find an apartment for us and your daughter. Meanwhile, organize yourself to leave Paris.

— Are you sure? I ask suddenly worried.

— I've never been so sure of myself.

— How long do you think it will take?

— A month. How much time do you need?

— I'm ready now, you know.

— I adore you, he says, hugging and kissing me. I will do my best to make it as soon as possible, I promise. Get ready, that's all.

— And what happens if you change your mind? I still wonder worried.

— I will not change my mind. You are the woman of my life. The one I have always waited for. You do not think I'll change my mind, now that I have found you, he says, kissing me as we arrive in our room.

— That's what you told me the last time we saw each other!

Olivier puts his finger on my lips and kisses me to shut me up. We make love all night and fall asleep each other's arms.

During the night, I dream of Samuel. We are at the opera. I am wearing a beautiful golden silk gown embellished with precious stones. Samuel is with me, very elegant and very attractive. We do not stop laughing. At the end of the opera, we reach the carriage that is waiting for us. We enter climb in and the coach driver advances the horses. In the coach, we continue to laugh. We laugh so much at one time, that our two faces touch. Samuel kisses me and I am mesmerized. I can not say no and return his kiss with passion. I am in a trance in his arms. This is something new for me. His kisses are of a haunting sensuality and I melt in each of his caresses. Eventually he finds an opening between my layered skirts and puts his hand high on my thigh. The heat ignites my whole body. I want him to continue but the coach stops. We quickly readjust ourselves so the maid will not suspect anything. We go to the Temple, where Samuel has an apartments. We get to the table where a sumptuous dinner has been already served. Samuel sends the maids away and takes care to close the doors. He takes my hand and invites me to get up in a very gentle manner. He lays me down on the couch and kisses me with infinite tenderness. I am his. He starts to put his hand on my thigh as he had in the coach. I want his hand to move even higher. I am a burning with desire that I have never known. Everything disappears around us and I give in go to the wonderful sensation of his caresses. I suddenly realize the enormity of what we are doing. I quickly free myself. He looks at me surprised.

— I want, my dear brother, that you forget everything that just happened between us, I say, readjusting myself.

— This will be difficult, my dear sister.

— I want you to promise me you will never tell anyone of what just happened. Promise me, please.

— I promise you, my dear sister.

— Promise me that you will never repeat what we have done.

— Will you be strong enough not to repeat it yourself?

I remain silent.

— You are right, I finally say. We must promise each other never to do it again or even speak about it.

— I promise, he says with a charming smile.

— I promise too. That's perfect, I say, getting up. Let's go now.

I wake up and suddenly realize that I have not called Samuel, as I had promised. I feel terribly bad. Olivier puts his hand on my shoulder and begins to caress me. I put outside my concern and surrender myself to his caresses. We make love slowly and I can't stop the tears running down my cheeks. He wipes them tenderly with his lips. I wish the time stops, but alas, it moves on and we must leave.

— We will soon be together, says Olivier in the car.

— I know, I say deeply moved.

— It will be okay, I promise.

The farewell at the airport is heartbreaking. Olivier finally leaves and I hurry to the car to abandon myself to my sorrow. I sob all the way back which is long time because of traffic jams on the highway. I calm down before arriving at Véronique's in the early evening.

— What happened to you? Véronique says, opening the door and hugging me.

— Olivier left, I say, beginning to cry again.

— How was it?

— Wonderful. He really is the man of my life.

— Why are you crying then? You'll probably see him again soon.

— Yes, I must go to Montreal to live with him in a month. Leaving him, only for a time is really painful. It's always been like that with him.

— I am very happy for you. If being with him is really what you want, it is worth the wait.

— I have to admit, I'm afraid it will not work. I'm afraid of never seeing him again. I think that's why it's so painful for me.

— This may be related to your past life, where you never saw him again!

— Yes, you're right, I say, while calming down. I realized yesterday that the last time we saw each other in our past life was at the Tuileries, and that's where we were reunited in this life. Isn't it crazy?

— It's the magic of reincarnation! You had to begin again something that was not finished. That amazes me to see how things are repeating and continue to evolve at the same time. This time, I really hope it will work for you, because you deserve to be happy, Kiera.

— Thank you, Véronique. In fact, I almost forgot what the most important is in all this. Where is my little sweetie?

— She made friends with the little neighbor girl who is the same age and she is at her place right now.

— Okay, this will give me time to pull myself together.

— I'll make you some tea and you can tell me all the details. Telling Véronique of all happened with Olivier allows me to refocus.

— What about Samuel? Véronique suddenly asks me.

— I love him, but it is not the same as with Olivier. Olivier consumes me and I can't miss the opportunity to be with him. If there was no Olivier, I would be for sure with Samuel. Anyway, Samuel knew I was with Olivier; I was supposed to call him and completely forgot. So I can tell you that I don't think he will want to talk to me now. He must have already understood everything with no need of any explanations!

Sophie arrives and rushes into my arms.

— Mom, mom. I missed you so much.

— Me too, honey, I say, hugging her. I can't wait you tell me everything you have done.

— I have a new friend. Her name is Nicole.

In the car, Sophie tells me all that has happened over the past four days.

After putting Sophie to bed, I make time to relax. I see the light of the answering machine blinking and I listen to my messages. I have two messages from Samuel and one from Olivier. In the first message, Samuel reminds me to call him when I get home. In the second, he says he is disappointed that I did not call him back and he drew the necessary conclusions.

Olivier's message is much lighter and makes me forget the previous ones of Samuel: 'I love you, Kiera and I miss you so much already. I will soon get on the plane and I know you are on the road, but I wanted to tell you how much I enjoyed the time we spent together. I can not wait to pick you up at the airport at Montreal. I'll call you tomorrow during the day. Good night, honey. 'I fall asleep on the couch listening to the message again and again.

Olivier calls me several times during the weekend to reassure me and tell me he spoke to Nora. By mutual agreement, they decided to separate and he began the steps to find an apartment for us. That encourages me to leave my own apartment and my job as soon as possible, which I do on Monday. The same evening, I announce the good news to Sophie, who is very excited by the possibility of being in the same country as her father again.

— When do we leave? Sophie asks. I can't wait.

— In less than a month, honey.

— Where will we live? At dad's house?

— You know that's not possible. But you will be able to see your father as often as you like. We'll live with a good friend of mine.

— Ah, the man we saw the other day at the park?

— No, someone I like even better.

— Is he nice?

— Of course, darling. He loves you a lot.

— So I'm sure I'll love him too.

The phone rings.

— I thought you would take at least five minutes to call me, says Samuel in a reproachful tone.

— I'm sorry, Samuel. I was very busy.

— Really? What's going on?

— I'm going to Montreal, I say, trying not to show my excitement too much.

Samuel takes a few seconds before answering.

— You could have called me to let me know!

— I'm sorry. I thought you would want to talk to me again and this just happened actually.

— Why are you going there? Olivier? Samuel asks calmly.

— No, it's work.

— Oh, what kind of work?

— Mom, mom, Sophie screams as she drops two eggs on the floor.

— Sophie needs me. We need to fix dinner. I'll call you as soon as I will make her to bed, I say, hanging up, relieved by the excuse that life just gave me to do so.

I clean up the mess, we eat crêpes, and Sophie goes to bed. I call Samuel back.

— You are going to be with Olivier, aren't you?

— Yes, I say surprised by my answer.

— You know, I would have come with you. I imagine that was not meant to be for both of us. Good luck, Kiera, he says, hanging up quickly not to show his suffering.

I try to call him back several times, but he does not answer. I leave him a message and I ask him to forgive me. I explain that if there were no Olivier, I would have been with him. I end the message by wishing him much happiness.

Chapter 4

Transformation

Sophie and I are in the plane and we draw our new life on sheets of paper. I leave my life behind me once again with no regrets. I am happy as I have ever been at the opportunity of being with Olivier.

When Sophie sees her father in the crowd of the airport, she rushes to him, excitedly. He opens his arms with a big smile. I find their reunion very moving: for a moment I feel as though I have stepped into my past. I did not think it would be so painful. Philippe sees my confusion and asks me if I want him to drop me somewhere. I thank him and go grab a cab.

I cannot wait to arrive at my new home and be with Olivier. I get out of the taxi in front of a beautiful house in Westmount, on Victoria Street. Olivier is waiting for me at the top of the stairs and rushes to kiss me. After paying the taxi driver and taking my luggage, we go up the stairs both emotional. I feel like living a dream while being awake. We enter the place. Olivier drops the luggage and gives me a tour of our apartment. I am amazed by the magnificence of it. The rooms are large and tastefully decorated with high ceilings and moldings in every room. Olivier has thought of everything to please me, even a fully equipped studio for me to paint.

— Do you like it? Olivier asks while looking at me.

— It's a thousand times better than anything I could have ever imagined.

— Come and see our room now. I hope you will love it because I want to spend a lot of time with you there, he says, taking my hand.

The room is decorated in shades of blue-green and brown. The bed is huge with cushions everywhere. The candles and the fire in the fireplace give the room an air of historical romance. I am transported to another time, outside time, where time does not matter.

— What about trying the bed, he says, rushing toward me and opening his arms to me.

I jump into them and we roll over the bed while kissing with passion. He undresses me with infinite tenderness. I surrender to his caresses and we make love more intensely than ever. We fall asleep in each others arms.

We are awakened at night by the doorbell. Olivier decides to ignore it and gives me a kiss but the doorbell is ringing with even greater insistence. We look at the clock: it is three o'clock in the morning.

— Who can it be at this hour? Olivier says, putting on his bathrobe.

He leaves the room and I hear the door open.

— Bastard, you lied to me! I want to see this whore, says a female voice.

— Calm down. I'm alone.

— Liar. Move over! I want to see for myself. I know she's there.

— Stop it. This is my place here.

— No. We still are not officially separated.

— You are losing your mind, Nora.

— Here is her luggage. I could have sworn it.

— Stop, you're hurting yourself for nothing.

I hear a slap on a face and steps in the hallway. Before I can do anything, Nora is in front of me. I pull the covers up to my neck.

— You're a whore and I'll kill you, she says, pulling a gun from her bag. Olivier's mine and you won't take him away from me.

— Leave the room immediately, or I call the police, says Olivier, who has not seen her waving her gun at me.

Olivier stops horrified when he sees the gun. He throws himself on Nora. A shot erupts and the bullet goes directly into the ceiling. Nora suddenly realizes what she has done and gives up any resistance. I take the phone to call the police but Olivier motions at me not to do anything. Nora begins to cry uncontrollably and Olivier takes her in his arms to calm her down, after removing the weapon from her hands.

I feel sick and go in the bathroom to throw up in the toilet bowl. I then sit down. Under the shock of what just happened, my body starts to shake violently. The cold of tiles invades my body. I feel like I am going to die here. My nightmare returns. A wheel on the cobblestone. An old wheel. This wheel is attached to nothing. Only a pin seems to push it. Some wooden steps. A frisson in the back of my neck. A terrible metallic taste in my mouth. Darkness. Silence. Death. I am afraid of death. An old wheel on the cobblestone...

To stop it, I decide to face my fear of Nora and return to the bedroom. There is no one. A deathly silence reigns in the house. I call to Olivier while going from one room to another. No response. I call on his cell phone. It does not answer. I do not dare to stay in the room, still traumatized by the scene that just took place. I go into the living room, where I anxiously wait for Olivier to return. I do not know what to think. I am lost. The nightmare is trying to return, but I put on some music, I light candles and I burn incense to not let myself being overwhelmed I succeed more or less, but I am panicked, deep inside myself. The slightest noise makes me jump. The sun begins to rise and Olivier is still not back. I am afraid something happened to him. What about, if, in a fit of madness, she killed him? She was capable of killing me. I do not know what to do with me. Panic orders me to leave, never to return, but reason advises me to stay there and wait for Olivier. I continue to try to call him regularly, but he still does not respond. The seconds seem to become minutes: minutes, hours; hours, days. I can not stand it anymore. I am about to call the police when the entrance door opens and closes. I rush to it. Olivier stands before me, his face impassive.

— You've ruined everything, Kiera. How could you do this to me? What were you afraid of?

— What are you talking about?

— She knows everything about us, in every detail. And she can only know it if you spoke to her.

— I never told her anything. I even never saw her until last night. How can you imagine that?

— I didn't imagine that. I saw your French phone number on our home phone. I saw with my own eyes.

— Why would I do this, I am asking you? You were with me!

— You were perhaps afraid that I wouldn't leave her. How did she know that you arrived last night?

— I have no idea. She must have tapped the phone. She tried to kill me! She is quite capable of tapping your phone, right?

— I can't stay in these conditions, Kiera. I no longer trust you.

— You will not do this to me, again Olivier? I am telling you that I am innocent. I haven't done anything

— You have ruined everything ...

— I did not, Olivier, on the contrary: I left everything to be with you.

— I am leaving you this apartment, so you decide what you want to do with it.

I am so stunned by everything that is happening; I do not know what to say.

— You have a real problem, Kiera. You need to see a doctor, he says while leaving the apartment.

I collapse on the floor and cannot stop crying. My life has stopped. The pain is so strong. I do not understand what I did to deserve such a punishment. I can no longer get up and I stay there. Hours, days, weeks, months, years? I have no idea! I lose track of time and space. I fall into an abyss of an intense suffering that I have never felt before. My nightmare even feels a greater comfort than what just hit me without warning.

I was the happiest woman in the world and I find myself the most unhappy woman in the world in one night. Even if I try, I do not understand the meaning of my life.

How can someone tell someone else how much one is loved one moment and deny it the next moment? How can this person make the other lives the most beautiful awaken dream and make it sink into the most terrible nightmares, then? How can one judge the other one without hard evidence and condemned to certain death without even giving the other one the chance to defend oneself? While I cannot find any answers to my questions, a feeling of déjà-vu overwhelms me so hard that I suddenly get out of my torpor in an instant.

What if that were true? What if I were the reincarnation of Marie-Antoinette? Was not she accused of the worst evils, while she was innocent? Did not she have an extraordinary life, followed by the worst downward spiral that can exist? I finally find a semblance of hope again. I go to the entrance of the apartment and look into my luggage to find all the Marie-Antoinette's books I bought in France: 'Marie-Antoinette, The Journey' by Antonia Fraser, 'Marie-Antoinette, L'Insoumise' by Simone Bertière and 'The Fatal Friendship' by Stanley Loomis.

I read the three books without stopping. Even if I am looking for answers to my questions, I can't find any: everything confirms that Fersen and Marie-Antoinette loved each other and he did anything possible to try to save her.

The answer must be elsewhere then. And if the answer was about Nora? I am looking in the books for a woman around Fersen. I finally find one, whose name was Eleanor Sullivan. This could be Nora: Elea-nor/Nora, it is pretty close. It is a bit too simplistic, however, and I continue my research.

Fersen had an intimate relationship with this woman while he was with Marie-Antoinette. Eleanor was not aware of his relationship with Marie-Antoinette as Marie-Antoinette was not aware of his relationship with Eleanor. Fersen seemed to love them both. I conclude, thanks to what I read, that Eleanor must have realized at Marie-Antoinette's death the real and profound attachment that she shared with Fersen.

In our present life, Olivier's heart still balances between us, obviously. Although, this time, I understand that he manages to save me in his way: he made me leave Paris for the New France, Quebec, which has the emblem of the royalty with the lily flowers on its flag. Olivier was maybe not meant to be in my life, but to save me like he wanted to do in his past life, making me leave France. As for Eleanor, I suppose he shows that he stayed with her for her in her past life because he is still with her even though I am still alive in our present life.

This is not the outcome that I have ever wanted for myself, but I feel soothed. Understanding the most probable unconscious motivation of Olivier amazes me and I can only feel privileged to see how perfectly the events are linked from one life to another, to know things beyond appearances and accept them whatever the circumstances and consequences are. With this understanding I suddenly realize the fatigue I accumulated all that time without sleeping and fall asleep immediately.

I wake up suddenly at night, totally excited by what I just realized. I was so absorbed in trying to figure out my relationship with Olivier, that I did not pay attention to a name that came up regularly in the three books I read: 'Artois'. After meeting with Samuel my mind did not say 'Artoi' (Stop) but 'Artois'!

I turn on the light and search this name and I find that Artois was Marie-Antoinette's brother-in-law and that they were very close to each other. They even acted plays when they were young. They went to the opera together. When I read this passage, I stop. I realize that everything has deteriorated with Samuel after we went to the opera together. It reminds me of the dream I had in Paris, where Samuel and I had flirted a bit in his apartment during our past life. I continue my reading, a little more to learn: the friendship of Marie-Antoinette and the Comte d'Artois was frowned upon by those around them and earned her the contempt of her entourage and the people. This dissipated friendship corresponded to the period when Marie-Antoinette was drawn to the balls and was going out all night without her husband. This behavior was unworthy of a queen. It was rumored then that Marie-Antoinette and the Comte d'Artois had an affair; Marie-Antoinette should have discontinued her relationship but she did not do it in time. This is why I couldn't distinguish between 'Stop', and 'Artois'. I rush to the phone and call Samuel right away. Surprised that he answers at the first ring, I hesitate for a moment.

— Allo, allo? he says. Who is calling?

— This is Kiera.

Samuel does not respond.

— I was wrong, Samuel. I'm sorry.

— What do you mean?

— I made the wrong choice. I should have chosen you.

— And you think this will be enough to make me run back to you? I thought about it a lot since then, you know. I had plenty of time for that, actually. I realized that since we've known each other, it's been only trouble.

— I know, I'm sorry. I did not anticipate that Olivier would come back!

— It started before Olivier actually. That's started when we went to the opera.

I remain silent.

— I would have given anything to be with you, Kiera. But now this is too late.

— I understand, I say disappointed.

We remain silent for a long time and Samuel finally hangs up. I collapse on the living room rug. Will I ever get out of this abyss? I feel that everything is taking me there all the time. And each time, I think I could escape, I plunge back even further. I am totally desperate.

I remain a long moment not knowing what to do. I finally get up and head to my studio. I choose a large white canvas 48 by 72 inches. I open my tubes and I let myself go. The time doesn't exist. I do one painting, two paintings, three paintings. I cannot stop. I happen to go through all the emotions: sadness, joy, anger, love, peace...

Painting has allowed me to find myself, to heal the wounds of my present life and my past lives and especially to find fulfillment. I have never been this far in my art and I find immeasurable happiness that I never expected. I am in front of my last painting, a woman in lotus in front of the ocean, when I hear footsteps in the apartment. Traumatized by the incident with Nora, I do not dare to move.

— It's me, Olivier shouts in the hallway.

I do not answer. I hear his footsteps coming to my studio. Olivier stops in the doorway and sees my paintings. He is full of admiration.

— You are really talented, Kiera. It's beautiful.

I do not say anything, still on the defensive.

— You are very thin, Kiera, Olivier suddenly realizes, looking at me. You have to eat. The fridge is full. I had filled it for us...

I still remain silent.

— I am really sorry for what happened and I want to help you if I can.

— I don't need your help, Olivier. You've hurt me enough.

— You did destroy everything by calling Nora and by telling our story…

— How many times do I have to tell you I didn't do it? Can't you see that she manipulates you.

It is Olivier's turn not to answer.

— In any case, she is strong: you went back to her, I finally say.

— Look, it's not about being back with her or not. I was totally committed to you, Kiera, and you blew it off. I have proof and you can not make me change my mind.

— I want to see the proof.

— That will not help. My mind is already made up. Anyway, I have not come for that.

— Really? And what did you come for? As you see, I'm doing pretty well without you.

— I want to set the story strait with this apartment. The lease is in my name, and I can change it to yours if you want. I can give you the cash for the rent for a few months while you find a job.

Surprised, I do not know what to say.

— Are three months enough for you? Olivier continues, handing me a wad of cash. I'll leave the furniture, of course. Although I would understand if you want to live in another apartment.

— I see you've thought of everything. Did Nora arrange everything you had to say in this meeting? I say, trying to contain my anger.

— No, but she wants me to kick you out and I am trying to find a compromise, that's all.

— I agree on one condition: you give me back the keys of the apartment immediately and you leave right away. By the way: you can keep your money, I am not for sale. I just want you out of my life. Now! I say, showing him the door.

Olivier leaves the room in silence after putting the keys on my desk. I hear his footsteps along the hallway and him closing the door.

To my surprise, I feel liberated. I take a shower, get dressed up and go out to get some fresh air. This is the first time since my return to Montreal I go outside. The sun almost blinds my eyes. I walk in the streets of Westmount.

— Kiera? What are you doing here? a voice calls from behind me. I thought you were in France.

I turn around. It's Selma.

— I have been back for some time already.

— Really?

— It's a long story, I say sadly.

— What about having dinner at my place tonight. It would do good on you, I think, she says, looking me up-down.

The evening is very pleasant with Selma and her husband. Selma makes me an offer to write articles on emerging artists for her magazine. She asks me to come and bring some of my paintings, so she can display them at her office and see if, from there, she can put me in touch with a gallery.

The next day, I begin research for my first article. I go to the library to see what style I will write about and I meet with two artists most closely corresponding to the post-Impressionist style that I chose to write about. The writing of the article is merely a formality.

A few days later, I show the finished article to Selma, who approves it, and it is sent to press for publication two months later. As life never does things by halves, Selma is equally enthusiastic with my paintings and exhibits them in her office. With this new visibility, customers call me regularly to buy me one.

At the same time I re-enroll at university to complete my studies in Fine Arts. This gives me more hard work and helps me in my grief about Olivier. Over time, I finish by being grateful for what he did and the direction my life has taken since then. I catch myself sometimes thinking about rebuilding my life with someone and let this new reality grow in me, slowly, without expectations.

When Sophie comes back home after her holidays with her father and his wife, she is amazed by her room and her private bathroom.

— Come on, we'll put away your stuff in closets, I say, opening the door, surprised to find beautiful clothes that I never purchased.

Sophie looks at the dresses as if she were in front of Ali Baba's cave. She takes them and tries them on one after the other.

— Who bought these dresses, mummy?

— It's the friend who was supposed to live with us!

— Where is he?

— He went far away and won't come back.

— Hey Mom, are we going to have a new dad with us one day? I have two moms now, and I would also love to have two dads.

I remain silent for a moment and then I take the opportunity to tell Sophie her story concerning her birth.

— In fact, you already have two dads...

— Where is my other dad, then. Is it the man who bought the clothes?

— No, this is someone else. His name is Thomas.

— Is this the man who took us to the pool where we saw the whale, when I was a baby?

— Yes, I say, surprised at her memory — I completely forgot that, at Thomas' insistence, I allowed him to see Sophie before we left Paris to go to Montreal. Sophie was just over one year old then and I never imagined she would remember this meeting.

— If he's my dad, why can't I see him?

I tell her the entire story and Sophie listens without saying a word.

— You know mom, I think I have always known what you are saying. I remember everything. I also remember that before I was born, I was someone else and I know who I was you know! My name was Charlotte, but you called me Mousseline. And back then, you were still my mom.

I look at her, stunned. Sophie continues not realizing what it does to me.

— There was another girl with me and I always was with her. She looked like my twin sister, but she was not. She was always dressed like me. I loved her a lot. Then one day, I don't know what happened. She was no longer with me. I was older. There were plenty of people who were mean to you and my other dad. We had to leave the castle. I liked the new one less. It was sad. We had less furniture and there were less people around us. I also had a little brother with whom I got along very well, but it was not the same as with my friend. We moved again and that was even less beautiful. Dad was no longer with us and Charles, my little brother had been kidnapped by police at a time, I do not know why. You were very sad and you cried all the time. The police came looking for you, too, one day I was left alone with my aunt. I was so sad and bored. After that, I do not remember.

I can't hold back my tears. Sophie looks at me, surprised.

— I don't want you crying like before, Mom. When my other dad was gone, you cried all the time like that and I felt very alone.

I hug Sophie.

— I love you, Mom, says Sophie snuggling against my chest.

While Sophie is playing in games at the park, I compare the information she gave me with all that I can find for Marie Therese Charlotte, the daughter of Marie-Antoinette, and realize that everything is consistent: Marie-Antoinette raised her daughter up with the child of one of her servants until the Revolution; she wanted to teach her humility and compassion for others.

After dropping Sophie at her father's and coming back home, I go to my studio to paint. I take three paintings by 30 inches by 24 and began a triptych. I am not trying to do anything special. I apply the colors just one after the other.

As my last painting is almost finished, I hear the door bell ringing. I open the door. To my surprise, I face a huge bouquet of red roses. I am wondering who could have sent me a bouquet like that and in a second find myself face to face with Samuel.

— Samuel? Is that you? How did you do to find me?

— I went to your office in Paris and I met Véronique.

— Come in, I say with surprise.

— That looks like you lost your temerity!

— Life broke me down!

Samuel doesn't answer. He enters and looks around in admiration. As I pass in front of a mirror, I realize that I have paint on my face, as it happens often when I paint.

— I am so glad to see you, Samuel, but I really need to take a shower, as you can see. I must admit I was not expecting your visit.

— You are beautiful by nature, with all these colors, I must tell you.

— Thanks. Make yourself at home, I say, pointing the living room.

— Take your time, I won't go anywhere.

— You can look around if you want.

— Can I admire your work? If that is as great as what I see on your face, this should be good.

— Of course, it's at the end of the hallway, I say, pointing into the direction of my studio.

In the bathroom, I can see even more the extent of the damage: I have painting everywhere on my face and hair. Much misfortune. In the shower, I am amazed by the synchronicity. I can not wait to be with Samuel again, but the paint is hard to remove. I finally go through it after a time that seems like an eternity. I dry myself and put on a nice wool skirt on and a cream blouse. I do my hair and put some make-up. I choose beige high-heeled shoes and some matching jewelry and voila: the chrysalis has turned into a butterfly.

I go to Samuel who is still in my studio.

— You are especially radiant this evening, Kiera. Paint becomes you!

— Are you kidding? Did you see how I looked? I reply, blushing.

— Yes, but the transformation is startling, Samuel sincerely replies. It was worth the trip. I had forgotten how beautiful you were.

— Thanks.

— I am pleased to see that life did not totally break you down. It would have been a waste.

— When did you arrive in Montreal, anyway? I ask to change the subject.

— This afternoon.

— Why didn't you call me? I would have picked you up at the airport.

— I wanted to surprise you and find a nice restaurant to take you to. I found one very close to your place.

— Which one is it?

— Surprise, I told you! You surprised me tonight. My turn now!

— Do not exaggerate, please. You're going to make me blush again! I say, laughing.

— It's already done. Come on, we're leaving. I won't bother you anymore until we arrive at the restaurant and until you explain your move here to me. All right?

Samuel listens carefully in the car. I decide to play the card of sincerity as I always did with him and tell him what happened with Olivier, deliberately omitting the episode on reincarnation. Samuel stops the car.

— Samuel! I say worried. What happened with Olivier is the best thing that ever happened to me. I realized so much about me, about my life ...

— It's true that you seem completely happy, he says, while getting out of the car to open my door.

— How do you know about the Japanese restaurant? I ask surprised. I don't remember telling you.

— When I learned about your address, I got all the information I needed from your friend Véronique, who is very charming and loves you very much. It made me feel much better to talk to her and hear her version. According to her, that Olivier was a manipulator and hearing it from her opened my eyes. Everything made sense then; I know how you can be naive!

I feel suddenly apprehensive. I hope that Véronique did not tell Samuel about my past life. I don't think so: Samuel would not be with me tonight.

— I want you to tell me how you decided to come to Montreal, I say, when we enter the restaurant, I try to put aside my anxiety.

— I was surprised that you called me to tell me that you would have been with me if Olivier were not in your life and to wish me 'good luck'. I felt your confusion. But I could not call you back, I was too hurt. You rekindled a flame in me I believed extinguished. I took the time to talk with your friend Véronique and think about the situation. Then, a week ago, I stopped thinking and decided to listen to my feelings. I didn't want to miss the opportunity to be with the woman of my life.

I listen to Samuel, tears in my eyes. At the same time I am reassured by his presence, I am completely overwhelmed by his authenticity.

— I beg for your forgiveness for anything I have done to you, Samuel. As soon as I saw you, I immediately loved you. At the same time, I was afraid to attach myself again to someone!

— I understand.

The lights of the restaurant are suddenly brighter and we understand that we must leave. Outside, Samuel takes me in his arms and kisses me. At home, we abandon ourselves to each other for a long night of love, as if we had left each other the day before. We end up falling asleep in each others arms in the early hours of the morning.

We wake up together and we laugh at everything, at nothing, at ourselves, by starting to make love. Still accomplices, we prepare breakfast together.

— You know, Kiera, I would love to do a painting together, says Samuel.

— What a great idea, honey. Do you have an idea of what you would like to paint?

— No, but I would like to do the research with you.

— Do you want to begin now?

— I'd love to.

I take his hand and lead him to the studio. We look in my books to discover what might app appeal Samuel to. He is finally attracted to the Asian art: he wants to paint a green background and three Japanese with encaustic.

With concentration, Samuel first draws the elements he has chosen. Together, we begin to paint.

— You have a real talent, Samuel, I say as we go forward in the painting.

— Thanks. I love it actually.

The smell of encaustic gives the day an ecclesiastical atmosphere and we do not see the time passing. We finish very late at night, once the painting is complete.

— You just have to sign now, I say, presenting him with the brush.

— I want us both to sign.

After his signature, Samuel hands me the brush, looking at me with great intensity. I hold his gaze.

— Kiera, will you marry me? Samuel suddenly says, while dragging along the brush a solitary.

I look at him, totally surprised.

— Yes, I would love to, I say. Oh, Samuel, this ring is really beautiful when he puts it on my finger.

— It will never be as beautiful as you, Samuel says while guiding me into the bedroom.

Samuel slowly undresses me and makes love to me tenderly. We do not even see that we get paint all over the bed. Nothing matters anymore. We care only about the fusion of our two souls.

Philippe brings Sophie back the next morning. When Sophie sees Samuel, she throws her arms around him, to our surprise.

— I knew Samuel was your true friend, mom, she says. Will you stay? she asks him.

— Yes, answers Samuel with a smile.

— We're going to get married, Sophie, and you'll be our little maid of honor.

— I am so happy, Mom. Will I have a pretty dress?

— Yes, the most beautiful dress. You'll pick it out.

The day continues as it has begun: in joy and good humor. As I have to finish a painting for a client, Samuel, still a child at times, takes care of Sophie. I am so happy to see them play together. Occasionally, they come to take my brushes and paint with me: there are endless fit of giggles.

As I put away my brushes, the phone rings.

— It's me!

— I told you never to contact me again, Olivier. Don't you think you have done enough damage?

— Don't hang up, please.

I wait in silence. I try not to feel the old emotion that I know so well when I am in touch with Olivier.

— I have you under my skin, Kiera and I want to be with you.

Samuel arrives in my studio at the same time, Sophie on his heels, stops when he sees my worried face. His eyes ask me if I am fine and I shake my head yes.

— It's too late, Olivier. I no longer trust you. For your information, I have someone else in my life and we're going to get married, I say, while hanging up.

The phone rings again several times and I do not answer.

— How do you feel? Samuel wonders, full of anxiety.

— Very good actually, I say, taking him into my arms. Won't I marry the most wonderful man?

— And won't you have the most wonderful girl as a maid of honor? Sophie adds while putting her little arms around both of us.

Chapter 5

Tests

Excitedly, I come to Samuel with the test in my hand.

— It's positive, honey. I'm pregnant.

Samuel draws me into his arms, overjoyed.

— I have been waiting for this moment for so long, he says, kissing me. After eight years of marriage, it was about time.

— You did plan everything, I remind you. My studies, my exhibitions and then the baby. If it had been up to me, we would have had that baby right away.

— I know, says Samuel. I wanted you just for me and that was worth waiting you, don't you think?

Sophie arrives in our room at the same time.

— Guess what, Sophie? Samuel asks excitedly.

— Mom is pregnant, Sophie says in the most natural way.

— How did you guess? asks Samuel disappointed.

— I don't know. Anyway, I am looking forward a little sister.

— I think it's a boy, you know, sweetie, I say softly.

— Let's say you have one chance to be right, Sophie says, while turning her hair around her fingers.

My pregnancy is progressing normally and I feel perfectly fine. Samuel and Sophie are very attentive and our life continues to flow in perfect harmony.

I feel I am expecting Marie-Antoinette's first son. I do not know why I am certain of that but that delights me.

Meanwhile, things deteriorate between Sophie and her step mother. My pregnancy has exacerbated Philippe's wife's criticism against me and Sophie does not accept it. The tension between them is so bad, that one evening, Sophie comes home in tears and announces us she no longer wants to go back to her father.

— What happened, honey? I ask, puzzled.

— She slapped me, because I tried to defend you. And Dad did not even take my defense. On the contrary, he made fun of me.

— I'll call Dad right away to see what I can do. This has gone on long enough.

I take a deep breath, stroking my belly to reassure me, and head to my studio.

— What is going on with Sophie? I ask, without preamble.

— It doesn't matter ... just a misunderstanding.

— Your wife hit Sophie, I am reminding you. It looks like a little more than a misunderstanding, don't you think?

— You always dramatize everything, Kiera. She did not hit her. She gave her a slap, because Sophie answered her inappropriately. Moreover, Sophie is rather hard to live with Lea.

— Do you know why?

— Because Sophie is jealous.

— No, because your wife says, when you're not there, very nasty things about me, like 'if your mother were to hit by a truck, it wouldn't bother me'. How can you say such things to a child?

— Sophie looks so much like you that Lea is certainly taking her frustration out on her.

— I don't see the correlation. I am surprised you don't say anything, though.

Philippe remains silent.

— But I don't understand why she is so upset with me, I continue. It's insane. I do not know her and I never did anything against her.

— You had Sophie and for her that's enough.

— And you?

— I think the same thing!

— That is why you let her treat your daughter this way, isn't it?

— I thought she was not my daughter. It would be great if you could tell the same version from time to time.

I do not know what to say and it is my turn to remain silent.

— Have you ever put yourself in my place for just one day? Have you ever realized all the harm you did to me? Philippe asks angrily. And you want everything to be forgotten because you are pregnant. That would be too easy!

— That's the reason. You are angry because I am having a baby with Samuel.

— Who knows? Maybe, it's Olivier's child. You still see him, I'm sure.

— You don't know what you're saying, Philippe.

— I believe what I saw and that's enough. Does Samuel know about Sophie? I'm sure he doesn't, otherwise he wouldn't be with you.

— He knows.

— What is wrong with you? Why do you tell everyone that Sophie is not my daughter, but you are glad to get the child support?!

I remain silent. Behind Philippe, I hear that Lea keeps asking him to hang up, which he finally does. I walk over to Sophie's room who is already in bed, but not yet asleep. I sit on her bed.

— I just talked to Daddy. I understand that this is not easy for him.

— His wife does go against us all the time. I love Daddy and I need to see him. But he does not defend me when she says mean things against us. That really hurts me, Sophie says, crying.

— I know, honey ... that's why I was wondering if that might be time for you to be in contact with your other dad, Thomas.

— Never, mom. I don't want it. Thomas is not my dad. Dad is Dad.

— I know. But, Dad is making you pay for something I did and that you are not responsible to. Maybe if you contact Thomas, you'd understand better what is happening and where you come from.

— Mom, I hate Thomas and I don't want to talk to him, Sophie says angrily.

— Okay, as you wish, I finally say, kissing her on the forehead saying Goodnight.

— Mom, I want you to stay with me until I fall asleep.

— Okay, I say, lying down next to her, while stroking her hair, as when she was a child.

When Sophie falls finally asleep, I join Samuel in the living room and tell him about my discussion with Sophie.

— I am not convinced that this is the solution, Kiera. In addition, it's been years that you haven't spoken to him.

— I know. But he always told me he would be there for us, no matter what. I thought of asking him to call Sophie at a time when I know she will answer.

— I think it will affect Sophie too much, honey. It is already difficult for her to have this situation with her father. Your pregnancy is also disturbing her now. Adding her biological father might confuse her more.

— I believe instead that this will give her some answers in relationship to what she is now going through.

— You may be right, I don't know, finally admits Samuel.

The next morning, I call Thomas after leaving my yoga class.

— Hi Thomas, this is Kiera.

— Wow. What a surprise! Is Sophie doing well? Thomas asks, suddenly worried.

— I want to talk to you about her actually. It has been very hard between her stepmother and herself and her relationship with her father has suffered.

— Ah? I didn't know you were divorced and he was remarried.

— And I'm also remarried and pregnant ...

— Congratulations, Thomas says, a lump in his throat. What I can do for Sophie?

— I would like you to call this evening after school. I'm sure if she has contact with you, she can better understand what she is going through with her father.

— No problem, Kiera. What time do you want me to call?

— Tonight at 6 pm for us, that is midnight for you in France. She will be back from school and will be doing her homework. I will arrange to be away from the phone, so she can answer.

— Okay.

— Thanks. By the way, what about you? What have you been?

— I am divorced like you and I lost everything. But I'm doing better now. I have an art therapy center.

— Congratulations!

— Thanks for calling me, Kiera. I look forward to talking to Sophie.

That evening, the first thing Sophie says after hanging up the phone with Thomas is that she hates him. This point of view has the merit of being clear: that allows me to focus the discussion right to the point.

— How can you say that?

— I don't like him, that's it, Sophie says, while crying. Daddy is my dad. He is the one I love. Thomas hasn't done anything for me ... he has never been there for me.

— But that's what Dad wanted. Thomas respected that, but looks forward to meeting you one day.

— I don't want him into my life, Sophie says, putting her head on my lap.

She finally calms down and falls asleep. Samuel takes her in his arms and puts her in her bed. She wakes up and Samuel speaks softly to her to try to open her to other possibilities.

— You know, Sophie, maybe you could keep this door with Thomas open just in case.

— But I don't like Thomas.

— You don't like him, perhaps because your father told you that if you saw Thomas again, he wouldn't want you anymore.

— Maybe, I don't know.

— Your father's not nice to you right now, Sophie. You don't need to do things to please him, when he isn't doing anything to please you.

— You may be right, Samuel, but I don't know.

— Think before you close the door to Thomas, okay honey?

— Okay. Thank you Samuel.

— My pleasure, baby, Samuel says while adjusting Sophie's covers. I know it's not easy for you, but you are lucky to have two dads ... so enjoy, says Samuel, kissing her and getting up.

— Okay, I'll think about it. Samuel, would you please leave the light on?

— Of course, darling. Sleep well.

Early the next morning, Sophie calls Thomas on her own to my great surprise.

— Sophie I'm really happy that you are taking things like that. I've waited for this moment for so long.

— I would prefer if we could exchange e-mails, Sophie suggests. I have trouble with the phone.

— It's a very good idea, Sophie. I will wait for your first message when you are ready.

Sophie and Thomas write to each other at least once a week and even manage to talk over the phone regularly. Over time, they get closer to the point that Sophie asks to go and see Thomas for the next holiday.

When Sophie arrives in France, she calls me from the airport to tell me that everything happens for the best.

— Mom, I love it. It's really beautiful. There was a friend of mine on the plane, there was a buddy of mine and I wasn't bored at all. Thomas was there at the airport. I gave him a hug. He is very nice. Now, we're going to the pool. Tomorrow, we'll see dolphins and whales and the next day, I'll meet his parents. I'm really happy. Thank you, mum, for suggesting that I see him.

— You're welcome, sweetie. I'm happy for you. Enjoy everything in the best way and take lots of pictures. Make yourself beautiful memories.

— Okay, Mom. I'll call you soon.

— I love you.

— Me too, Mom.

Sophie calls me several times, as it becomes more difficult for her to spend time with Thomas.

— Mom, I can't stand him touching me. He is nice, but it seems that I want to hurt him, Sophie confesses.

— Do you know why you do that?

— No ... Perhaps because I feel I am hurting dad being here.

— You are with Thomas today because Dad was not nice to you. Try to talk to Thomas about what you feel, your blockages. You don't know him, after all. That is normal what you are going through. I'd like to talk to Thomas.

— Okay. I love you, Mom.

— Me too, honey, and my heart is with you.

— How is it going? I ask Thomas.

— Fine. Sophie is lovely, even if she has a strong temper... like you, I must say. It's like being with you again fifteen years ago. I admit it's disturbing.

— Don't tell me that. Philippe told me the same thing.

— It's probably because it's true.

— I don't think so. There must have been some truth in fact. You know, I have changed a lot since I've been with Samuel.

— I feel it.

— Sophie has just told me that it was not easy for her and it's hard for her to get close to you.

— Really? She is a good actress because she is very affectionate with me in fact.

— Good. But she said she finds it difficult to accept that you are being affectionate with her. I would like you to try to talk to her about that. You should take your time to get to know each other. After all, it's also new for you than it is for her.

— You're right.

— Thanks again for all you do for her.

— Thank you for having sent her to me. I love having her with me. It is a wonderful gift.

When Sophie returns from France, the first thing she tells me is that she was hard on Thomas during her stay.

— Mom, I feel terrible, but I couldn't help it.

— What did you do? I ask, worried.

— I wanted to do what I wanted all the time. When he said no, I had a melt down.

— Really? And how did he react?

— He always did what I wanted so I didn't cause a problem.

— Why didn't you tell me?

— I don't know.

— Did you appreciate your stay, anyway?

— Yes, but I don't want to see him again. I don't really like him.

— Let the time work for you, darling.

— Mom, dad is my dad and I miss him terribly. I am going to call him to tell him I want to see him.

Sophie goes to her father's on the following weekend. Samuel and I are worried about what will happen, but we have no choice but let things go. We decide to go for a ride on Samuel's motorcycle in the Laurentians so we can think of something else. We spend a lovely day together and we listen to our messages on the answering machine in the evening. Philippe says that he will keep Sophie with him for a week. I find this message a little cavalier, because Philippe did not ask my opinion, but Samuel sees the positive side that Philippe may want to get closer to his daughter again.

Surprised not to receive a call from my daughter in the following days, I try to reach her, in vain. I am shocked when, at the end of the week, I receive a cold message from her, asking me to bring her clothes to her father's, without any comment. I make Samuel listen to the message. He immediately calls Philippe to get an explanation.

— We want to keep her an extra week, that's it, says Philippe.

— But you didn't ask us our opinion, Samuel replies.

— I don't have to. From now on, it works in my own way and you have nothing to say, says Philippe and he hangs up.

— We'll find a solution, don't worry, says Samuel. The important thing is that Sophie is not in the street.

— I'm going to lay down, I say when I feel my belly tightening.

I can't help but expect for the worst from my daughter, even though I know that nothing can happen to her. I am so afraid of never seeing her again. It is an irrational fear, but it is stronger than I am. The old feeling comes back to me: A wheel on the cobblestone. An old wheel. This wheel is attached to nothing. Only a pin seems to push it. Some wooden steps. A frisson in the back of my neck. A terrible metallic taste in my mouth. Nothing. Silence. Death. I am afraid of death. I take a deep breath to stop it. I take one of my books on Marie-Antoinette and seek for an answer. I finally find it: the separation of Marie-Antoinette with her children has always been brutal. Marie-Antoinette lost her first son after a long illness when he was seven. She had not been able to mourn him the way she would have liked to because he died June 1789, just before the storming of the Bastille and beginning of the French Revolution. Four years later, Marie-Antoinette and her family were imprisoned in the Temple, Louis XVI was guillotined on January 1793. In July of that year, her second son, Louis Charles, was kidnapped brutally from his mother, his captors wanted to beat him of his royal privileges. Marie-Antoinette was taken from her daughter the next month, when the revolutionaries came to take her and lock her into the Conciergerie, the prison that she left only to go to her death.

The next day, after informing the school principal, Samuel and I present ourselves at school to find Sophie. When she sees us, she looks around as if to escape, but realizes she can't do it. I see the disappointment in her eyes and I am badly shaken.

— We are leaving and you are coming with us, says Samuel to Sophie.

Sophie reluctantly follows us. In the car, she does not say a word. Samuel is now entering the discussion, once we get home.

— So what happened, so your father did not want you to come back home?

— Nothing, Sophie responds with downcast eyes.

— Something must have happened, Sophie. You know you can trust us!

— Nothing happened. I just wanted to stay another week with them.

— So why didn't you say it in a simple way by calling us?

— I left a message.

— It was very cold, Sophie! Have you ever asked yourself how your mother would feel hearing a message like that?

— I needed my stuff, that was it.

— Your mother has always been there for you. What happened that you treated her so badly?

— Nothing!

— Look. There is only one possibility it is that your father was told that you went to France to see Thomas. Did you tell him?

— No!

— You're lying!

— Calm down please, Samuel, I finally say softly. Look, Sophie. We believe you spoke to your father. It doesn't matter. We just need to know what happened. Then, if you tell us that you prefer to live with him, we will understand.

— I told Dad ... I couldn't help it, admits Sophie crying.

— Don't feel guilty. I always told you the truth and it's normal that you do the same.

— I was close to Dad and I felt so guilty having seen Thomas ...

— I understand, honey.

— I'll call Philippe to tell him that Sophie is with us, says Samuel while leaving the room.

— What happened, Sophie, so that dad didn't want to give you back and convinced you to stay with him?

— He told me that you were not a good mother and it was time for him to handle things.

— Did you believe him?

— Yes.

— Do you still believe him?

— I don't know, Mom.

— You'll stay with us for awhile. If, afterwards you still decide to move in with him, there won't be problem. All right?

— Okay.

Samuel returns, after his call to Philippe, and Sophie leaves the room to watch TV.

— Philippe is furious. He wants to talk to Sophie. I told him it was impossible and she would take two days to think about all of that before making a decision where she wants to live.

The phone rings and I answer automatically. I am surprised to hear Philippe yelling at the other end of the phone.

— I'm tired of this story, Kiera. It's time to stop it. I want to do a paternity test, I'll let you find the DNA lab and take care of the formalities. If Sophie is my daughter, I'll demand the custody. Otherwise, I'll stop paying child support. It is as simple as that. It's time for you assume your mistakes! He says while hanging up.

I suddenly begin to feel sick. My belly makes me suffer terribly. I try to hide the anxiety that grips me and tell Samuel that I need to take a shower. I go to the bathroom and undress, when what worries me comes true: there is blood all over the floor. I scream in fear. Samuel runs to me and sees the blood. He opens the tap and helps me settle down in the shower. He comes out and calls a neighbor to come over to care for Sophie. I let the water run, without reacting. Samuel comes back and helps me get dressed.

We leave the house for the emergencies. In the car, I can't stop crying. Samuel tries to reassure me by telling me that it is perhaps not a miscarriage, but just an insignificant blood loss. At the hospital, the tests continue, I lose a lot of blood before a gynecologist is available to examine me and stop the bleeding. Samuel stays with me all the time and helps me not to despair. Finally, when we go out of the hospital, twenty-four hours later, I am exhausted.

I am very confused by everything that has happened and the loss of all that blood continues to haunt me. Samuel is also badly shaken and we close ourselves off from each other in our suffering, instead of sharing it. The days are a living hell for both of us. I decide to return to therapy to try to save my marriage.

Although I am very depressed, I also take care of the appointments for the paternity test. I don't know if I would have the strength to get through all this because a paternity test is not just for Sophie and me a saliva sample that is taken to obtain a result; it is also the conclusion of a long journey towards truth and freedom from our past.

I finally go and see the therapist, that Selma advised me.

— I really can't understand why the baby has decided not to be born, I say, after explaining my situation and my work on past lives, without talking about the life of Marie-Antoinette.

— I see that this child was your first son in your past life. Much was expected of him, but he died young.

— It's true, I say surprised.

— Your life with your husband gives you the calm and freedom to give love and do what you deeply want in your soul that you could not really live in your past life. The loss of this child has upset your balance, just as it has affected your life over. I will help you to clean everything.

Rose makes me lie down and works around me with energy coming from her hands. I can feel the heat coming out of them. I find myself in an instant in the body of Antoine. We walk, my family, from Notre Dame to St Louis to get to mass. During the journey, the crowd welcomes us with a silence full of hate. So as not to collapse, I look for my son's eyes and finally see him at a balcony plagued by illness which prevents him moving by himself. He was placed there so he could attend the parade in his own way. I give him a discreet wave and he replies with a weak smile. I feel him leaving us more every day and that simple idea consumes me little by little. I would die with him and escape this world that is so hostile to me. I want to shout my love to him and give him the last strength I have left to ease his pain so we can keep him with us longer. I fear his impending death will propel us into an endless abyss, which nothing can get us out from. I try to leave these anxieties in order not to faint in front of everyone and I pray intensely for the salvation of my son, when we arrive in the Church of St. Louis.

Although the crowd was silent as we passed in front of it earlier, the bishop now harangues his followers by denouncing the waste of the court. I try not to let myself be affected by his words, by concentrating more on my prayer. But when he specifically speaks of the construction of my hamlet as a childish imitation of nature and the congregation applauds, I feel attacked in the depth of my being; I would like them to understand that I am not playing a game, but that I am looking to give more authenticity, openness and humanity to a life that is lacking all of them.

Coming back to my son, who is even weaker since the last time I saw him, allows me to recover from these repeated affronts. I am relieved to see he still manages to have fun listening to his tutor's riddles. Seeing a smile on his face ravaged by pain is a real source of happiness for me.

When Louis Joseph sees me, he stretches his arms slightly towards me. I sit on his bed and put my head against his chest. I make a superhuman effort not to let myself be overwhelmed by sadness and enjoy the few moments that life still gives us together. I stroke his hair. While I know that death will be a great comfort to him, I do everything to keep him close to me as long as possible by giving him all the love and attention I can.

Despite my efforts and my presence, my son gives his last breath in my arms several weeks later and I collapse on his bruised little body.

— Kiera, Kiera, says the voice of Rose in the distance.

I remain silent, locked in my suffering.

— Five, four, three, two, one, zero. You now come back in the present moment.

I try to come back, but I can't. The pain inside me is stronger than everything.

— I can't go back, I say weakly.

— Tell me what's stopping you.

— If I let my son go, I will have to relive all those horrible events that took everything away from me, I say, sobbing. I don't have the strength to lose him and all who are dear to me, again. I'd rather die with him right away.

Rose lets me cry without intervening.

— How do you feel? Rose wonders when I open my eyes.

— Peaceful. It's like a big weight on my chest is gone.

— You have associated the death of your child with the loss of all that is dear to you. Unconsciously, you thought that the loss of your child in this life was the announcement of the most horrible disasters like in your past life.

— What about my husband in all that? Why should he live that, too?

— He was very close to you, says Rose, closing her eyes, to concentrate. I see that he was your brother, without being really your brother. You had kind of an adventure together, but that looks like you ended it.

— Yes.

— There is a story of an illegitimate child, too. A rumor about yourself, actually. People even said that the man I am talking about was the father of your son at the time, because of your close relationship. They used the child's death against you. Something broke in you and that's what you need to restore, if you don't want the same mistakes to happen again.

— What can I do to stop this chain of events?

— Try not to react to what happens. We cannot change the way things happen again and again, but you can change the way you respond to it. This is the key.

— Is this going to be enough to keep Samuel and I together?

— I don't know. Although, it is important that you know if that happens that you don't have another child, you will find the one you just lost by chance and you will recognize him later as the son of your past life.

I come back home. Samuel is in the living room working.

— So how was your session? Samuel asks me, without even looking up at me.

I sit by the fireplace and tell him everything that just happened. I tell him about my discoveries concerning him, without giving the names of who we were.

— You know that I am open to everything, Kiera, from the moment it does not concern me. In fact, from now on, I'd appreciate it if you don't talk to me about those things.

— Okay, I say, while getting up not to show my disappointment.

— I must tell you that I sometimes wonder where all this will take us. Your beliefs are far from mine and the more you go there, the more I am away from you. I have to admit that it scares me.

I leave the room without answering and go to bed. I feel alone and abandoned.

The next morning I find a note from Samuel on the kitchen table. 'I need some fresh air. I can no longer manage all this. Your stories of reincarnation and the paternity test bother me at the highest point. I feel that my life is no longer mine. I'll call you later. Samuel'. Under his letter, I find an opened envelope. I take it and see it comes from the laboratory that did the paternity test. I am nervous. I go back fifteen years ago. I read the results: Philippe is not Sophie's father. In a way I am relieved because that confirms my intuition, but at the same time, I fear all that will result from it: Samuel's reaction does not bode well. I slide to the ground.

The nightmare returns: a wheel on the cobblestone. An old wheel. This wheel is attached to nothing. Only a pin seems to push it. Some wooden steps. Cold frisson in the back of the neck. A terrible metallic taste in the mouth. Nothing. Silence. Death. Then it starts again. I cannot stop it. I come back to myself when I feel someone taking the letter from my hands. I open my eyes and see Sophie reading it in silence. She starts to cry. I get up and try to hug her, but she pushes me hard.

— You have ruined my life, Mom. I hate you.

I don't react, because I understand the pain that tears her apart.

— Now, dad will no longer want me. I'm so angry, she says, taking a lamp and throwing it against the wall.

— Sophie, calm down, please.

— I don't want to calm down. You're not even capable of recognizing the right people for you. Dad was right: you're not good for me!

— Enough, Sophie.

— Look, Dad was good and you cheated on him. And even worse, you had me.

— You're the best thing that ever happened to me, Sophie.

— Why couldn't you try to protect me then?

— What do you mean? I ask, surprised.

— Samuel abused me, Mom! Sophie responds with a rage that I have never seen in her.

— Sophie, you're angry and you don't know what you're saying.

— I know very well what I'm saying. How do I know that he has a birthmark on his penis, then?

I remain speechless. I look at Sophie, not knowing what to do. She eyes me, her arms crossed. I try to understand the inconceivable. How is it possible that I have not guessed what was happening under my own roof? I lose my bearings. My whole life is collapsing. I try to take Sophie in my arms again, but she pushes me even harder than last time and I fall down on the floor. She leaves the room and I hear the front door open and close. I stay lying down, completely appalled by what I have just learned. I lose track of time. The nightmare returns stronger than ever: a wheel on the cobblestone. An old wheel. This wheel is attached to nothing. Only a pin seems to push it. Some wooden steps. A cold sensation in the back of my neck. A terrible metallic taste in my mouth. Nothing. Silence. Death. I am afraid of death. I cannot stop it and the nightmare continues to turn in my head. My cell phone rings constantly, but I am so lost in the maze of my subconscious that my body remains motionless. Suddenly I feel very strongly shaken and I hear my name over and over again. I gradually return to consciousness.

— Kiera, Kiera...

When I realize that it is Samuel that is calling my name and shaking me, I completely emerge from my lethargy and jump on him like a fury.

— How dare you, you bastard?

— Kiera, calm down. I just slept over at John's. I needed...

— How dare you touch Sophie. I want you to leave immediately. I never want to see you again, do you hear me, I say, pushing him towards the door.

— What happened to you, Kiera? Did you lose your mind or what?!

— My mind is fine, on the contrary, and I want you to leave immediately, I say, continuing to push him toward the door, as he continues to resist.

— At least I deserve an explanation, don't you think?

— You abused my daughter and I'll never forgive you.

— It's not true, Kiera. She told you that to punish you for the test.

— Really? And how does she know about the birthmark on your penis, can you tell me that?

— I did nothing, I swear, Kiera, Samuel says, very pale. Your daughter just wants to destroy you, as she believes you have destroyed her.

— Get out, Samuel, I say calmly. Now!

Samuel looks at me, completely dumbfounded. I feel weak inside, but determined to be strong outwardly. I see he hesitates. He then leaves the house without a word. I slide on the floor and cannot stop crying, I do not know for how long. I hear the front door open and close, and Sophie stands in front of me.

— Where is Samuel? my daughter asks with disdain.

I do not answer.

— Where is he, Mom?

— He's gone. I kicked him out.

— It hurts, huh? she says angrily. I hope you suffer as much as I do.

I do not know what to say and remain silent, consumed by pain.

— I wanted to go to dad and he didn't want me, she tells me. I'll stay with you and I assure you that you will pay for all the harm you did to us.

— I'm really sorry, Sophie, believe me.

— And you think that's enough to be sorry. Do you even realize what you did to us?!

I do not answer. Sophie continues to pour out her anger on me and I let her do it. I can not react to anything anymore. With Samuel's departure and our own suffering, I want to die. The nightmare is superimposed on the fiery words of my daughter: A wheel on the cobblestone. An old wheel. This wheel is attached to nothing. Only a pin seems to push it. Some wooden steps. A cold sensation in the back of my neck. A terrible metallic taste in my mouth. Nothing. Silence. Death. It is unbearable. I lose all sense of reality and faint. I leave my body and see Sophie stop talking, suddenly aware that she went too far. She shakes me to bring me back, but I find myself drawn into the body of Antoine. I just finished writing my last letter. I lie down on the bed. I stand there, my head and my heart empty. Rosalie enters the cell with a bowl of soup. I change my dress. Men arrive. One man ties my hands behind my back and cuts my hair. We are moving towards the exit. Outside, the cart is waiting for me. The guards open the gate and the people are there, silent. I ride in the tumbrel. We are moving very slowly. I am cold. From the top of a window, the priest gives me the sign of the cross. We arrive in front of the guillotine and the executioner helps me down from the cart. I climb the few steps of the scaffold. We settle on the board. I see the basket on the ground. I hear a loud noise. I feel the cold on my neck. A horrible metallic taste floods my mouth. I cannot breathe. Nothing. Silence. Death. I remain there, prostrate, over my body.

— Mom, Mom, please, Sophie says, shaking my body. I didn't mean what I said. Mom, mom, she continues.

I finally come back to my body. I open my eyes painfully. Sophie takes me in her arms and starts crying.

— Sorry, Mom.

— I am so sorry, Sophie.

— Mom, I have to tell you something.

At the same time, the doorbell rings. I look at my watch.

— Oh, damn. It's the customer who's supposed to pick up her triptych, I say, getting up hastily. I completely forgot. Sophie, will you take her to my studio while I get ready.

I go to the bathroom to refresh my makeup, put on another dress and go to my studio. My client, Annie, is there waiting for me. As soon as I see her, I see her previous life: she was Indian and her entire family was wiped out under her eyes. I sit, trying not to show my confusion. She looks at the triptych, dumbfounded.

— It's beautiful, Kiera. That's exactly what I wanted.

— I'm happy you like it.

— Are you all right? she asks me suddenly, a concerned look on her face.

— Yes, of course. I have a question for you though. Do you believe in past lives?

— Not really, why?

— Because I saw your previous life as soon as I saw you.

— And what does that say? Annie asks, curiously.

— That you were Indian and that your family was killed in front of your eyes. You had five children then. Two girls and three boys.

— That's exactly what I would have, says the woman very moved.

— You were left for dead, but you survived. You died shortly afterwards as a result of your injuries, however. Gangrene apparently infected your left arm.

Annie rolls up her sleeve and shows me the birthmark that covers her whole forearm.

— What does it mean? she asks, worried. I don't understand.

— What would you say to yourself if you had lost your five children, suddenly?

— I think I would have suffered so much having lost them I would be unable to have other children. Oh my God. Is that why I can't have children, then?

— That is possible.

Annie remains silent for a long time.

— What can I do to have children now that I know that?

— It's going to happen naturally and I would not be surprised to see you pregnant soon.

— Thank you, Kiera.

— It's my pleasure.

When Annie leaves the apartment, my pain comes back to me in force. I lie on the couch and think about what Sophie has told me: I sink further into the abyss that I thought I had escaped. Sophie asks me if I need something. I answer weakly that I will be all right; I just need time to get over all that has happened.

— Mom, I really want to talk to you.

— Later, honey, I say, closing my eyes. Sorry.

I would like to be there for my daughter, but I cannot. The pain inside myself is stronger than anything. I later try to find answers to my misfortune in books about Marie-Antoinette. I realize then that I am the same age as Marie-Antoinette, thirty-seven, when she died. Everything fell apart in my life on October 16th, the same day as the date of her death. This gives me a glimmer of hope for my own life. If I was indeed Marie-Antoinette and I experienced so much trauma on the anniversary of her death, things in my life should calm down now. I barely come to an understanding of these ideas, when my daughter enters the room, in a bad mood.

— Why are you still reading this story about Marie-Antoinette, Sophie says pushing a lock of hair behind her ear. Don't you have enough, she says, taking the book from my hands and throwing it across the room. You see, however, it does not work; we have that problem because of that!

— I'm sorry ... I say.

— It's not true. You don't care about anything, Sophie replies angrily. You don't even take care of me anymore. There is nothing else beside yourself and your pain. But you aren't the only one in pain, I hurt too.

— Talk to me in a different tone, will you? I say getting up.

— I will speak in a different tone and I'll come home when you have decided to stop reading these stories about Marie-Antoinette, says Sophie leaving the room.

I hear Sophie leave. I run after her in the street, but she has already disappeared. I go back home. I do not know what to do. An inner dialogue starts in me.

— I want to die. I can't take this anymore!

— I cannot believe no one is interested in my cause, and they will leave me like this. I will die alone and without being rescued, says Marie-Antoinette in echo.

— I feel so trapped in my situation I do not know from where to take it. I do not know what to do. I want to die. I'm at the end of it.

— We should have left before. Now that I am in this cell, I do not see how it will be possible to get out.

— Should I leave? Should I stay?

— All is lost. That almost worked out. My God, we were so close to the exit and I am back to the starting point.

— I am sick of my suffering. I do not see how I can get out.

— At my trial, I am sure that everything was decided in advance.

The phone rings and gets me out of the vicious circle I am in. I run, thinking that it is Sophie. It is Selma. When she hears me crying over the phone, she says that she will be at my place very soon. She is with me several minutes later. I tell her everything that just happened and that I don't feel strong enough to pull myself away from it.

— You will get out of it and I will help you. Let's go look for Sophie, offers Selma.

— I think we should start with Westmount then go downtown, I say taking my jacket on the back of the chair.

— You're right ... Selma says in a hurry to leave.

I close the door behind us, after leaving a note for Sophie on the table.

We walk on Sherbrooke street at a rapid pace, then take the car and go to St. Catherine street in Montreal. We stop every vagabond that we meet to see if Sophie could be among them. Most are so drunk or on drugs they do not even react to our presence.

— Maybe we should go to Saint-Denis street, Selma offers.

— That's a good idea. She is always around that area with her friends.

We cannot find Sophie. I can hardly hold back my tears and Selma can clearly see it.

— We won't go home until we've found her, says Selma to reassure me.

Selma drives fast, too quickly, to Saint-Denis street. I don't dare say anything and cling to my seat. We park the car and go back and forth on the street, in vain. It is late, now. Three hours have passed since we left the house.

— Perhaps Sophie has gone home in the meantime, I say exhausted.

— We have already called several times and nobody answered, says Selma.

— I can't stand it anymore, Selma. It is not worth it. She may have gone to a friend's. Let's go home. It is almost morning. If she's not at home, we'll start the search again tomorrow.

We return to the car, without a word, and Selma drives slower this time. On the way home, we continue to inspect the streets to see if Sophie could be somewhere.

— Thanks Selma, I say, when we arrive in front of my apartment.

— I can stay with you if you want me to.

— I'll be ok. Thank you again, Selma, I say getting out of the car.

At home, I head for Sophie's bedroom, hoping to find her. The room is empty. I find the energy to brush my teeth and put my on nightgown. I slip in my bed where I am surprised to see my daughter asleep in the middle of my bed. I am so relieved that I start to cry with joy, hugging her. Sophie, startled by the touch of my skin, goes back to sleep immediately. I finally loosen my grip to watch her sleep, wait and fall asleep with her, reassured and determined to get my life completely back under control.

While I am preparing breakfast, Sophie enters the kitchen and puts her arms around me.

— I'm sorry for what I said last night, mom, she says, while pushing a lock of hair behind her ear.

I hug her back, tears in my eyes.

— It's already forgiven, honey. Do you want toast with your eggs?

— No thanks. I'm already late for school. Will you take me, Mom? Sophie pleads.

— Okay, I tell her while getting up to follow her.

In the car, Sophie suddenly says:

— Mom, I'm sorry for what I said yesterday, but I'm serious for the rest: I really want you to stop all that.

— All what? I ask surprised.

— The past lives, Marie-Antoinette. I don't believe in it and all I can see is that it only harms us. If this were true, we would be happy, don't you think?

I stay quiet and thoughtful to the point that Sophie has to ask her question again.

— Promise me, Mom. Please! This is destroying us.

— I promise, I finally say reluctantly.

— Thanks. I have something else to ask.

— What is it?

— I would love to move out of Montreal and go to another country. I can't stand to be here anymore: I have too many bad memories. Everything reminds me of dad, says Sophie in tears.

— I'm so sorry for everything that happened, darling.

— Do you agree, then?

— Yes. In fact, I was thinking about it too.

— Oh Mom, I love you I love you, I love you. When can we leave, then?

— We should start by knowing where we would like to go, don't you think?

— Ca-li-for-nia, here we come, she says, singing Phantom Planet's song. You always said you wanted to live there.

— That's true!

— I want to go where there is the big Ferris wheel on the beach.

— In Santa Monica? This is where I would go too.

— Since you believe in signs this is a big one!

— You are right! I say dreamily.

— When are we leaving then?

— I don't know. Give me some time to organize things.

— Oh Mom, I love you, Sophie says, hugging me as hard as she can.

— Gently, darling. We'll have an accident, I tell her, while giving her a kiss.

A few weeks later, as I get back home, I am surprised to see Annie on the porch waiting for me. When she sees me coming, she opens her coat and reveals a slightly rounded belly.

— I'm pregnant and it's thanks to you, Kiera, says Amelia, hugging me. You have no idea how grateful we are, my husband and I.— Congratulations, Annie. I am very happy for you.

— My best friend, Nathalie, tried everything to help me during all those years when I could not have children, Annie continues, sitting down in my living room. She referred me to therapy and alternative medicine, in vain. I told her what you told me. She was blown away. I talked about your work and the paintings you made for me. She has a gallery and she asked if you would be interested in exhibiting your work. She loves your art as much as I do. She would love to see if your gifts are linked to your paintings.

— That is so nice, I say very touched.

— Her gallery is in Los Angeles, Annie continues.

I look at her, completely dumbfounded.

— What's happening? Annie asks me, surprised.

— It's amazing. My daughter and I are talking about moving there and I was wondering how I could make it happen. We thought of going to Santa Monica actually.

— This is where she is!

PART III

Chapter 1

Recognition

We are on the plane heading to Los Angeles and my neighbor starts to talk to me right away.

— Is she your daughter? he says looking at Sophie putting her head against the window.

— Yes, I answer simply.

— She really looks like you, it's amazing.

— That's what everyone says. Do you have children?

— Three.

The man has just finished his answer when he seems to disappear before my eyes. The setting dissolves and I see an army officer on a battlefield ordering his men to go into battle. I sense that he knows the battle is already lost. I hear a voice repeating 'It's not your fault'.

— Are you ok? Wonders the man while touching my shoulder lightly.

— Oh, yes. Excuse me.

We both remain silent for a moment.

— Can I ask you a question? I finally tell him.

— Of course.

— Are you in the army?

— No. I'm a financial advisor.

— Ah? I say, the image of a man in uniform still in my mind.

— Why do you ask me that?

— It will seem strange to you.

— In my job, I hear a lot of things.

— Do you believe in past lives?

At the same time, I get a light tap from Sophie. I look at her and she returns to her music without insisting. The man gives me a smile.

— I don't necessarily believe in it.

I don't answer, still badly shaken by the images of the battle that I continue to see.

— But I am open and very curious! What were you about to say?

I remain silent, bothered by the presence of my daughter. The man understands and doesn't insist. We return to our respective reading. When Sophie gets up to go to the bathroom, my neighbor asks me the same question again.

— I saw your previous life, I say.

— You see that kind of stuff?

— It happens!

— I'm interested in knowing more! I don't know why, but I trust you. I'm ready!

— I saw you on a battlefield. You were an officer and you ordered your men to go to the fight when you knew very well that the battle was already lost. Everyone, including yourself perished, but you had time to see all your men slaughtered. You felt much guilt about this. It keeps telling me in my head that this was not your fault.

Sophie returns to her seat at the same time and we stop the conversation. She kisses me on the cheek, tells me she loves me and returns to her music and reading.

— It's amazing what you just told me, whispers my neighbor. I have nearly two hundred battle games at my place and I am trying to sell them. It was my passion. Tell me how you know this stuff?

— I don't know. I see it, that's all.

— It is a gift, anyway. You should do something with it. Write a book on the subject, perhaps!

— It's a good idea.

— I recognize talent when I see it and I can tell you that you have a lot of it. It would be a shame not to use it.

— Thanks. Can I ask you another question?

— You're frightening me, the man says jokingly.

— Have you lost a child in this life?

— Yes, how did you know that? he asks, amazed.

— Ah... That's why I keep hearing the sentence 'It's not your fault'. You think it's yours, when it is not, as well as the men that died in the battle, who were like your children. It was not your fault. You had to follow orders, that's all.

— And why did I lose a child in this life, if I had to lose all the soldiers in the previous one? Says the man, holding back tears.

— Because there is still a karma that is attached to that story: that of obeying orders and have had men killed, when you knew they would die.

— Why did I continue to do battles with all these games I had, then?

— Because subconsciously, you were trying to change the course of the battle that you lost.

The man remains silent and begins to cry quietly. He takes my hand.

— Thanks for the wonderful gift you've given me, Kiera. You took a huge weight off my shoulders, you have no idea.

We remain silent for a long time.

— What is your name, anyway?

— Kiera. And you?

— Luc.

— Will you give me your e-mail, Kiera? I would like to continue to be in touch with you. It is no accident that we met today.

— That would be a pleasure, I say, while writing down my contact information on a napkin.

— Where do you live, if I'm not being too personal?

— We used to live in Montreal, but we are going to live in Los Angeles today. What about you?

— Montreal.

We continue to talk like two old friends, until we get to Cincinnati airport. Sophie wonders what happened with this man as soon as he walked away.

— Nothing. We just talked and it was nice.

— Do you like him, Mom?

— He is married, but I like his soul. I feel like I know him!

— What do you mean 'I like his soul'?

— We could become friends.

Palm trees and blue sky give us back some energy when we finally arrive in Los Angeles. Nathalie welcomes us and takes us to the apartment she is letting us use, three blocks from the beach. We agree that we will stay there while I paint and prepare for my opening.

After setting in, Sophie and I take the time to rest and spend some time together. Every morning I go to the beach and I am happy to watch long beaches, endless waves, dolphins jumping, cormorants, which dive and surfers who dance in the waves. In this heavenly setting, I run, do yoga and meditate. All afternoon, Sophie and I swim in the ocean and lie down on the sand. After two weeks of holiday at this pace, I start painting and writing, as Luc suggested to me. I enroll Sophie in school. She is very proud of going to a middle school that looks like those on the TV shows she used to watch with her friends in Montreal.

After receiving a lot of e-mails from Luc, I take time to answer him.

Subject: Finally!!!...

Luc,

What a beautiful meeting for both of us. I don't know what links us, but there is surely something. I did not see it in past lives! That is not something I can control. Does the period of the French Revolution mean anything to you?

Big Hugs

Kiera

Subject: Re: Finally!!!...

Good evening Kiera,

I am so happy you finally answered my e-mails. Concerning our meeting, yes it was beautiful. I understood quickly that an enriching relationship was in the air and that I strongly wanted it. My philosophy is to contribute to the life of others and to hope to receive the same in return. It is what I experienced with you. Perhaps that's what's links us?

Past lives, perhaps, especially after what you told me in the plane. I understand your curiosity, because I also have the feeling we have met before.

The French Revolution is one period that always horrified me, all those people massacred for a yes or a no for the amusement of the crowd, it's so ugly. I have the same feelings about the Inquisition. They are parts of History that I always avoided as much as possible, be it articles, books or films. I do not know why these in particular; I don't have the same loathing for the Holocaust for example which is in fact quite worse in terms of victims and ugliness, of human darkness. Then yes, the French Revolution means something to me and I undoubtedly lived a quite sad story at that time. My choice was to defend my homeland, not to kill defenseless people.

I believe that's what links us, it's the present, it's our path towards Love of life, the Universe, in other words towards God. You enabled me to recapture my faith, it's not insignificant. Since then I find myself wanting to give even more to those around me.

You told me on the plane that life is easy, that it is made of simplicity; what links us, at least for the current part of the path, is perhaps as simple as that. Perhaps also that I am tired, it's almost midnight, and I'm going to bed.

Take care,

Luc

Subject: Re: Finally!!!...

Luc,

Thank you for this lovely message!

Meditating on the beach this morning, I saw us together. I felt very emotional and overwhelmed, and that confirmed certain feelings we have towards each other. What is strange is that I saw you in several past life regressions and I didn't recognize you in the plane, although the resemblance is obvious. I imagine I had to be ready. You have to guess if you ever have certain elements! I already have many and they all coincide well. I certainly don't want to influence you!

Big hugs.

Kiera

Subject: Past life

Hello Kiera,

I have the impression that we have been in harmony since our first meeting and we will soon arrive at something amazing.

Concerning our common past life, you feel emotional and overwhelmed. When I read this passage, tears came to my eyes. I was emotional and overwhelmed too.

I had already shared with you in the plane my feeling that we had known each other in one such life; without the excluding it completely (who can?) you had answered that you did not see it and that you had, however, seen several of yours. So, I told myself that it was probably an illusion. Since, I rejected several images around this past life and consequently I did not explore it.

Two surprising and deep emotions come up while reading your message: one is immense sorrow and the other is a relief to be recognized, finally. The surprise is struggling, my throat is knotted while writing this, and it is intense. It is amazing.

I understand that you don't want to influence me; it is the only way to have a positive verification. I'll tell you here, what I remember of the images I received. In my case, it's not like a film; it's emotions, feelings or impressions, and images. I am far from having your expertise in this type of research.

I often had flashes in which we lived as husband and wife, or as lovers, or as father and daughter, but also sometimes as mother and son; could there have been more than one past life? Why not, if one is possible? And are we always the same sex? I am uncomfortable with that as if were not possible. In the majority of these lives, simplicity and love dominated.

The life that moves me the most is when I see you going up a wooden structure, my eyes full of tears, your gaze is looking off, to the horizon, it's a beautiful day, the crowd shouts, you look at me, your eyes full of concern and of endless love, I can do nothing, I can only look, your face expresses a profound peace.

I do not see our exact relationship at that time. I don't even know if we knew each other before but I have the impression that we did. I know too well what this scene suggests.

That scene has been very persistent in the last month. But sometimes, in this same scene, I am the one climbing the wooden structure but what I observe of you remains identical to the first description. I don't remember anymore which scene came first. But I feel that it is the one where you go up. In any event, the connection between us is identical in both cases. Is this the little boy who sees his mother going up on the scaffold and who would have wished change places with her? When I write that, I have a very strong pressure on my chest.

For two days and this is new, I see us losing a child, our child; but I do not know if I am the father or the grandfather. But I was with you at the death of that child. It is blurry, though.

Following that memory was a scene from my current life where, in losing my son and taking care of my wife, I saw 'another failure'. I forgot the child and concentrated on my wife. I had a strange feeling at that time; today I know that it was an impression of "déjà-vu"

I have to stop here.

There, I've told you everything, I feel fragile, as naked as I ever was. Whether it corresponds with what you have or not, truth is better than doubt. I only hope that it is not a "mentalization", as Hawkins says. But taking into account the associated emotions, I doubt it.

We'll see if something else comes to me in the next days.

Love,

Luc

Subject: Re: Past life

Wow... you have it and I can tell you that it is not mentalization. I can give you the following elements because I myself verified who you had been. You had been my father in my past-life. and you died when I was a child. I knew that we had deep love for each other and that I had considered it unfortunate that you left so quickly.

The structure that you see is indeed the scaffold!!! ... And it is what makes me say that I can tell you more. You were the emperor François the 1st of Lorraine (I did not know his first name but when I saw it I understood that I had good information since it is the first name of your lost son). I wanted to know what he died of but I couldn't find anything. In my opinion it was of heart disease, because I feel that it was very quick. A woman with whom I made a regression had spoken about it: she had seen this loss and how much it had affected me. She told me that it was necessary that I cure the sorrow which I had had following the loss of my father when I was child in that life, because still today it affected me very much. She asked me whether I had any memories of it. I told her that it was very vague, because I felt that he had died when I was young, without really knowing the story. Yesterday I finally checked. I had never done it until now concerning my father and I don't know why. I wasn't ready maybe or I had not met the person and I did not have the links yet. Often they arrive afterwards. I felt so vulnerable since I've told you, that I understand why I was not ready before. On the other hand I also knew that it was the key.

Check and see whether you find yourself in that life. For me, the resemblance is amazing. Besides, I think that when I was guillotined, your spirit saw me and came to take me (I feel that it is true as I have tears in my eyes writing it!), because you had died long before and you stayed with me when I went to accompany my son until his death. That's certainly what you have seen.

Every time I went into past life regression, people saw the guillotine on me even before I start the session, since that's the life I came to settle and let me do what I do now.

For the other lives, I agree with you, even if I don't know them at all. What's crazy is that since I'm in California I told myself that if I had a son I would call him François. That did not last but that was very strong and I wondered why. Now I understand: that first name announced your return in my life!

I feel so relieved that you felt things without me having to tell you. I met many people from that past life. My ex-husbands who were my brothers-in-law (I established the links afterwards). I also met other people. Some know it. It's marvelous because all these meetings confirm the unfolding of what did happen. My daughter is of course my daughter then and now.

I'm really anxious that you check and tell me what you feel.

Happy to have found you finally! Thank you for your open mind and all that you share with me! I really feel very privileged for all this.

With all my love,

Kiera

Subject: Re: Past life

Wow, Kiera, wow.

I don't know where to start. Thank you, thank you, and thank you for your message.

First of all, I feel a great relief. I am moved but am not upset. It is as if I had just arrived from a long voyage. I understand things so much better now; it is like a mental jostling. I have the impression that we are solving a puzzle together but that you place ten pieces for each one of mine. I looked at the History. There are several rulers named François 1st. Please, tell me if he is really the one that lived from 1708 to 1765, born in Nancy and died in Innsbruck, François the 1st of Lorraine, Holy Roman Emperor.

When you were guillotined, you write that my spirit was there. You're right for three reasons, first is the surge of emotion while reading your text, second is the persistent impression that I always saw the scene from several angles or points of view, the third is the strong intent to protect you. You provided an explanation. For my part, it's not the little boy who would have liked to save his mother, but rather the father to save his daughter, that sounds so true (I have the tears in my eyes as I write this).

Concerning François 1st, you say that the resemblance is telling; can you explain in what way? Tell me more. I cannot say that I recognize myself there. For the moment there a few things that come to me, except the desire for a big family (I would have had as many children as my wife would have wanted), an interest as you know for military things and a strong interest for politics although I stay away from it, they really have no creativity nor courage, at least that is my impression. I'll see if something else comes me. I get an impression that I was noble by accident!!??

The first time I saw you, I sensed your vulnerability and worried temporarily. I put aside this concern because I did not know you. Moreover, I fought against a strong feeling of love for you as we were talking on the plane and I denied it because my life is with someone else, whom I adore. Now, I understand where it comes from and of what this love is made of. It becomes easy to accept and express.

Also, I remembered in this context: A thing that I found funny and strange at the same time, I found that you had a noble posture and, a name affectionately came to me for you and it was Marie-Antoinette, oh yes, and I have no idea why. Then when I looked at François the1st, whom I did not know at all and I saw that he was Marie-Antoinette's father who was approximately ten years old when François died and that she was guillotined, I was startled. Does that have any significance for you? Does it make sense? Are you that person? If so, then it does not matter what will come, it will only be confirmation.

Me too, I feel privileged.

God, to talk with you and to touch you physically, what joy it would be with what I know now. Or what if this bubble should burst?

Luc

Subject: Re: Past life

Luc,

What a beautiful reunion…

I'm glad, happy and filled with wonder with the situation and that you have felt so much connected from the beginning. You are the third person of that life who is conscious of it and that has really strengthened me throughout the passing years. Because it's not easy being in contact with a past life and not being able to talk about it. At the beginning, it was a woman psychic who saw my past-life

When I spoke about the resemblance, I spoke about the portrait of François the 1st; you are right it is the right one. You felt that your noble title was an accident? It's true in a way: even if you were already noble by your birth, you were crowned emperor so your wife could be Empress!

For Marie-Antoinette, the people who are close to their soul know it when they see me. There are even people who call me quite naturally Marie-Antoinette instead of Kiera.

People have always thought I was German, like her, because I am a tall blond with blue eyes.

What do you mean when you say if a bubble should burst?

Much love,

Kiera

Subject: Re: Past life

Hello Kiera,

Reading what you and I wrote again make other things come to me.

Concerning François 1st, there is indeed a physical resemblance. For the remainder, I'll see in meditation.

When I saw you, I had the impression that you were of German origin, afterward came the name of Marie-Antoinette.

Tell me, am I dreaming or does this make sense?

Regarding the bubble, it refers to a person who is in his bubble, therefore cut off from the external world, and consequently sometimes cut off from reality; and when one breaks the bubble, one returns to earth!!?? I could just as easily have written: "I wish that all were true."

Tell me the things that you felt too.

You said: I didn't have anyone to share this story with up to now. With my wife I can't do it either. When I told her about our meeting on the plane, I told her that I found you extremely beautiful, physically as well as spiritually. In so doing, you became a dangerous rival, even if I reassured her many times, I was awkward. She knows that we communicate, she doesn't like it but she accepts it. When I spoke to her about past lives, I felt that it would be better to avoid the subject. For her, like many, it's rubbish.

Today, a friend asked me why I had such a big smile my face, I told him that I had found my daughter and that we had lost each other in a past life, thus my joy. I limited myself to that concerning our identities; he's a long time friend, but I have to hold back. You know, once, as I gave some of my friends my impression of you, they were very anxious that I would continue my life with you. When they admitted that to me, I was astounded.

I avoided the subject afterwards, it was energy wasted unnecessarily. So, you see, even these two people, so close to me,

I won't speak to them about it. Thus none, for the moment; but do I need to talk about it?

What should happen, according to you, when one opens such a door?

Much love,

Luc

Subject: RE: Past life

Luc,

I think that we have all the elements to accept that our shared past-lives are real, because we've confirmed each other's circumstances.

This discovery that you have been my father in my previous life and that you accept it, is, I feel it, very important for me. It enables me to make peace with my past life completely.

I felt so alone at the end although you were there — perhaps that's where my connection with the dead and the spirits and these levels of energy come from. I don't want to ever go through the loneliness and the suffering of the end of that life. It was hard for me to be so alone, but it must have been hard for a father to see his daughter undergoing these atrocities without being able to do anything.

I'm trying here to establish links of that life with the battle we have seen; would the link be the inability to change destiny? I feel there might also be something else.

It's true that it is hard to talk to people about reincarnation. Most are skeptical, especially when it comes to historical figure because they idealize nobility or royalty. If they had had to live those lives, constrained by etiquette, they wouldn't make much of it. When one is in there, it's clear that there is nothing to envy. Because these lives can be lives of misfortune. I wouldn't wish to anyone what I endured there. To have it all and to lose everything. All these extremes, what a nightmare! Having no other choice but to endure everything.

In my current life, it is the freedom that I have to experience because that past life had been a true gilded prison! It is important to know that a lot of people think they were a historical figure: those figures are the landmarks to find a past life that happened at the same period.

Before ending, I want to let you know, that I followed your advice that you gave me in the plane: I have started to write my book about reincarnation. It is not easy, but I think that it is what I am supposed to do. You were right.

Much love,

Kiera

Subject: Our past life and some answers

Hello Kiera,

Your message and your answers were very inspiring. Thank you for sharing that.

I do not doubt anymore, I reread our emails, and there are too many connections. It is a gift of life to discover you and also to discover myself. There will be doubts, they will disappear; the gift will remain. Moreover, for me also it's working all by itself.

When I feel what you, my daughter, have undergone in that past life, I must contain a powerful wave of emotions; because I want to observe them and because they are very upsetting, I must not forget reality. There is revolt, an ocean of tears, rage, intense love, revenge, prayer, frustration, regret. And I feel that I saw that daily. And when I went to get you at the end (while writing a scene of tenderness comes and corresponds to an image which I had on the plane but I had rejected it out of context), a desire to protect, to surround you with affection, to place you in safety dominated my thoughts. Very quickly after that, an avenging surge came; to destroy this nation capable of such cruelty. The battle then, the bond which came: Elite soldier, young talented officer, natural leader, to fight, to obliterate the torturers, to avenge the homeland, sees this time the price of his rage (still a lot of emotion here) during the events themselves, that is to say the massacre of his soldiers (his children) and decides, "never again", and understands that it is never the right reason for combat. Combat is a giving of oneself, not a taking of another; when one goes to combat, one must see himself already dead in the name of universal good and that at the very beginning, one can then give everything to succeed with serenity and competence, if not, it is the downward spiral to the abyss.

Through our exchanges, I suddenly understand why I have a difficult time offering my services. I do not deserve success; I lost children, I could not protect my children, especially you, I had my children (soldiers) killed in a bad attack, I lost children again in this life; it's hell! If that exists, that's what it is.

It's important, tell me how our discovery frees us from that life; I feel that it brings back in the past on the contrary. You see, I remember, when I first met you, one of the feelings that I had very early towards you, was a need to protect you. This need grew with time. When we left each other at the airport, I felt something break, but a healthy break.

Perhaps my release comes from the fact that I've found children I lost, is that it? Have I paid my debt? (It's hard to continue, the emotion is too intense, I have a very bad headache).

Much love,

Luc

Subject: RE: Our past life and some answers

Hello Kiera,

Yesterday, at the end, I suffered. It had to stop.

From the beginning, I had an impression that you were my guide. It's confirmed. The guide shows the path and I take the path. I want to settle things, to find harmony again that I already knew or wished for in one or other past lives. I must understand that this discovery of ours will allow me to heal. Of all the children that I had, I know well that one of them lived a horror with full awareness of what was happening, and that was you. I felt a responsibility and helplessness before it. I now understand my intense search for serenity; I want to transcend these events that I did not know but that I know now. I want to find inner peace and to continue my progression while acknowledging that this discovery of our bond is a very important step. In any event, whether I succeed or not, I am richer now. So, how does one free himself from that life? Is it by finding links, by using meditation or something else? Can one do it alone? When I was in a hurry to go forward because I felt something of major importance was coming, I wonder whether it was not my past life.

I am very happy that you have already started your book. I feel that it will be the beginning of a great adventure for you.

Tomorrow, I offer you a phone call. I will call you on your cell around 4pm my time, that is 1 pm yours. Please, let me know if it is a rendezvous.

Love,

Luc

Subject: RE: Our past life and some answers

Luc,

In fact, it is not the debt that is important, but rather the emotion attached to it. It's what I learned in a dream. It's what brings us to a better understanding of oneself and of others, with more compassion and unconditional love. I learned also in another dream that countries have karma: the Second World War would be the consequence of the French Revolution; what the revolutionaries did to people at that time, they would have had to relive it in the camps! That is why the country we are born in and the parents we are born with are very important: they are there to reactivate the karma we need to deal with so we can heal.

I think that we can never completely release ourselves from our past lives in one life since we came to free ourselves from them, because they are part of us, part of our essence. Only time and links can appease them! Gradually one manages to rise up beyond the pain, consciously, if we stop reacting to circumstances, I guess! Meditation helps for sure.

I have been very tired since yesterday. Painting and writing my book everyday are overwhelming. With Sophie, it is not always easy too. She is a teenager! Fortunately I like the sea and for me it's a place to re-energize!

No problem for tomorrow. It's a date!

Much love,

Kiera

Subject: Our conversation

Hello Kiera,

I loved our conversation yesterday, especially the small hesitations at the beginning. You laughed a few times in such a way that I've never heard you before. I found that very pleasing. Our relationship goes to another level and I will help it grow with you. Thank you for being there. Thank you also for debt versus emotion. The answer is still love.

And since my two or the three previous emails where I felt much emotional, there is now much inner peace. One could say that a search, a tension, has disappeared. I realize that I did all I could for my children and even more. A relaxation thus settles in, and I then have the impression of finding my way again. I forgive myself. After that, yesterday, I then realized that if this life took one child from me whom I never knew, it's now given me back another one to love that I already knew, it is magical, magical.

I am focused on what I have rather than on what I don't have. Life is beautiful. I sense my little François smiling.

Love.

Luc

Subject: Re: Our conversation

Luc,

I have to admit that I was not as at ease as I would have liked to during our conversation. Sophie was around and I did not want to ask her to leave the room because she was on the internet. She is against everything that is close to reincarnation and does not want me to talk about it, as you may have noticed. I promised her that I would stop, but our meeting has changed a lot of things. I am sure you have felt the difference when she left the room.

Regarding laughing, I am somebody who adores to laugh and it is something that I found again here, completely, because I feel a lightness here in LA. The sun, that helps.

I wanted to share a quote that I love with you:

God give me serenity,

To accept the things that I cannot change.

The courage to change the things I can,

And the wisdom to know the difference.

Thank you also for being by my side; that makes my heart feel totally at peace too!

Love,

Kiera

Subject: Since our conversation

Kiera,

Since our conversation, I have received only gifts. It's like a fairy tale. I have enormous energy and I tackle things that gave me pause before. I express my love very easily to the other people when I feel that they are receptive.

For a very long time, I was seeking you without knowing. A hidden memory came. When I was a young man, at the Polytechnique de Montreal, there were hundreds of students, only a few girls, imagine a college for boys only and a few girls come in; but for the first time I take time to look at one. She is tall, fair, thin, quick-witted, vulnerable, with very soft eyes and I said myself: "She reminds me of this Austrian, Marie-Antoinette ", a flash already at that time.

You were only two years old; I was already looking for you.

I remember a sentence that I want to share with you: "What one does for oneself is forgotten, what one does for others is immortal."

Much love,

Luc

Subject: RE: Since our conversation

Dear Luc,

You told me I was two years old and you were looking for me already. I think my nightmares began at that age, after my forehead was cut open for a fall. This is as much as I remember. In a regression, I saw myself being born, my head emerging from between my mother's legs. After Marie-Antoinette's beheading, her head was put between her legs. When I saw that I was nauseous and I no longer wanted to be born. The doctor had to use the forceps at my birth so I no longer had a choice! Today, I have no regrets.

I must tell you: I love you very much, Luc! It's really intense, but also very peaceful and very serene. Very hardcore too! Like a daughter and her father!

I realized something important through what I have with you: connection. I have it with my parents in a certain way but it is not expressed and I need to guess it.

Talking of my parents has reminded me that I had to find out who my father was in my past life. I have had the name 'Barnave' in my head for years. I just checked on the internet. That was about time after all those years. I have to tell you that Barnave really existed in time of Marie-Antoinette: he was a revolutionary and a very good speaker (I can see that in my father too) and wanted to find a balance between the monarchy and freedom. He wanted more control over the revolution because it was too violent for him. He escorted Marie-Antoinette and her family back to Paris after the failed escape to Varennes. He really appreciated her. After that he tried everything to save her, in vain. He died, guillotined like Marie-Antoinette, shortly after her. I can tell you that when I read that, I realized that even if I am not close to my parents physically, I feel very close to them on a spiritual level, and that is what is important to me.

I hope that the fact that I understand the question of karma and I agree to deal with it, will help me transcend everything, have faith in life again and come back to God to be one with Him.

Our relationship has cured me of the abandonments in my previous life, but my daughter doesn't look like she wants to benefit from it. She is making things harder on me. She feels things are changing and she doesn't want them to change. I am praying for things to get smoother for her and for us.

Hope my daughter will receive this too and will stop rejecting me and my book.

Much love.

Kiera

Subject: RE: Since our conversation: Peace and Serenity

Kiera,

I feel humility in front of your serene courage for what you're going through and what you've been through, you inspire me. You almost always have one positive interpretation of what's happening or what happened. You always see what you can get from it and you make use of it to go forward. It is fascinating and I wonder 'how does she do it'.

I like how you jump into life, how you consider others, how you love, how you embrace your sensitivity. It is with humility that I try to follow in your footsteps. You are my guide. Simply to communicate with you, in writing or otherwise, nourishes me.

What I feel for you is so intense, so strong, I don't know how to classify it. I feel that it's a level of positive emotion that increases in every life we are close to each other, we enrich each other and that empowers those I love in both of my lives.

For this reason you are an example of the most beautiful of what life offers and for several months, I thank God for your existence and to have allowed our paths to cross. What a privilege!

What you write on the souls that meld in one is so beautiful that it can only be true, real, ineluctable. This helps me to integrate in my life what I feel for you.

Thank you, Kiera, to be so beautiful, inspiring and loving. Thank you for everything you do for me.

What I feel about you now is an increasing simplicity towards your life, towards the life. You spoke about this simplicity without naming it but you did not live it. Now I feel that you do.

Your new life, I feel you approach it with confidence, and I like what I feel in you. Sometimes you will undoubtedly fall. You need to know that I am always there to help you raise you up. There is no fear there, only faith. You are not alone anymore.

For your daughter, I am telling you again: it's normal that she's rejected your book and everything about reincarnation. She wants to keep control over you because you are the only person she has. She does not believe that the story about her father had anything to do with past lives and that's why she blames you. Give her some time, but do not allow her to plant the seed of doubt in you about who you are and what you do. Let her believe that you've stopped reading and researching about Marie-Antoinette, but let's continue our discussions, even if you must hide them. Continue your book. This is the key, I feel it. I am convinced that your book will complete your liberation.

I love you.

Luc

Subject: Somebody loves you!

Kiera,

I don't have any news from you and I am worried. I hope you did not give into the pressure from your daughter. I hope you are doing well.

Here is what I would like to write to you. Your power. What makes a flower grow? Force or power? And yet what is more fragile and vulnerable than a flower? One cannot force a seed to germinate and become a flower. On the other hand, with a little water and sun… I am convinced that it is the power of Life. Your power is the same, it is that of your Life and it is all the more impressive because of your fragility and your vulnerability. Force requires many resources and exhausts those that use it. Power is unlimited, inexhaustible, and immortal.

With you, the discovery of past lives shows me our immortality, that we are from the Source, that we are pieces of God, that we try to return to our Source, it is our goal on this earth for each one of our lives; all the rest is illusion.

You once told me that my sensitivity was a force, but I thought it was the equivalent to fragility and vulnerability, until I understood that it was in fact a power. To be able to radiate love while being ready to receive what comes, is very powerful because it is very True. And it is very Beautiful. That attracts people who seek the Truth.

I wanted to share this quotation of John Keats with you: "Beauty is truth, truth beauty, that is all ye know on earth, and all ye need to know". In addition to your power, it is your intensity which makes it radiate.

Thinking of you, Kiera.

I love you.,

Luc

Subject: RE: Somebody loves you!

Luc,

It looks like the problems with Sophie are back again. Hell. I cannot stand it anymore. That's why I couldn't write. A thousand apologies.

I am trying to get out of my past-life patterns and my daughter has decided to dive into them. Her pain is so strong and her rage so powerful that I can no longer function. I had to cancel my opening. I do not know what I am going to do: my daughter exhausts me.

While I make my living with painting, I can't do it anymore. I can't stand it. I realize I have not stopped since my separation with my husband and life is eating me up: I can't escape. My daughter doesn't want me to. I have to deal with everything I had to go through with what happens to my daughter and me.

Please, do not worry if I don't write you for some time. I feel that I need to step back from all that intensity that we have just experienced, in order to focus on my daughter and me and to help us manage what is happening. I have said no to destruction, but it seems that Sophie has not said no to it and I have to help her out. I think that she's fighting, because the information has changed for her: in our past life I was dead already and in this life I continue to live and be with her. I changed the data and Sophie must change hers to evolve: I feel the two are connected!

I love you too.

Kiera

Subject: RE: Somebody loves you!

Kiera,

I understand what you are going through. I am here for you and will always be, whatever happens. Do not hesitate to contact me whenever you need me. ESPECIALLY do not give up. You are almost there.

I love you, Kiera.

Luc

Chapter 2

Nightmares

It is late and someone knocks on the door. I open it and Sophie comes in suddenly. I am shocked by the spectacle she offers me: her clothes are torn, her hair is wild, her pupils dilated and she is shaking violently. I put my arms around her for a long time and she eventually calms down.

— What happened, honey? I ask quietly, putting a blanket over her shoulders.

— Nothing, answers Sophie in a very dry ton.

— I am here to help you, I say gently. Stop looking at me as your enemy, Sophie, and tell me what just happened.

— Three guys tried to rape me on the beach, Sophie finally articulates.

— Oh my God! We have to call the police immediately.

— They came when I managed to escape ... but I couldn't wait. I was too scared.

— Do you want to go now?

— Oh no. I can't bear to see those guys again.

I take Sophie in my arms to console her.

— You've been drinking and smoking marijuana, haven't you?! I exclaim in surprise.

— No!

— Don't lie to me. You smell like alcohol and marijuana.

— I just smoked a joint.

— We both know that this is not true. You know it's dangerous to do drugs on the beach especially at night, I say without being able to contain my fear any longer. Look what just happened. In addition, you are under age!

— I'm sorry, says Sophie, crying.

She starts to tell me everything that has happened. I feel projected into her story and I see it as a movie: around a large fire, young people, unconscious, dance in silence punctuated by laughter, voices distorted by the waves and bottles clinking together. Smoke rises now around the moving shapes. A strange smell fills the air, as if a skunk passed by a short distance away. Among these young people, I can see a tall and beautiful blonde girl whose gaze looks completely lost. She does not stop laughing. In a strong altered state of consciousness, she rolls herself in the sand, tracing a whale in the sand with her toes.

— A whale! Alert! A whale! She screams, writhing in the sand, followed by others who do the same.

The euphoria lasts about ten minutes and gives way again to silence punctuated by the sound of waves and the crackling of the bonfire. Sophie finally gets up to warm her hands in front of the big fire she and her friends have built. In the distance, two dolphins do a split in the air and hit the water with a great splash, under the astonished eyes of Sophie, who has now approached the ocean. Alice, a childhood friend comes close to her.

— I really can't believe you're still fascinated by dolphins and whales.

Sophie gives her a sideways glance and simply agrees with a nod. She seems very far away.

— You've already been very lucky, Sophie, to see them together. That's never happened to me ... continues her friend while trying unsuccessfully to build a pyramid in the sand.

— Onewhaletwowhalesthreewhales... jokes one of her friends, joining them.

— Stop laughing at me, Bobby.

— I'm not laughing, he says, laughing and giving a joint to Sophie. Now, you can see them together. I always see them together when I'm high.

Sophie takes a puff and they laugh together.

— That's it, says Sophie by rolling on the ground. I see so many whales that I can no longer count. Wait, I try. One, two, three... how many again... damn I have to start over, she continues, looking forward. Oh, I really need to pee.

— Why not do in the water.

— No, it's too cold!

— Do it behind the life-guard station, then.

— No ... I really have to go to the restroom... are you coming with me?

— You have to loosen up, Sophie, you're really too shy, Bobby says with a laugh. The others join in.

Sophie finally gets up painfully.

— Well, I can tell that no one wants to help me. Too bad, she says, falling into the sand. Oops, I really have to go if I don't want to pee in my panties, she says, laughing.

She staggers away, still trying to count the whales.

— onewhaletwowhalesthreewhales...

Sophie is so under the influence of drugs and alcohol she does not notice the three young people who begin to follow her since she left the group.

— Hell, they don't stop moving and I can't count them, she continues.

The three young men, covered in tattoos, approach, laughing. One with a black cap and very muscular arms talks to Sophie, while touching his genitals through his pants.

— I think you'd love to see my whale. It is really big, you know.

Shocked, Sophie returns to herself in an instant and tries to get back to her friends, but the guy blocks her way. She tries to escape but the guy with multiple piercings in the ears prevents her.

— Where do you think you're going like that? he asks roughly, stroking her shoulder.

— Help, she shouts in the direction of her friends who cannot hear her.

The three young people begin to jostle her while kissing her neck, shoulders, forehead, cheek. Sophie defends herself by pushing them away hard.

— Oh, but she has character, says the third by removing his shirt to show his muscled abs and shoulders. She is even more exciting.

— I saw her first. She's mine, says the first guy. You'll love my whale, he says, while unbuttoning his jeans and while the other two guys holds her.

— No... Sophie desperately screams.

— No one hears you. Look at your friends. They are too far away and too stoned to help you.

The young men push Sophie in the sand and the one with the black hat tries to remove her jeans. Sophie struggles and screams.

A tall young man arrives suddenly and calls for help while throwing himself at them. Sophie manages to escape, but the first young guy grabs her leg and causes her to fall into the sand again, head first. She continues to struggle while screaming, while the tall young man continues to fight with the other tattooed men. Sophie manages to give her attacker a big kick in the face. Overcome by pain, the young tattooed guy lets her go harshly.

The police, making their rounds, arrive at the same time. Sophie, totally panicked, runs breathlessly home.

When Sophie finishes telling me her story, I come back to reality. Images of Marie-Antoinette's rape are trying to get in the way, but I manage to push away these thoughts strongly concentrating on Sophie.

— You need to relax after all you had to go through. I'll run a bath ...

I kiss Sophie on the forehead, stroke her cheek and go to the bathroom. Sophie follows me. She looks at herself in the mirror and starts to cry. She dries the tears running down her cheeks, while I run water in the bathtub. I pour the bubble bath and light some blue candles while Sophie looks at me blankly. I take her in my arms.

— I'm so scared, Mom. I thought they would do it. It was awful ... I wanted to die.

— I know...

We remain silent and cry together softly.

— Take your bath and it will get better, I finally say.

I put her robe on the sink and close the door gently behind me. Images of rape are trying to dominate my mind, even more strongly, but I resist in order to be there for Sophie: I focus on the sounds coming from the bathroom.

In the bathroom, Sophie drops her clothes on the floor and immerses herself in the bath. Her head remains under water as long as possible. She would like to stop breathing, so she will not remember what just happened. She wants to die. She stays under water then emerges to take deep breaths. She begins to tremble with cold and runs more hot water to warm up the bath. The water is so hot that it burns her skin. She does not react because she needs to materialize outside the pain that she feels inside. Her skin becomes very red and she finally turns off the tap. She thus remains still for several minutes without moving.

— How are you? I ask through the door.

Sophie does not answer. Concerned, I repeat my question a little louder. Sophie comes out of her torpor and says she will come out in a few minutes.

— I'll wait in your room, Sophie, I say very gently.

Sophie lays down on her bed. Her room is decorated with posters of singers and American actors. She stuck a lot of magazine pages up on the walls. Several pictures of Sophie and her friends are all on a wall near her bed and gives the room an atmosphere of the seventies that is very friendly. I feel that Sophie has a really good taste in assembling disparate things, into something harmonious. I lie down beside her.

— I haven't been laying on your bed for a long time, I say.

— I missed it, Mom, says Sophie snuggling on my chest and crying softly.

I caress her hair in silence.

— Hey Mom, I'd like you to sleep with me tonight, Sophie tells very sadly.

— Of course, darling.

— Thank you mom. I love you, Sophie says, closing her eyes.

— I love you too. Sweet dreams, I say while diving under the covers.

Sophie turns on her side and falls asleep immediately. I stay awake for a while, wondering how I will approach the subject of drugs and alcohol with her. I watch her sleeping. I notice that her shoulders are much more prominent than before. I am worried for her, because I am afraid she is using drugs other than marijuana. After turning over the problem in every way and fighting against the images of rape of my past life, I fall asleep.

I wake up in the night completely traumatized by the nightmare that I had. In my dream, I am in the 1970's. I see a woman covered with needle marks. The dream told me that this woman was around Andy Warrhol. She looked very happy to be around him at first, but her life went wrong and she died of an overdose. Even if I do not know who this woman was, I know she is my daughter today.

I now understand her suffering and cry softly while looking at Sophie. I go into my office and sit at my computer trying to find on the internet the woman I have seen in my dream in vain. Sophie comes up behind me and asks me what I'm doing.

— Research, I answer evasively.

— Reincarnation, I bet, says Sophie angrily.

— Sophie, we need to talk about marijuana, alcohol ...

— I have nothing to tell you. I'll do what I want. Leave me alone, she says leaving the room, furious.

I do not know what to do. It is early in the morning and I decide to go running on the beach. After doing my jogging, yoga and meditation, I come back home. A message from Sophie's counselor waits for me on the voicemail: she tells me that Sophie is not at school and she has been absent for the past three weeks. I am devastated. I call Luc to ask him what I should do. He tells me to wait until she gets back home and not to worry.

— She's taking drugs, Luc. How can I not worry?

— You have no choice, Kiera.

— Do I have to call the police?

— That would make things worse. Wait, that's the only thing you can do.

— I can't... I feel so anxious.

— Continue to write your book.

— I can't. Sophie takes all my energy with her mood swings and her dysfunctional behavior. I must do something for her.

— That must awaken something from your past life, don't you think?!

— Luc, worrying for a child does not necessarily refer to a previous life, I say impatiently. I'm tired of having all this information. It doesn't really help me to solve my problems with my daughter. On the contrary, it makes things worse.

— Excuse me. I feel so much a father to you. I just want to help you...

— And I feel you are my father as well, Luc. I'm sorry. Excuse me.

— She'll come back, don't worry. She made you think she was at school these past three weeks. She'll do the same today, don't you think?

— You're right. Thank you for being with me. I don't know what I would do without you.

— Call me anytime.

— Okay.

I cannot hang up and remain silent for a while. Then, to my surprise, I begin to cry without knowing why. Luc hears it and asks what is happening with me. I finally tell him that Sophie's attempted rape has aroused my own memories: Marie-Antoinette's rape by three guards. He listens to me with great respect and compassion and that calms me down immediately.

We continue to talk a little bit and I hang up because I feel writing is calling me.

I am so focused writing about Marie-Antoinette's rape in my book that I do not notice the time passing. I startle when Sophie comes up behind me.

— Mom, I thought you had stopped all this stuff. You promised.

— I'm writing a book, Sophie.

— Reincarnation again? Don't you get tired of living in a world that is only the fruit of your imagination.

I remain silent for a moment while focusing on my goal: helping Sophie to solve her problems.

— Where were you, Sophie? I say quietly to change the subject.

— At school. Why?

— Because the school called me to say that you weren't there.

— They made a mistake. That's because I was late.

— Why were you late? I remember you left early…

— The bus broke down.

— Really? And the day before, the bus broke down too, right?

— Nope. Why?

— Because you have not attended school for three weeks, Sophie.

— Who told you that?

— The school called me, I just told you!

— They have a problem with their computer system, Sophie replies, not at all flustered.

— Sophie, stop telling me stories.

— I'm not! That happens to a lot of my friends. The school calls parents to tell them they are not at school when they are.

— Sophie, you've lost a lot of weight and that worries me. You're doing drugs and that's why you don't go to school, right?

— You don't know what you're talking about, says Sophie furious.

— When you're aggressive like that, it's because you are under the influence of drugs...

— You're really crazy. You should be hospitalized, Mom.

— Sophie, I want to help you.

— How can you help me, when you're not able to help yourself. You've ruined my life. You're a whore, Sophie says, screaming and leaving the apartment.

Stunned by what my daughter just told me, I do not know what to do and collapse on to the floor. The nightmare returns: A wheel on the cobblestone. An old wheel. This wheel is attached to nothing. Only a pin seems to push it. Some wooden steps. A feeling of cold on the back of my neck. A terrible metallic taste in my mouth. Nothing. Silence. Death. Rape.

The phone rings and brings me back to reality in an instant. It's Luc.

— Has she returned yet?

— Yes and she has already left. She was awful and called me a whore.

— The revolution, surely ..

.— Really?! It's true you're right, I said suddenly quieter. I had forgotten, that Marie-Antoinette was said to be a whore. Although, it doesn't excuse my daughter. It's awful what she said and it makes me very sad..

— She didn't meant it. She only repeated what she has recorded in her previous life. I am sure she is taking drugs to forget this period, and more recently, what happened with her father.

— I'm afraid that something will happen to her.

— She is strong. Have faith.

I spend the night waiting for Sophie. I develop all sorts of possible scenarios in my head, each one worse than the next. I decide that this situation cannot last anymore: my intuition tells me that she is taking drugs and her lies do nothing to reassure me of the opposite.

Exhausted by my thoughts, I fall asleep and my nightmare returns: a wheel on the cobblestone. An old wheel. This wheel is attached to nothing. Only a pin seems to push it. Some wooden steps. The feeling of cold on the back of my neck. A terrible metallic taste in my mouth. Nothing. Silence. Death. Rape. A woman in a trance lies before me and prevents me from me moving. Her head is resting on my breast. I want to help her and call her parents to spare me from the pain at the same time, but I am immobilized by her. Suddenly she emerges from her trance and says, 'I see the knives on your neck'.

I wake up crying and the scene of Marie-Antoinette's rape comes back to me immediately. I feel the icy knife-edge on my neck. I am trembling with cold. I feel disoriented and at the same time relieved. I had no choice but to let them rape me because of the knives in my neck; those knives, which were only there to prepare me for the blade of the guillotine. The pain could not express itself, because this traumatic event prepared me to die on the scaffold, as I was already disconnected from reality. I remember the visions of my father in my prison and that calms me down.

I stand up to see if Sophie has returned. She has not. I take a shower while trying to think of something else. I leave the bathroom in my bathrobe and I am surprised to see that Sophie is waiting for me on my bed.

— Sophie, I can't continue like this. I can't stand it anymore. It's killing me.

— I'm sorry, mom, Sophie says, crying.

— What is happening to you? Why are you doing this? I say, taking her in my arms and crying with her.

— Mom, you were right from the beginning. Your dreams were telling the truth. I'm sorry that I lied to you. I took drugs, but I assure you, it's over now.

— How come it's over?

— I think I may have overdosed last night.

— Oh my God! I say horrified.

— It's all right Mom. I had to experience that to stop it, I guess.

— What happened?

— I spent the night with my girlfriend Alice and I apparently lost consciousness. I turned blue and my tongue was out of my mouth. Alice almost called the paramedics, but I came to me in the meantime. We were both scared and we vowed never to do it again.

— What kind of drug was it?

— Cocaine ... I'm sorry, Mom, I assure you.

— But when did you start all this?

— After the DNA test, I think. I had lost my dad and I didn't know what I was doing, you know!

— I am so sorry, I say, holding my daughter very tightly in my arms. What can I do to help you really get out of it?

— I told you, Mom, I stopped.

— But how can you do that alone? You need help.

— I was so afraid that I was going to die, I don't want to do it again, I promise you.

— I want to believe you. Ok. Now I have to take you back to school and you promise to stay there.

— I don't want to go, Mom.

— You have no choice. The school was very clear on this. If you don't go, we will have to go to court. It is only a matter of months.

— Okay, says Sophie finally.

— I'm counting on you, Sophie. I don't want to hear about this stuff, anymore. It's about you and your future.

In the meantime, I drive Sophie to school. On my way back, I call Luc to tell him everything that just happened.

— I'm happy for you and Sophie. You know, there may be something that could help your daughter. I just found a movie that recently came out on video, 'The Factory Girl', and apparently it's about Andy Warrhol and a girl he knew. I feel you should see it.

— I'll do it right away. Sophie told me she's stopped drugs but I have to remain vigilant.

I sit at the computer, full of expectations, mixed with apprehension. The film is about a young woman, Edie Sedgwick, who was Andy Warrhol's muse and actually died of an overdose. I do research on this young woman and it is very difficult because I feel the suffering and pain of my daughter in my every cell. I compare the pictures of Sophie with that of Edie. They correspond. The way they dress, hold their cigarettes, drink and party are the same. I am so impressed with what I found. I save all the information in a folder to show to Sophie.

Sophie arrives home from school, as I finish it.

— How was school?

— I can't wait not to go. I can't stand it. I hate this school.

— Look, Sophie, I have something for you, I say, handing her the folder.

— What is it?

— Look.

Sophie looks at the photos and then reads about the two lives that I have compared.

— I don't understand, she finally says while giving me back the folder.

— Don't you think you look like her?

— Ah, that again! But, Mom, it has to stop, you're crazy.

— I thought it would help you understand your problems with drugs and quit once for all.

— But Mom, this is not what I need. You don't really understand anything, Sophie says, slamming the door.

I run after her and ask what she needs. She stops and comes back to me.

— I need you to be normal. I need a normal life, Mom. I've had enough of this paranormal life, which exists only in your mind. You don't even work anymore because of it. What are we supposed to do for money? I wish I knew.

Suddenly, Sophie comes closer to me, her face completely transformed by hatred.

— I need money now and if you don't give it to me, I'll kill you.

I look at her transfixed; completely panicked. I leave and go to my room. Sophie follows continuing to threaten me, but I do not hear anything. I roll over on my bed and close my eyes not to react and especially not to inflame the situation.

An old wheel on the cobblestone. This wheel is attached to nothing. Only a pin seems to push it. Some wooden steps. A cold sensation on my neck and then a horrible metallic taste in my mouth. Black. Silence. A long corridor, the corridor of the Conciergerie. I see the light at the end of the tunnel. I arrive at the gate. As we are about to leave, the guard turns to me suddenly.

— I want more money, he says very threatening.

— Sir, we have already given you the money you requested and you will receive what was agreed as soon as I leave this prison, I say gazing at the gate.

— You don't understand. I want more money now.

— Anything you want, sir, once we get out, I say trying to keep my composure.

— I can't wait. I want it now.

— As you know, I do not have any money with me. I promise you I will give you what you want as soon as we get out of this place, I say again as calmly as possible, without understanding that he does not realize the seriousness and emergency of the situation.

— No money, no way out, he continues.

— I have to get out to be able to pay you, sir, I say, starting to panic inside, but trying not to show it. I beg you, sir. We must move quickly now. We have an agreement.

— You see, I have a family... And we risk a lot if I let you out...

At these words, I think of my children and I understand his confusion. This man is right. I cannot allow him to take the risk of penalizing his family, as I cannot take the risk of penalizing mine.

What would happen to this man and my children if I manage to escape? The revolutionaries are capable of anything. They did not hesitate to kill my husband. I look at him without a word and decide to stay. Relieved, I turn around and walk silently back to my cell. I get the test that God gives me without any resistance, I agree to stay for my children and to sacrifice myself for them to live, I rely on God completely. I return to my cell, totally transformed to the depth of my soul. Even if I am in prison outside, I have never felt so free inside. I curl up in a ball on my bed and savor this moment of bliss that I am living, as a gift of God.

Sophie shakes me to make me come back to myself. Paralyzed by emotions, I start to cry without being able to stop. Sophie finally realizes that I am not going to react to her threats and her insults.

— I'm crazy, Mom. You have to make me locked up. I don't know why I said all that. It's really awful.

— You're not crazy, on the contrary, I say, clasping her in my arms and crying with her.

Sophie looks at me, surprised. She opens her mouth to speak and I interrupt her to avoid the hot topics of past lives and reincarnation.

— I need to get out to get some fresh air and clear my head.

— Let's go to the 'top of the world', Mom. You'll see, it's amazing.

We get to Sunset Boulevard, but Sophie can no longer find the street leading to her 'top of the world'. We turn in circles. At one point, we turn around in front of a meditation center. I then see the name of Yogananda, and I do not know why but the name sounds familiar. I propose to stop for a moment to discover the place. Sophie reluctantly agrees.

— We can ask where the street to the 'top of the world' is, I say stopping the car in the parking lot.

We are moving towards a vast green lake; it's beautiful. The vegetation is lush and we walk in silence around the lake. It feels like home to me. We stop to meditate a few minutes in an old windmill that has been converted into a chapel. The feeling I experience is extraordinary: I feel like I am reconnecting with a part of me that I had forgotten. I am overwhelmed by the emotion of the reunion and cannot stop tears from running down my cheeks. My meditation is deep and I feel completely revitalized and refocused as I walk out of the meditation room. We continue to walk around the lake. Sophie is amazed by the magnificence of the place, too.

— I do not believe in God, Mom, but if I had to come somewhere, this is where I would come, she says, showing me the individual stones where each of the world's religions is listed. Did you see, they have all the religions!

— I think I'm going to come back here often, since my meditation seems to be much stronger here than anywhere else.

We arrive at the visitor's center and I ask the man standing at the door if he knows how to go to the 'top of the world'. He gives me directions and I ask him more details about where we are. He tells me that this place is called the 'Lake Shrine' and has been given by a wealthy producer to Paramahansa Yogananda.

— Who was the Para ... Yogananda? Excuse me. I'm having trouble remembering his full name.

— Pa-ra-ma-ham-sa Yo-ga-nan-da, says the man kindly. He was a spiritual Hindu teacher who came to teach Kriya Yoga in the Occidental West.

— What is Kriya yoga?

— It is a meditation technique that, if practiced regularly, releases you from your karma.

— That's exactly what I need. I'm interested. I want to learn about the teachings of this man.

— Mom, let's go, please, Sophie asks impatiently.

— Give me a moment and we can go. You can just go for a little walk.

— I suggest you read his book 'Autobiography of a Yogi', says the man, showing me a book after Sophie left. Then you can take the lessons if you're interested and get initiated in Kriya Yoga later.

— My God, I say surprised. I've had this book for at least ten years, but I've never read it.

— It is still yours: I'm offering it to you.

— Thank you, I say, touched.

— Do you believe in reincarnation? asks the man suddenly.

— Yes, I say surprised by the question, after looking around me to see that Sophie is not in the vicinity.

— Don't take it in the wrong way— I'm married — but I feel like I know you. This is the first time this has happened and it's really strong.

— Ah, I say without lingering, because Sophie is back beside me.

— Here's my card. My name is Bob. Call me if you need me.

— Pleased to meet you, Bob. My name is Kiera and this is my daughter Sophie. Thank you again for the book, Bob, I say as I walk away with Sophie.

— He's a little strange, this guy, don't you think? Sophie says, taking the card from my hands. Here, he's a business coach. Maybe he could help you with your work, Mom.

— Maybe you're right. In the meantime, let's go to the conquest of your 'top of the world'.

The view of Los Angeles and the ocean from the Sophie's 'top of the world' is breathtaking. We sit there waiting for the sun to go down.

— It's amazing how we are nothing. Can you imagine if there was a tsunami here? Everything would disappear.

— I think that where we are right now, nothing would disappear. We're too high.

— Tell me Mom, would you rather die or survive? Sophie asks curious.

— Die. I would not want to have to face the famines, the epidemics.

— Well, I'd rather live because we could start the world off again on more human values and less capitalistic ones. We could stop polluting and killing our planet as we currently do.

— Wow, Sophie, you impress me, I say looking at her, thinking, without actually verbalizing it, that in our previous life, she was the sole survivor of the family. I'm really proud of you.

— You know, in my course in astronomy, they say that we are all one, Sophie adds after a moment of silence.

— So we're nothing or we are one?

— Well, if it goes beyond the atom, there are waves of energy that suggest that behind the material, there is energy. Now we are energy. Together we seem very small in the universe; but we are all the same unique energy.

— It's really interesting. What does that mean then: if we die, our bodies are reduced to dust, is that right?

— Mom, don't start, please.

— I just want to make you think, without trying to convince you. Okay?

— Okay!

— So, answer my question, please.

— Yes, our body is reduced to dust.

— Beyond the atoms, there is energy. That would mean that we are energy. What happens with this energy, when the matter of our body disappears?

— We return to the universal energy, I guess.

— And what do you do with the individual energy?

— I don't know, Mom. Let's go. I'm cold, Sophie says, rising.

Chapter 3

Healing

I arrive at the Lake Shrine, full of hope. Bob is waiting for me and hands me an envelope. I look up at him, surprised.

— It's a gift. I registered you for the kriya lessons, so you can start them as soon as possible.

— Thank you, Bob. It touches me deeply.

— Come on, we'll sit down and you can tell me what brings you here. Know that I will do everything in my power to help you.

— Thank you so much, I say, walking with him. I'm curious Bob. Why did you mention reincarnation the other day?

— Because I feel like I know you.

— It's special that you say that. I work a lot on past lives. I am writing a book about reincarnation. I have been in contact with my past life for longer than I can remember. I resolved a lot of my life's issues with this work, but curiously, I have never earned much less money since I have been in the USA.

Then, suddenly, I realize that the American Revolution had been financed secretly by Louis XVI and had increased the debt of France considerably. The nobles and the people had attacked the monarchy, accusing Marie-Antoinette and her way of life for their misfortunes. Thus, my soul must have associated the United States as a source of debt.

— Are you alright? Bob asks me anxiously.

— Oh yes. Excuse me. I just came to understand something about my past life. Where was I?

— You said you have earned much less money since you have been in the US.

— Indeed. I cannot paint anymore, because I have to take care of my daughter. She's been doing drugs and I'm not sure if she is still taking them. I don't know what to do to get back on my feet. I saw that you were business coach, so I'm wondering if you could help me.

— Do you do other things apart from painting?

— I write, as I told you.

— How do you make a living?

— In Montreal, I sold my paintings. But here, I cannot do anything, except write. The situation with my daughter is very difficult, I must say.

— Can you do something else for a living?

I don't have time to answer him as a tall ageless blonde woman interrupts our conversation. I am surprised by the resemblance she has with me. Bob has to be thinking the same thing too because he looks at both of us, stunned.

— You are a man who likes to help, lead, and control, says the woman, turning to Bob without further preamble. You are very disciplined and have a job related to helping others. Then she addresses me directly. As for you, you are in great transition. You are completely blocked in one of your past lives and I have come to help you heal both your present life and your past life.

I remain speechless. Bob looks at me, surprised

— If you want to know more, I'll see you at the parking lot in fifteen minutes, she continues as she is walking away.

— I want you to come with me, Bob. I'm not sure if I want to be alone with this woman. It bothers me that she looks so much like me. I don't understand.

— The resemblance is striking, it's true. She looks like your sister, your mother and your daughter all at the same time. It's as if she has no age. As if she came from another planet.

— This is exactly what I was thinking.

— You know Kiera, in all my twenty years at Lake Shrine, I've never seen anyone with the ability to attract things like you just did.

We head to the parking lot where the ageless woman is already waiting for us.

— My name is Marie.

— This is Bob and I'm Kiera.

— I wanted to prove to you that I would meet you, she says, showing me a page from a magazine.

— But, that's my past life, I say bewildered, seeing the article on Marie-Antoinette that Marie is handing me. How did you know?

— There are no accidents and it's certain that you are related to Marie-Antoinette, but to say that you were Marie-Antoinette, there is a difference, says Marie with a sweet smile. Historical figures are a reference which allow us to place ourselves on time line. That's why I wanted to show you this page.

I do not answer and I wait silently for her response.

— I'll do your session in the park near here, if you don't mind.

— Alright.

At the park, Marie tells me all sorts of things that happen to be completely right: my two divorces, my daughter, and my financial problems. Her way of connecting to me is very special: she closes her eyes, takes my wrists and describes the images that come to her mind.

Suddenly, she bends over to look at my neck, stands up and looks at me, surprised, without saying a word. She looks at me again, completely stunned.

— You are right, she finally says. You are Antoine, I mean, Marie-Antoinette.

I don't know what to say.

— You have a beautiful aura, but it's completely blocked by the jealousy of the people who surrounded you at that time. It is this jealousy that blocks your life today. You have also hurt a lot of men. They were all in love with you and you tended to play with their feelings, even if you were faithful. Men have been hurt and still blame you for their feelings today. I will clean your aura and teach you how to protect yourself. This will allow you to improve your gift of clairvoyance, which is very strong, and go on with your mission. I'll have to give you a therapy with light and candles. I need a quiet place where we will not be disturbed.

— You can do it at my house, Bob proposes spontaneously.

At Bob's, we light the candles that we bought for the ritual that Marie is offering to do: seven candles of different colors, one color per chakra. She seats us around the candles and begins with some incantations. She then asks me to light the first candle; the candle's base chakra is red. I light it, repeating the prayer that Marie gives me. I use this candle to light the second candle, which is orange; that of the sexual chakra. I am not able to light it.

— That's what I thought, says Marie. You are disconnected from this chakra. It may be that you were raped in your past life and it affects your present life.

I look at her, totally shocked.

— I saw that Marie-Antoinette had been raped in regression but I have never found confirmation of such event.

— I'll confirm it, but don't worry. I'll readjust this in your energy.

We continue the ritual with the candles. I manage to light each candle for each remaining chakra without difficulty. Marie ends with several ritual chants in Sanskrit. I feel much lighter, although I am very tired. I then accompany her to her house.

— What you've done for me is priceless, I say, stopping the car. So that's it: I thought I only had $100 on me but I also found in my pocket $60 when we were with Bob. I can give you all knowing that it is well below your worth, I say giving her the money.

— If I haven't mentioned my fee before we start, it's because it is out of question. I am here to help you, that's it! says Marie while getting out of the car. If you agree, I would like to do rituals in different temples around Los Angeles, to help you heal from this past-life.

The next morning I am awakened by an astonishing dream where my parents told me that they knew since I was born that I was Marie-Antoinette. My mother asked me where were the jewels that I had wanted saved. I then answered that I had no idea.

Luc calls me when I wake up.

— So how's your jewel? he asks me bluntly.

— Excuse me? I say totally shocked.

— Well, yeah. How is your book?

— You will not believe my dream. My parents told me that they always knew that I was Marie-Antoinette. My mother asked me where were the jewels that I had wanted saved. I then said that I had no idea.

— It's amazing. Something told me to call you this morning and to ask you that.

— We are really connected, that's clear. It makes sense that my book would allow me to get the money, which I gave away in my past life and was unable to save me.

— It seems that this book will do even more. It will save you!

— You must be right, I say, looking at the time. Luc, sorry, I have to go right now. I have to pick up someone.

I jump in the shower and get dressed. I'm off to Marie's in a jiff, totally elated by my conversation with Luc. I pick her up and she guides me to a beautiful Buddhist temple. I feel immediately at home surrounded by these energies of gratitude and profound joy.

I follow the instructions Marie gives me dutifully: I pour water at the foot of the boddhi tree, walk around it, pray, put my head on its trunk. At this moment in time, I'm almost in a trance because the energy of the tree is so strong. With this energy, I follow Marie inside the Buddhist center and we meditate together. I totally lose track of time and space. A monk comes to talk to me after the ritual and tells me that it seems I find it easy to meditate and that I must get better by meditating more often. He gives me water from the temple, which Marie and I later pour around the Lake Shrine's trees.

Marie and I repeat the same ritual the next three days in three different temples. Each time, I feel like I know the procedures to be followed, although I have never learned them.

In the last temple, the one located in Malibu, I feel completely transported; it feels like we are in a Mayan temple, without having to leave California's lands. It's cold and normally I cannot stand the cold. Marie notices it and says a prayer: I am not cold anymore. I can now enjoy the ceremony with the monks in its entire splendor. Monks chant mantras while moving from one deity to another and allowing us to participate. In the end, they give me a Buddhist rosary to help me improve my meditation and develop my gifts of clairvoyance. I am deeply grateful. I remain permeated with all the energy that emanates from this temple for a long time.

When I bring Marie back to her house, she gives me a little book that she advises me to read that evening; which I hasten to do as soon as I get home. I am baffled by the simplicity of these few untitled pages. They say that when God wants to bring us back to him, he starts by taking everything away from us. It is therefore advisable to accept losing everything and abandon everything to make this real meeting with God: it is in this abandonment that we can find complete faith. I find that these writings are completely consistent with what I am experiencing: I don't have a penny and yet I am very happy because I have met God as I have never met him before.

After reading the book, I go to bed serene. During the night, I am awakened by the cold that has totally taken over my body. I try to get up and hit my head on something hard. I then find myself in Antoine's body, when she hit her head, when the police had come for her to transfer her from the Temple prison, to that of the Conciergerie. I hear myself saying 'nothing can hurt me now'. I see my last conscious moments after the trial and before the guillotine, when I no longer had hope and had to wait for the end to come. I feel cold. This cold seizes me and takes me back to that memory, as soon as I am in contact with it.

I had managed to master the cold during the ritual thanks to Marie's prayers and afterward in the car through my prayers. But now it seems that despite the blankets and all of my prayers, it is necessary that this cold memory of the last moments of my past life unravels within me. I cannot do anything but let it happen. I relive everything very intensely: the setting, the sensation of cold, my hair, the cap on my head, my nightgown, the bed, my renunciation, the abandonment, my despair, and my acceptance. I wait for the process to end without resisting it, while telling myself that this is my last night spent this way. I do not fight it and I fall asleep when it's over.

As I wake up the next morning, I feel relieved. My dream comes back to me: I'm in a lighthouse, with a number of people, one of whom is Samuel in his casual clothes. We are expecting someone. There are vintage cars and improved remodeled cars that people have placed around as a background. All of a sudden we see a huge wave on the screen. We know that none of us is going to make it. I cry out. The wave engulfs us. I find myself in a cafe where Marie is watching the disaster unfold on the screen. She asks me if the senator Samuel passed away. I say yes, pointing out that I was there and saw it all. She says that she knows and no one seems surprised that I am there although I had just died: I resuscitated instantly.

Chapter 4

Confirmations

I am walking down Robertson avenue, checking out some galleries with Marie.

We enter 'French Gallery' and start looking at the paintings with great enthusiasm, because it is a style that definitely comes very close to mine. I realize then how much I miss painting. The gallery owner comes toward me and asks me if I am German.

— Non, je suis française, I reply.

— My name is Georges, he answers in French.

— I'm Kiera, I say while shaking his hand. And this is my friend, Marie.

— It's a pleasure. I thought you ladies were sisters.

— That's what everyone says, I smile.

— Are you both artists? George asks us.

— Not me, but Kiera is, answers Marie, walking away.

— I did a lot of exhibitions in Montreal, but since I have been here, I haven't really felt in the mood.

— What style of painting do you do?

— Encaustic abstract. Magazines have critiqued my paintings to be organic because of the way they resemble nature, in an abstract way.

— I would really like to see your work. Do you have a studio?

— Yes, but I don't currently have anything to show you. Only the ones that I made to hang in my house. I could show you my portfolio although, if you'd like.

— We can start with this and if I like what I see you could maybe do some more for this gallery.

— That's a great idea!

— I could come by next Wednesday, in the morning.

— Alright.

After having given him the directions to my house, I leave the gallery, pleased with this serendipitous meeting.

— It looks like it's your time to shine, says Marie smiling.

— What do you mean by that?

— I can't tell you more. You will see for yourself later.

— Always so mysterious! There is nothing I can do that would make you tell me, I say, a little disappointed. You know everything about me and I know so little about you. Yet I feel as though I know you, because of how much we are alike on different planes. It's a very weird sensation.

— You will know everything, when it's time. For now, savor our friendship. That's all that matters to me.

I do not answer but I squeeze her arm tightly to confirm that our friendship is reciprocal. We continue to walk in silence and turn left on Melrose. We find ourselves in front of an esoteric bookstore named "Boddhi Tree". I have heard a lot about this place but I haven't visited it before.

— What don't we go inside? Marie suggests as she leads the way up the stairs to the bookstore. Something tells me that you will find the answers to your questions in here.

I follow her, then Marie goes in one direction and I go in another. I am moving forward more so to impregnate myself with the special atmosphere of the place then to look for something. I secretly hope to find my lost inspiration. All of a sudden, I feel a strange force imposing me to stop where I am, which I do. I look at the bookshelves, intrigued, and to my great surprise, I read 'reincarnation' on one of them. My gaze is attracted by a book with the title 'Return of the Revolutionaries' by Walter Semkiw, which I take and turn around to read the back cover.

This book does not talk about the French revolution, as I expected, but about the American Revolution. "Walter Semkiw, M.D. asks a startling question in this provocative book: 'What if the key figures in the American Revolution were back with us today, reincarnated in new bodies and personalities, and just as interested in supporting social change and spiritual awakening?' I browse through it, looking for a sign, as I read: 'Much of the world is hostile to reincarnation. This resistance is present, in large part, because acknowledging the reality of reincarnation requires a traumatic reevaluation of belief systems.' As I continue browsing through the pages, I see that the author has compared the portraits of characters from the American Revolution with portraits of their current life reincarnation. I am surprised that I did not think to do this with all the people I have re-discovered in Marie-Antoinette's life. I buy the book, without hesitation, despite my restricted budget. I feel that this book is an important new key in helping me in my path towards reincarnation and in finding my inspiration again. Marie joins me with a knowing smile.

We leave the bookstore and stop at Urth Caffe's patio, which is nearby, to sip on some iced chocolate drinks.

— You knew I was going to find this book, am I right? I ask Marie, curious.

— Yes. It will give you the confirmations that you need to reassure yourself and continue your work more serenely.

— Do you know the author?

— No.

— Walter Semkiw works with a medium, Kevin Ryerson, who has worked with Shirley MacLaine for 30 years. Shirley MacLaine is the author who opened my soul to spirituality. Walter has found that the spirit guide that Kevin channels appears to be able to make accurate past life matches.

— Everything happens for a reason, you know this.

— I know, I say as I survey the book. Look, this book says the same things I have received intuitively.

— Really?

— It says that we reincarnate ourselves with our soul group, that we have the same character and the same physical traits from one life to the other.

— Maybe you should contact this Walter guy? offers Marie with a smile.

— I wouldn't dare, I say, suddenly scared.

— If you got together a file with all the people you have found in your past life, I am sure he would be willing to meet with you.

— And what good would this do?

— It would allow you to believe more in who you were in your previous life and to trust more your intuitions in your present life.

— You may be right. But, I am not sure I would be capable of meeting this man, actually. I am not ready to bring all of this out the open, yet.

— I can do it for you if you want. Once you are done making your file.

— You'd do this for me?

— Of course. I'm here to help you, you know…

— I know, but I am not sure I know why you are doing all this for me.

— Because I find your story amazing and exiting.

— Will you tell me, one day, who you were in this past life? If you are helping me this way, you must've been there at the time when I was Marie-Antoinette, no?

— I cannot tell you for the moment. You will discover it by yourself, when you're ready.

— There are time when I would like you to be less mysterious, you know, I say, pretending to be disappointed.

I spend the next three days building up the file of my past life and that of my entourage. It is very easy, considering I know who, in my present entourage, was who, in my past life. I then only have to search on the internet for the portraits and stories of the people from my past life and compare them with the people from my present life. The result is breathtaking: all the pictures of the people from my present life correspond with those of their past life portraits. I then compare their lives with the data I have and then again, the results are impressive: the events, the personalities, the talents, the dates, everything coincides.

Confident in the light of all this newly found information, I send Marie an email with the attached file. She then contacts Walter Semkiw, telling him she has an anonymous case that is quite interesting to submit to him, without really telling him anything more. To my great surprise and to Marie's great satisfaction, Walter answers back the following day, telling her that he is interested in learning more.

Marie then sends him the complete folder. He answers that he is very impressed by my work and that he would very much like to meet me in San Francisco. Afraid of being alone in this adventure, I ask Marie to come with me. I call Tania so she can keep an eye on Sophie while I am gone; which she accepts right away.

I met Tania the previous year, through Bob, whom, I discovered later, was the reincarnation of the Abbé de Vermond, Marie-Antoinette's early confident and tutor. Bob wanted to introduce me to her when he saw the paintings hanging in my house. As Tania is herself a painter, Bob thought our connection would be great. When we met for the first time we spoke exhaustively, as if we had known each other forever. As she was leaving she complimented me on my studio. I offered her the opportunity to paint there for as long and as often and as she desired. She cried in joy and told me that this was the most amazing gift I could give her. And this is how our story started.

Tania came over to paint practically every day following our first meeting. Every chance we had, we took some time to talk and get to know each other. It seemed that I was re-creating the conversations heard in one of Marie-Antoinette's salons. One day, during one of our numerous discussions, I got the intuition that Tania had been Elisabeth Vigee Lebrun, Marie-Antoinette's portrait painter. Tania was older when I met her, thus I had no means of knowing if she looked like a younger Elisabeth Vigee Lebrun or not.

One day, Tania showed me pictures of her as a young woman and I compared them with Elisabeth Vigee Lebrun's self-portrait. The resemblance was breathtaking. Tania even recognized her sister from her present life in the portrait of her daughter from her past life. Furthermore, their lives corresponded perfectly: Elisabeth and Tania both had taken portrait courses and both had had husbands who were gamblers. Their art was very similar, although Tania had concentrated on abstract art instead of portraits in her present life: the backgrounds of Elisabeth Vigee Lebrun's paintings had become Tania's main axis in her current paintings. Tania suffered a lot from not being recognized as an artist in her current life. Knowing that she had been successful in her previous life allowed her to accept herself. As a struggling artist in this life, she works for herself and not for others, as Elisabeth previously did.

Meanwhile, Georges comes to see my paintings and I show him my portfolio. He likes my work a lot and offers to have an exhibition in his gallery as soon as I produce a dozen paintings. I am enchanted with this opportunity, after I wasted the one with Nathalie. This allows me to offset the difficulties I am going through with my daughter. Indeed Sophie, who is dreading my departure, blames me for my research in the reincarnation domain.

— You told me you had stopped, Sophie tells me angrily. You lied to me again.

— Again?

— Yes, you lied to me about my father.

— I have always told you the truth. And it's still the truth today. Look at all these pictures, I tell her while handing her the file I had prepared for Walter Semkiw.

— How do you want me to tell you this? I could not care less! She says as she grabs the folder and throws it against the wall.

Sophie slams the door as she leaves the house. I run after her but she is nowhere to be seen. I return to home and call Luc, to have his advice.

— Why do you need to prove this reincarnation stuff so much anyway? It's affecting your daughter, can't you see? Luc reproaches me.

— Yes, but I know it's related to her past life. She is reliving the same anxieties as Charlotte, but she doesn't have the memory of the events.

— And what is going to happen if Kevin Ryerson tells you that you are not Marie-Antoinette? How are you going to feel, after having invested so many years of your life into this project? Don't you think it is better that you don't know?

— I need to know. I need a confirmation from a reincarnation expert, like Walter Semkiw or Kevin Ryerson, to enable me to move forward. And then again, you've seen as I have that the resemblance of all these portraits with the pictures of the people from my present life is very striking. You've seen your portrait. You've seen as well that you used to take care of the household's expenses for the Austrian family and that now you're a financial advisor. You had weight issues back then and you still do today…

— It's true that all of this is very disturbing. Anyhow, you are very courageous, Kiera. I am proud of you.

— Thank you. I don't really have a choice, actually. I have come so far I can't go back. I need to finish this.

— You're right.

— What should I do with Sophie, now?

— Wait until she comes back. As always, she will come back, don't worry. You are way too connected in both your present and past lives to not continue on this journey together. She is a teenager right now and it's normal that she is rebelling against you. But if she chose you, there is a reason and I am sure she knows that, even though she is standing up for herself.

— Thank you, Luc, for being in my life. What a joy it is to have met you, to have found you again. Sorry for repeating it so often.

— I can't get enough of it, Kiera. All the pleasure is mine, you know it!

— Who are you talking to? Sophie shouts as she enters the room like a fury. Aren't you sick of all these made up stories that don't make any sense?

— I'll call you back Luc, I say, hanging up. Sophie, don't talk to me like this. I've told you so a hundred times.

— You're crazy. So, I do what I want.

— Sophie, let me show you something ...

— Your file with the pictures? I don't want to see it, I've already said so.

— Let me show you, and if you don't believe it, I'll stop everything. I promise.

— You've already told me the same thing and you haven't kept your promise, she points out.

— This time it's different. Look, please, I said handing her the prized folder.

Sophie hesitates and reluctantly takes the folder. To my surprise, she lingers on it and sits down to get a better look.

— Is it true, then? Sophie says, crying.

I remain silent and sit next to her while she takes the time to look at the pictures one by one to compare.

— Dad looks so much like his past life, it's crazy. The Comte de Provence! He was your brother in law so he was my uncle, right?

— Yes.

— Why did you do this to him?

— What this?

— A child with another man in this life. What did he do to you in that other life?

— He didn't help during the revolution, that's clear. But I feel that the answer lies elsewhere and I have not found it yet, actually ...

— Where are Marie-Antoinette's other children if this is true, then?

— I think your step-sister today was your brother at the time, Louis Charles. Look, they look so much alike.

— It's true. That means we can change sex?

— Yes. We had to dress Louis-Charles as a girl to escape during the flight to Varennes. We were caught and had to return to Paris. He died in prison four years later. Louis-Charles may have kept this memory and chose to be reincarnated as a girl in this life to succeed in escaping from his past life.

— And the others?

— I don't know yet. I think Louis Joseph is Baptiste, you know, the little boy we met a few months ago with his parents on the Promenade. You remember?

— Yes. I remember they had to move to France because of his illness.

— Right.

— Why would it be him?

— Louis Joseph was Marie-Antoinette's first son and was very sick. He died of tuberculosis at age of seven. He started getting sick when he was about two and a half year old, as Baptiste has, and they both have the same symptoms of illness, at the same age.

— Why would Baptiste come back with the same disease, just to die again?

— I don't know ...

— Did you have any other children?

— Yes, a little girl who died at eleven months. Her name was Sophie, too. It's your first name!

— And do you know who this little girl is now?

— I don't have the impression that she has been born yet.

— What about me? It's true that I look like her, says Sophie, looking more closely at Charlotte's picture. This is Charlotte, right. It's a pretty name.

— Charlotte was the name we wanted to give you before you were born. But we went to a meeting in spiritualism by chance just after your conception and we were told that your name would be Sophie.

— What is a spiritualism?

— It's a session where you invoke the spirits for answers. I studied spiritualism after this, and I learned that it is advisable to be careful when you do it because it can attract negative spirits who encourage you to do things that are not necessarily good for you.

Sophie stays silent for a long moment as she looks at the portraits.

— What do you think? I finally ask her.

— There are many things that seem true, but I don't know if I still believe in this completely.

— What are you missing?

— I still don't understand why you didn't have me with Daddy.

— And if we find out why, would you believe it?

— I think so, says Sophie, hesitantly.

— Once you are ready, we'll search together in all the books we can find. Is that okay?

— I'm not sure I want to know, Sophie says dreamily, looking at the portrait of her past life.

The day after, Marie and I arrive in San Francisco in late afternoon and we easily find the restaurant where we are to meet Walter Semkiw. Arriving at the door of the restaurant, I cannot move forward.

— Marie, I can't. I'm too afraid... I'm not ready.

— It's no problem, Kiera. You want me to cancel?

— No, I want you to go without me.

— And what are you going to do?

— I'll drive around San Francisco. Call me a little bit before you are done so I can come and get you.

I immediately recognize Walter sitting at a table, thanks to the picture of him I had seen in his book.

— You look a lot like Marie-Antoinette's portraits, Kiera, says Walter standing up and warmly shaking my hand.

— I'm Marie, pleased to meet you, I say.

— Oh, I'm so sorry. I thought you were Kiera, says Walter.

— I am not surprised. We do look a lot alike. Everyone thinks we're sisters, although I was her therapist before becoming her friend.

— Kiera couldn't make it?

— At the last minute, she got cold feet and decided to drive around San Francisco.

— I understand ... Tell me how you discovered that Kiera was Marie-Antoinette.

I tell him about my meeting with Kiera at the Lake Shrine and how, in a daydream, I'd been told to go to this place to meet her and offer my help. I tell him about the cares I gave her, her childhood nightmares, her visions, her emotions and events in her life, including those around the paternity of her daughter. After more than two hours of conversation, Walter is convinced.

— The fact that Kiera has met many people from her past life strengthens her case. We need to see what happens in a

session with Kevin. Although, do you mind if I check with Kevin Ryerson tomorrow?

— Of course not. On the contrary.

— Does Kiera agree?

— Of course.

— You could go with me, if you want. It would give you the opportunity to meet with him, too. Normally he would only see me, but I think he would make an exception, since you're therapist.

— I'd love to, I say enthusiastically.

I leave the restaurant very excited because of what just happened. I call Kiera, who is already waiting for me outside the restaurant. I get in the car.

— Have you been here for a while? I ask, surprised.

— I couldn't do anything. I was totally paralyzed by fear. How was it?

— Great. Walter is a charming man. He is open and supportive of your connection with Marie-Antoinette. He will discuss your case in his session with Kevin Ryerson tomorrow.

— Awesome. That's exactly what I needed.

— You want to come with me?

— Oh no ... although, I want you to tell me everything.

Kiera drops me off at the corner of Kevin's street and leaves. I walk to his house and ring the doorbell. Walter welcomes me in as warmly as the day before. Kevin is waiting for us in his office with a big smile on his face. We introduce each other and Kevin sits in a chair and closes his eyes. He breathes deeply and begins to speak in a very strange voice. He then presents himself as Ahtun Re, a priest from Ancient Egypt. He is able to read the Akashic Record to learn about individuals past lives.

— Hello Ahtun Re, says Walter. We are here more specifically to verify the previous life of Kiera Hermine and some people from her soul group. Is it possible to have some answers?

— Yes, it is.

— Is Kiera Hermine, born in Bondy, France, and living in Los Angeles the reincarnation of Marie-Antoinette?

I hold my breath. Thirteen years of Kiera's life will find its culmination point, or not, in a few seconds, depending on Kevin's response.

— Yes, she is.

I cannot stop the tears from rolling down my cheeks, because the emotion overwhelming me is so great. I close my eyes to savor the moment that Kiera has been waiting for, without knowing it, all these years. I want to call to tell her the good news, but am unable to move.

— She's very emotional and that's normal, continues Ahtun Re through Kevin. Marie is connected to Kiera and that is very good because they need each other. Do you understand?

— Yes, says Walter.

— Do you understand, Marie? Ahtun Re asks me through Kevin.

— Yes, I reply timidly.

— Few people really know Marie-Antoinette. She was a mystic and helped Mesmer for many years. All that she learned then and that we do not know about her now will surely help Kiera in her current life. Do you understand?

— Yes, I answer, while taking notes.

Kevin remains silent. Walter continues.

— Is Sophie Loringini, born in France and living in Los Angeles with her mother Kiera Hermine, the reincarnation of Marie Thérèse Charlotte, the daughter of Marie-Antoinette, known as Madame Royale?

— Yes, she is.

— *Is Sophie also the reincarnation of Edie Sedgwick born in Santa Barbara and egery of Andy Warhol?*

— *No, she is not. She had a similar fate at the time she knew Andy Warhol and died of an overdose too. That is why Kiera felt she could be Edie. In this life, she has to overcome this problem. She does not need to know her lives between her life as Charlotte and the present one, because they are too traumatic. Do you understand?*

— *Yes, I answer while writing down what Kevin just said.*

— *Is Philippe Loringini, born in France and father of Sophie, the reincarnation of the Comte of Provence, brother of Louis XVI? continues Walter.*

— *Yes, he is.*

— *Is Samuel Parbes, born in France, the reincarnation of the Comte d'Artois, brother of Louis XVI?*

— *Yes, he is.*

— *Is Olivier Fertari, born in Montreal and working as an interior designer, Comte Hans Axel de Fersen?*

— *Yes, he is.*

— *The last for today: is Thomas Innesref, born in France and owner of an Art-Therapy center, is the reincarnation of Louis XVI, King of France?*

— *I cannot say anything more. Kiera must discover this for herself. But it will be obvious to her the next time she sees him. Do I make myself clear?*

— *Yes.*

— *Do you have any questions, Marie?*

— *Yes, Kiera asked why she has done so much harm to her ex-husband, Philippe Loringini?*

— *Because he betrayed her in their past life! A clairvoyant actually already told her so once.*

— *That is why Kiera has a child with her lover!*

— *Among other things.*

— *Could you be more specific?*

— *I can't tell you anymore. She will discover the truth when her daughter is ready to receive such information. I feel you should both focus more on the fact that you and Kiera should finish your book on Marie-Antoinette's reincarnation. Do you understand?*

— *No, not really. Actually, Kiera is writing a book on Marie-Antoinette's reincarnation, but I am not. I'm helping her with her work, that's all.*

— *You have accumulated a lot of data about her and Marie-Antoinette and your contribution will be helpful for the publication of this book. Kiera, in a very near future, will be afraid of the consequences of the book's publication and she will close up and retreat, once at the publisher's. You will then have the choice to finish that book instead of her.*

I don't know what to say.

— *Has this been of help? finally asks Ahtun Re*

— *Of course.*

— *I must withdraw now. Thank you for your attention, says Ahtun Re through Kevin.*

We remain silent. Kevin then returns to himself, shaking his head. He then drinks a large glass of water, looking at me with a smile.

— *So do you have the answers to your questions? He asks me with a lot of empathy in his voice, which has now returned to its normal pitch.*

— *Yes, thank you, I say with a smile, tears in my eyes.*

— *Everything is going to go very well for you, Marie, do not worry, he says, getting up.*

Walter and I leave the room in silence. Walter offers to eat at a restaurant at the marina. In the car, I call Kiera to tell her the good news. She is silent and I just have time to tell her where I am before she hangs up. We finally arrive at the restaurant.

— Could Ahtun Re have been mistaken? I ask Walter once we sit at the table

— In my experience, Ahtun Re is accurate but I always try to validate the statements through historical research and I perform my own assessment. You will need to do that also. Similarly, regarding the book, Ahtun Re made the suggestion, but you will have to decide for yourself whether you want to proceed. .

I remain silent

— This will be so good for Kiera to be supported by rational people like you and Kevin, I say trying to keep my own fear under control.

— You do seem to have psychic abilities, as does Kiera. I think it would help Kiera to continue what she started. You can help her.

— How?

— Kevin told you. Marie-Antoinette was a mystic. I am under the impression that Kiera needs to continue what she started, even if she does not want to finish her book, and you must help her to find what the historic books do not tell us. You did not meet each other by accident, and it is your work in common that will allow your research to deliver and this book to be published.

— You must be right ... Can I ask you a question that has been haunting me ever since I have read your book, Walter?

— Of course, Walter responds in a friendly manner.

— In your book you talk about 'split', that is to say a single soul who could have embodied different bodies at the same time, to address several problems at once. I admit that I don't believe it ... This is beyond my comprehension! Could you explain how it works to me?

— When you look at an octopus, it has a head and several tentacles. Imagine that the head is the soul and the tentacles are the lives that the soul has decided to live. It's the same head and therefore the same soul that controls the tentacles which are the different lives. Is this more clear now?

— Yes, but I admit that it's a concept which I will have to get used to.

— Generally souls who can have split incarnations have had a great deal of experience incarnating on the Earth plane. Even for people who are pretty advanced, the idea of split incarnation can be pretty mind-boggling.

— I understand ... I said, thoughtfully.

— Are you thinking of a 'split' in particular?

— No, not really ... I just feel that understanding the reality of the 'splits' will allow me to continue more effectively on my own path.

On our way back to Los Angeles, Marie finishes telling me everything that Kevin Ryerson, Ahtun Re and Walter told her. I feel that there is something she is holding back, and as much as I keep insisting, she says that she has told me everything. To clear my head, I call Sophie to tell her the good news about Marie-Antoinette.

— Mom, that's great. I'm really happy for you! Did he confirm Dad, Thomas and the others?

— Not all of them, but the main ones, yes. Except Thomas.

— Thomas was not my father, then?

— He told Marie that it was important that I discover it by myself.

— Oh!

— I'll be there in about four hours. See you soon, sweetheart.

We drive in silence. I think about everything that just happened. I keep thinking of the session with Kevin that Marie described to me and feel a new energy manifest itself in me.

When I get home I am exhausted. I need several days of intense sleep to incorporate this new reality within me that I am indeed Marie-Antoinette's reincarnation. I feel that this past life, which I experienced but did not truly understand and accept, has now, little by little, integrated every facet of my life. I finally feel complete.

PART IV

Chapter 1

Comprehensions

I write the word 'END' at the bottom of the last page of my manuscript with a lot of happiness. I've enjoyed the effort I put in for almost a year to finish my book.

Soon after, Marie tells me about Marie-Antoinette's exhibition at the Grand Palais in Paris. I immediately feel I want to go, because it would allow me to meet with the publisher recommended by a friend at the same. I don't not know how this would happen. I need a miracle, because I invested all my time and money I earned with my paintings in my book. A very tough little voice told me to trust and that something would happen before April 19, anniversary of Marie-Antoinette's marriage by proxy.

Joyfully savoring a rare moment of idleness, the phone rings.

— It's me, says a voice.

— Who me? I ask surprised.

— The Pope, the voice responds, laughing.

— Thomas? What a surprise! How did you find me? How did you get my phone number?

— The magic of the internet ... How is Sophie?

— She's fine. It was a difficult time, but she got through it, thank God.

— I find it reassuring. I just heard about a man in his thirties who was in a relationship with a girl Sophie's age. I was so disgusted I wanted to be sure she was okay.

I told him everything we had been through since our arrival in the United States: Sophie's drugs, her repeated absences at school, our arguments and finally a reprieve since meeting Marie and Walter.

— Why didn't you call me? I may have been able to help you.

— The last time I spoke to you, you did not really help us, I point out. You offered that you would pay child support after the DNA tests and you did not make it. This entire DNA story was the reason Sophie started taking drugs.

— What are you doing in Los Angeles? Thomas asks to change the subject.

— I just finished a book.

— That's great. Congratulations. What is it about?

— Reincarnation.

— You're kidding?! I always believed in reincarnation, but I have never told anyone because I was afraid that people would say I was crazy. Have you found a publisher?

— Possibly.

— Where?

— Paris.

— Why don't you come to France, then. I'll pay for the ticket. I think your project is fabulous. I want to help you.

— Thanks. That's nice, but I can't leave like this; I have to pay my rent and my bills. I'm pretty late as it is.

— How much do you need?

— $4,500.

— I will send the money and you then only have to decide when you want to come.

I spend the next two days organizing my departure. I ask Sophie to come with me, but she has to go to school and does not want to miss her classes. I ask Marie to come over and take care of her, while I am away, but Marie prefers to go to France with me to see Marie-Antoinette's exhibition. I then ask Tania who is painting at my house that day, to take care of Sophie and she accepts, without hesitation: she has always enjoyed drawing and painting with my daughter. They are both great artists.

Once in the plane, I realize that I am leaving Los Angeles, on April 21st, the anniversary of Marie-Antoinette's departure from Austria. That day, in fact, she left her homeland to travel to France and marry the Dauphin Louis Auguste, the future king of France, in person.

I am very serene at my reunion with Thomas. Because of what I know about his possible former life, I see him differently now. Everything is an excuse for me to observe and find confirmation of my intuitions.

Thomas and I meet Marie at the entrance of the Grand Palais. She has arrived early and already has the tickets in hand. I introduce her to Thomas and, although he doesn't say anything, he is blown away by our resemblance.

Marie-Antoinette's exhibition is divided into five periods: her childhood in Austria, her life at Versailles, the Trianon, the revolution and the guillotine. Thomas opens the discussion by saying that the portraits of the young Marie-Antoinette are strikingly similar to Sophie. Although it is true that is easier to see Sophie in the portraits of Marie-Antoinette and that Sophie and I really look much alike, I cannot recognize myself in any of the portraits of Marie-Antoinette. Although, I find myself seeing Marie in the portraits too.

— Is it possible that if I were Marie-Antoinette, you were one of my sisters? I finally ask her.

— Who knows? Marie replies evasively.

— There are times when I would like you to help me a little bit more, you know.

— This is what I do, but there are answers that you have to find by yourself, she says with a smile. This is not against you. It is rather to help you strengthen your gifts. If I give you all the answers you won't develop the ability to look for them.

I walk away without a word, frustrated not to have answers to my questions. I continue to make progress in the show, disappointed not to see myself in the portraits of Marie-

Antoinette. I do not know what to think. Is it possible that I am deluded and either Sophie or Marie is Marie-Antoinette? Is it possible that Ahtun Re made a mistake, too, about my past identity?

The further I go in the show, the more I am obsessed with those questions. The more I ask myself these questions, the less I feel I could have been Marie-Antoinette. Although, I have no problem recognizing Philippe, Samuel, Olivier and even Thomas.

Beset by doubts, but amazed by the ingenuity of the exhibition, I try to keep moving through the different phases of Marie-Antoinette's life with detachment.

When I get to the section that represents Marie-Antoinette's life at Trianon, I have a shock: I must grab on to the door frame and breathe deeply not to lose consciousness. My legs begin to tremble: I feel like my body and my mind are trying to dissolve in the atmosphere. I sit down to avoid falling. My mind tries to join the two realities, that of Trianon and that of today, at the same time. My body is not able to handle the huge influx of energy that results and I feel like I will implode. I close my eyes and stop resisting. I am floating and I think that if that is death, I accept it without hesitation. I let myself be in the moment. There is an ethereal reality that is superimposed to my physical reality. I do not know where I am: real in this exhibition, ephemeral at Trianon or dissolved into the universe. Actually, it doesn't really matter. I am now at the Trianon and walk with delight. I see my bedroom, my garden, the grotto.

— Kiera, Kiera, what's happening? I hear in the distance.

In an instant, my mind comes back to the reality of the exhibition. The feeling of expansion of my body and my mind is still strong but I can open my eyes. I smile with happiness.

— What's happening? Thomas asks me, panicked. You've been acting really weird since you got here.

— I don't know, but it's very nice! I say with an ecstatic smile.

— Have you taken drugs or what?

— Don't talk that loud, please, the noise is very difficult for me right now.

— I'm whispering. I'm really worried now!

— Let me take care of her, says Marie, who arrives at that moment.

I remain silent and close my eyes again. I feel my soul trying to leave my body and I am ready to let it go.

— Zero, one, two, three, four, five, says Marie with a snap. Open your eyes, your eyes are wide open.

I open my eyes immediately. My body is still between two realities. I want to let myself go into the sweet sensation that calls me, but Marie calls me back to reality constantly, with little success. I come back in a second, when she finally puts me a small jar of smelling salts under my nose.

— What is your reincarnation book about exactly? Thomas finally asks.

— Why do you ask? I ask with difficulty.

— I need to know. That would help me understand what is happening with you, since we've been here.

I cannot answer.

— What is the book about? asks Thomas to Marie. I wish someone would tell me.

— Kiera has to do it, not me, answers Marie.

— I guess it's about Marie-Antoinette, right? Thomas asks, angry. The more I look at her, the more I think Kiera looks like the portraits of Marie-Antoinette.

I don't know what to say. I just want to close my eyes to escape the hostile reality and sink back into that wonderful sensation of detachment of my soul when I was at Trianon.

— Come on, Thomas says, forcing me to get up. We'll walk a little and you'll feel better.

— Wait, I can't, I say, closing my eyes. Give me a few minutes, please.

I close my eyes and let my body take over in that delicious feeling of life at Trianon. 'Here I am myself'.

— Aum, Marie repeats endlessly, until I return completely to me.

I get up. The feeling continues to be very present but I can walk, even if I have the strange feeling that my body is no longer mine and I feel as though I am floating rather than walking.

Walking allows me to gradually come back to the present. In silence, Marie, Thomas and I come to the part of the exhibition that represents the corridor to the guillotine. I cannot stop the contractions I feel in my body, while the wonderful floating sensation persists. I look at all the objects in display with detachment. When I arrive before an unfinished portrait of Marie-Antoinette by Alexandre Kucharski, I finally recognize myself. Thomas and Marie are at my side looking at me, dumbfounded.

— Well, I need to know what is going here. What's the story with Marie-Antoinette? You were her or what?

— You won't believe me if I tell you!

— Look, you don't have to convince me. I think you look a lot like her. Sophie and Marie, too. This is insane.

— Two psychics and Marie told me I had been Marie-Antoinette in my previous life, and I have been doing research for years to learn the truth.

— Look, there's no need to search. It's obvious. And Sophie, who was she, then? And me?

— Sophie was already my daughter and you, I think you were Louis XVI. I'm not sure though. I asked for a sign and I am waiting for it.

— That's strange, because I'm more interested in the Napoleonic period, not the French Revolution.

— I told you, I am not sure. You look much more like Louis XV, I think. Why don't we go to the bookstore to check it all? Maybe if you read about Louis XVI, you will know.

Fascinated by my story, Thomas buys us all the books we need to continue our research on Marie-Antoinette. He also buys a book on Louis XVI for himself.

We finally go outside and the fresh air helps, but the feeling in my body lasts a few hours more before gradually disappearing. Marie leaves us to find a friend at St-Germain. We will see her again the next day at Versailles; she wants to be by my side when I come in contact with the elements of my past life, to be able to help me if I need it.

— I forgot how life was rather extraordinary with you, Kiera, says Thomas, while taking my arm, as we head to the car. What a pleasure to be with you again.

I do not know what to say and continue to walk, silently.

— Have you ever loved me? Thomas asks me in the car.

— I met two other men and I can say that I've really loved them. As for you, that was something else! Karma surely, I guess.

It is Thomas' turn to remain silent. We drive in silence, each one of us lost in our thoughts. As we arrive at the Conciergerie, Thomas stops the car.

— Do you really need to meet this man now?

— Yes, it's important.

— Is he one of the men you were deeply in love with?

— No, he is not.

— Call me when you're done.

— Do what you have to do, because I will have to be with him for a while, I say once I am out of the car.

I meet Bastien in front of the gate of the Conciergerie. I recognize him in the raincoat that he often wears in Los Angeles.

— I am so glad to see you, Kiera, he says, hugging me.

— Tell me, Bastien, it puzzles me: why did you choose the Conciergerie for our appointment?

— I don't know. I wanted to and I didn't ask myself why, he says, as we enter the prison.

— How is Baptiste?

— Not very well. He can no longer stand up on his own. Although, he is very positive, always smiling and you have no idea how precious he is!

— Good. And you, how are you doing? Sincerely!

— I'm holding up. I am with my son as much as possible and don't think about the future. Have you already been to the Conciergerie? Bastien asks me as we enter the guard room.

— Yes. When I was a kid, my mother brought us here. I very vividly remember the Marie-Antoinette's cell. Very small, very dark, the walls that ooze moisture. A small wooden table with a chair. I would recognize among a thousand, I say, although I must confess that I don't feel anything strong right now.

— It's amazing the memory you have. How old were you when you came here?

— I don't know. Nine years old, I guess.

— Impressive! I have no strong memories from that age. Speaking of Marie-Antoinette, the e-mail you sent me regarding Baptiste as the reincarnation of Marie-Antoinette's son was very interesting. It is cool to know that my son was a little prince. I look forward to learning more. Did you find me by chance?

— You would have been Antoine Allonville, Baptiste's tutor when he was Louis Joseph. You were like a father to him.

— That's beautiful. That is why he's my son in this life, then?

— Yes.

— So do you recognize it? Bastien wonders when we arrive at Marie-Antoinette's cell.

— It's weird, I say shocked. Not at all. Yet I still remember very accurately in my mind. As if I were there...

— Look, Bastien says, pointing to a small sign. This is not the cell where Marie-Antoinette was, but a similar cell. Her cell is now apparently the chapel.

— Ah, I say continuing to look closely inside the cell, to match my memories with what I see today.

I suddenly realize that if the cell I remember is not the cell that I visited with my mother, it must be my memory of the time of Marie-Antoinette. That upsets me a lot. Bastien realizes something is wrong and takes my arm gently to comfort me.

— Don't tell me that you were imprisoned here, anyway?!

— Of course not, I say, trying to regain my senses and to fight against the desire that my body has to dissolve into the universe as it did at the exhibition.

— Let's go for something to eat, Bastien says leaving the room. I know a really nice restaurant near St. Louis Church.

— Good idea, I say following him robotically.

I feel good being outside, even if the light dazzles me. I have memories of when Marie-Antoinette came out the Conciergerie: the same glare, my surprise at the cart, the horses rearing up, the crowd being silent... I step back with fear without realizing it and stay there as if I were hypnotized by the scene of the past.

— What is happening to you, Kiera?

— Nothing, everything is alright, I say, shaking my head. Walking will make me feel better.

— You know, you never told me who you were in Baptiste's time, when he was a little prince. I'm sure we knew each other!

— I will tell you when we have verified you and Baptiste! All right?

— Ok!

Bastien and I are walking, while talking. I am amazed by our natural complicity. At one point I look up to a balcony and I suddenly remember the faint smile of Baptiste as my son. In shock, I stumble and almost fall down. Bastien grabs me in time and looks at me, surprised to see my eyes full of tears.

— What's happening Kiera?

— I just remembered a regression that I had when I saw m ... uh ... your son on this balcony, I say, pointing upwards to show him the place.

— We should start a tour company called 'Qui-Erra Erre-Mine-De-Rien' (who wandered casually wanders), Bastien says, laughing.

I look at him in surprise and I burst out laughing with him.

— It's my turn, continues Bastien. You can tell me how I do ok?. Now I see the crowd around us. They are silent and look at us with hatred. I am afraid they'll kill me. I sit before you to protect you, oh My queen, he says, suiting the action to the word. You manage to run away, but the crowd is attacking me and killing me and I cannot do anything, finishes Bastien, collapsing to the ground theatrically. What do you think?

— I think you are very talented, I say, holding out his hand to help him up!

— So I passed the test?! We are partners?! Bastien says, laughing.

— It's clear!

— Let's celebrate, Bastien says as we arrive at the terrace of a cafe.

We order two 'kir royal' and toast, laughing. It feels good to be with Bastien.

Bastien's phone rings. His wife is on the line and he walks away to answer her. When he returned, his face is dark.

— My wife is already mourning Baptiste and that gives me great pain. She wants us to have another child, when I just want to spend my time taking care of him. I am so disappointed that she has given up.

— She is suffering, you know, and sometimes it's easier to cut the suffering than going through it. How is Baptiste doing?

— You know, of the three of us, I think he's the strongest. He completely transformed me with his way of dealing with the disease. He is very young and while doctors have condemned him, he always smiles. I feel he is aware of everything.

— What about making the comparisons between your son and Louis Joseph, to try to understand what is going on?

— Good idea. I'm listening.

I take the pages concerning Marie-Antoinette's son that I compiled from different websites when I did my research.

— Louis Joseph is a bright child who has a quick mind.

— Absolutely Baptiste.

— His illness began with a high fever when he was two and a half years.

— This is exactly the age when Baptiste's high fevers began.

— Two years later, high fever resumes and spine begins to curve. We see a little later he has trouble walking.

— It's amazing. Baptiste can no longer stand because his spine can no longer bear it, says Bastien very moved. What does all this mean? Why does Baptiste have to come back with the same disease?

— I don't know, really. Maybe we'll discover why together. We cannot go further, now, because Baptiste has only these symptoms for four years.

— How old was Louis Joseph when he died?

— About seven and a half years.

— That's about Baptiste's life expectancy. Do you think we can still do something to save him?

— There are things that we can change when you know the past lives and others that we cannot change. Maybe he was just there for you and your wife to transform.

— It's already done. Beyond all hope. And what about him in all this?

— He has his own karma. He must be an evolved soul if he returns with the same disease.

— Why did he choose ma as a father if he was Marie-Antoinette's son?

— You were his tutor and you were together at all time and therefore very close. You played with him and invented all kinds of games to amuse him.

— It's fun. It's still what I do now in some ways, since I have my own toy company.

— You have been awarded of the Order of St. Louis and we are on the 'Ile St Louis'! It's special.

— The first tour we will create for our company, Bastien says, smiling.

— Good idea, I say in the same tone. It is also said that Antoine Allonville was awarded of the Cross of Malta when he was 50 years old, I said, looking at my notes.

Bastien, surprised, unbuttons his shirt and shows me the cross he wears around his neck.

— For my fiftieth birthday, I bought myself the Maltese cross. I did not know why, but it was very important that I had it. Today, I understand. Would that mean that all of this is true, then? Bastien asks, still in shock of his discovery.

— That must be!

— What about my wife? Who was she?

— I think she was the Duchess of Penthièvre.

— Her name sounds familiar.

— She was one of the richest women of the court and was married to Philippe d'Orléans, who was involved in the revolution and voted the death of his cousin, Louis XVI. His vote had the power to change the destiny of the royal family.

— Do you think they were lovers, the Duchess of Penthièvre and Antoine d'Allonville?

— History does not say, but certainly you've rubbed shoulders.

— And what is her relationship with Baptiste? Why would she choose to be his mother?

— She was the mother of several children and maybe had been shocked that the beginnings of the revolution, orchestrated by her husband, did not allow Marie-Antoinette and Louis XVI to be with their children. Louis Joseph died just before the Revolution, June 4, 1789, and his parents could not mourn the child, because of the events that precipitated the French Revolution! The death of Louis Joseph was really the bad omen of all that followed.

— But why should we be his parents?

— Maybe, she believed you were the perfect man for her children, when she saw you taking care of Louis Joseph when he was sick. Moreover, you gave your life for Louis XVI and Marie-Antoinette, during the events of August 10, 1792, while her husband took their life. By both giving life to that child, you unconsciously tried to change the course of past events.

— So we ended up together because we had and still have the same beliefs and aspirations. It's beautiful! And who were you into all of this? Are you going to finally tell me?

— I was his mother! I answer simply.

— I knew it, says Bastien at the height of excitement. And what is your role in all this?

— Marie-Antoinette never recovered from the loss of her son who died at the beginning of the revolution. She was also very much affected by the kidnapping of her other son by the revolutionaries. I think I had to find them again in this life, to make peace with the fact that I could not be there for them when they needed me the most.

— So I guess Sophie was your daughter at the time. And your other son, where is he?

— He's a girl and she's the daughter of Sophie's father.

— What I still do not understand is why Bastien has the same disease?

— I don't know, I said, flipping through my notes. Look, maybe this: Marie-Antoinette said, 'If my son were the son of an individual, he would have been saved.'

— He's telling us that it was his destiny, Bastien says, tears in his eyes, and nothing can change that. Right?

— Yes, and even today, despite all the improvements in medicine, we still cannot save him.

— I would love for you to meet Baptiste but my wife refuses. I'm sorry.

— Things are repeating, unfortunately. I was denied the right to see my son at Marie-Antoinette's time. This is still the case today. Don't worry, I have learned to detach myself, because I know through reincarnation that our children do not belong to us and I will see them again.

— What you've said is beautiful.

— It would be maybe too difficult to be again all together today after having lived such traumatic past lives, and we would maybe not be able to get through. I know that I love my children, despite the distance and the trials and they are loved by their parents. As there is no death and because love transcends death, what now could I want more?

— You're right. I just wish that Baptiste could see you, Kiera. Can you imagine how powerful that would be?

— That might be too powerful, in fact, Bastien. Life always knows better than we do what we need to evolve.

We continue to talk all night, without stopping and without being aware of time passing. It is a moment stolen in time that takes us out of time. We walk along the banks of the Seine and witness the sunrise.

Thomas picks me up outside of the hotel of Bastien.

— So how was it? Thomas asks me when I get into his car.

— Extraordinary. We found lots of answers to our questions about Baptiste's disease and existential questions that we had.

— Do you think the child will be saved?

— No, but what we found allows Bastien to accept the situation with more detachment, even if it is still not easy to see your child dying slowly. Now that Bastien believes in reincarnation, he is open to other perspectives and this can only be positive for him and his son.

— What are the prospects?

— Accepting to let go his son, by knowing that is what is supposed to be. Bastien is a very combative businessman and he thought he might be able to save his son, simply because he wanted to, when it is something that is beyond success and failure. At the level of the soul, there is no failure or success; there is only perfection in everything.

— My God, that looks like this night was intense for both of you.

— Yes, I say dreamily.

— Did something happen between the two of you? Thomas asks off the cuff.

— Not what you think, but much more: we have communicated at the level of the soul and it was wonderful.

— Good.

— Look, I have not slept all night but I feel great to go to Versailles now. Knowing Marie, I am quite sure she is already there.

— At your service, majesty! Thomas says in a tone of humor. I would not miss it for anything.

We arrive at the gates of the château and there is a big crowd to get tickets. I join the line and call Marie. She says she is caught in traffic and she will be late. Thomas goes somewhere in the château to find out how to obtain tickets for the château, the Trianon and the Hamlet so as to save time.

When I see Thomas going into the château, I receive a shock: I immediately recognize his clumsy and lackadaisical gait when he was Louis XVI and I was Marie-Antoinette. I watch him disappear into the building and wait to see him come back to see if the feeling would still be the same. It is. I'm excited to tell him about my discovery.

— I have no doubt that you were Marie-Antoinette, but I am not so confident with me being Louis. I don't feel special affinity for this man. I don't like his cowardly and indecisive personality. At the same time, I believe in your intuition, because it makes sense. Perhaps the book on Louis XVI will tell me more, when I read it!

— Surely.

— By the way, they say we have to wait two hours to get our tickets.

— What about going to the 'Petit Trianon', then? I say, while taking my phone to call Marie.

— Good idea.

— Marie, where are you?

— Right behind you.

We all go to the 'Petit Trianon' through the gardens and the 'Little Venice'. The place is beautiful and seems familiar, especially with the boats on the water and people picnicking on the edge of the lake. I feel at home. We continue to walk when I see the sign 'Grand Canal'. I stop, surprised. I realize then the perfection of life: I now live in California, thousands of miles from Versailles, on the Grand Canal, the same name as the place of my past life, without having planned anything whatsoever. What are the chances of that happening to me?

We continue to advance and reach the 'Grand Trianon' quickly because I do not really like this place and I cannot wait to be back at the 'Petit Trianon'. This decision, however, allows us to buy our tickets. We arrive at the 'Petit Trianon' and learn that it is closed for renovations. I cannot believe I made a journey of ten thousand miles to find a closed door. Disappointed, I look at Marie who smiles at me without a word. I do not understand.

— It's fate, says Thomas, when we are in front of the building.

I do not listen and choose another destiny. I climb over the fence. I am inside the Petit Trianon! I tread carefully among the tools and scaffolding. I am afraid of being discovered. There are music, lights and work but not workers. I take this opportunity to visit the Trianon, from top to bottom and bottom to top. I take all the steps and visit all the rooms without interference. I am excited to be back home. My body tries to dissolve, as before, to re-enter at the moments of my previous life. I remember the main staircase, the bull's eye window, the view of the gardens. Even if the walls are white and empty, I see the curtains of the time, occasional tables, chandeliers, fireplaces, furniture, mirrors. I even remember the smell. I see the flowers that I asked to have everywhere to make this place more welcoming. Time does not matter anymore. I take time to enjoy every second here, where I loved to be so much.

Suddenly I feel I must leave and I head towards the exit. By the time I step over the barrier, a worker comes in and looks at me, surprised.

— I couldn't help it, I say with a smile.

— We won't say anything, he replies, smiling at me.

Thomas is waiting a little further away, Marie at his side.

— That was wonderful. I had the Petit Trianon to myself. I remembered everything as if it were yesterday, not two hundred years ago. My body seemed to remember too. It was as if the past and the present were not separated, as if I were in two simultaneous realities.

— I'm really happy for you, Marie tells me contentedly.

— I feel like my body went through something very intense, like an important energetic alignment.

— You emanate it very strongly indeed, confirms Marie with a smile.

— You really took the opportunity that the universe has given you, in any case, Thomas says, very excited. Congratulations. I must admit I was nervous when I didn't see you coming back for more than an hour. Marie kept me from going to get you!

— Were you afraid I would disintegrate into the past, right?

— Something like that, Thomas answers with a smile.

— Well, I really have to walk if I don't want to go crazy. My body and my brain are completely in turmoil and I feel like I will explode.

We walk toward Marie-Antoinette's theater. It is an architectural gem. What happiness for me to be there. I remember playing with Philippe and Samuel on the stage. Thomas is there watching us from his chair. How many laughs we had! The same laughter I had with Samuel in my present life. I think of him suddenly. I miss him. Everything is so confusing and intense that I cannot hold back my tears.

I loved that period so much. I was so far from knowing what would happen then. I remember the crowd that arrived at Versailles. An old wheel on the cobblestone ... I take a deep breath so as not to be caught in negative emotions and spoil the wonderful time I am experiencing.

— I need some fresh air, I say, leaving the theater.

— This place is so beautiful, says Thomas. I have a feeling of intense déja-vu.

I remain silent and gradually return to my senses. I soon find the pleasure of being in the moment again. Marie takes my arm and we walk in silence toward the gazebo and the grotto. I let her guide me, although everything seems so familiar. I seem to follow an invisible thread, that of my past. The locations have been not erased even after more than two centuries of my absence.

We enter the grotto and sit on the small stone bench. I close my eyes to better enjoy the moment. I think of Louis Joseph's death. I miss that child. Meanwhile, I am happy to have found him again and to know that Bastien and his wife are taking care of him so well. I remember all the events that have just happened. Suddenly, a man interrupts my thoughts and tells me that I must return to the château quickly. I get up. Marie asks me quietly what I see and I suddenly come back to reality. I open my eyes.

— I saw the last time I was here. I didn't know it was the last time. I am so happy to be here today, you have no idea. It feels like a resurrection!

— You know it's weird, I feel I know this place, too, that I've been here before, says Thomas, who sits down next to us. What's crazy is that I often visited the château of Versailles with my family but I never came here.

— It must be your past life memories recurring to you, then! I say with a smile.

— Yes, says Thomas moved, and I want to thank you for that. Thank you for this great experience. It's so precious.

We all remain silent.

— What about going to the hamlet? I look forward to seeing it again! I say, smiling.

Thomas and I leave the grotto, arm in arm, a new complicity creating itself between us, as if by magic. It is Marie's turn to follow us in silence. We continue to walk as we talk. Thomas is turned upside down by our reunion and our escapade to Versailles. He would like to resume our relationship where we left off. I gently make him understand that my life is in California with my daughter and not with him. We had to meet again to turn our karma around and heal it. Furthermore, what we are experiencing right now belongs to the past and allows us to make peace with this traumatic period.

— Do you think I could really have been Louis XVI, then? Thomas suddenly asks me.

— I feel so strongly about this ever since I saw you in the paved entrance earlier. Look, here is the hamlet, I say, pointing towards it.

— This place is really special. It's beautiful! I have never seen it before.

— Oh my God, I say suddenly surprised. You know what? I'm realizing that this place looks very similar to the Lake Shrine, where I usually meditate in California.

— Really?

— It's amazing ... I realize now that when I first learned that I could have been Marie-Antoinette, the psychic brought me here. And the second time, when I met Marie and she discovered my previous life, that was around the Lake Shrine, which looks so much like this place, I say suddenly completely overcome by emotion. I look around for Marie, who is right by me and takes my hand to calm me.

— It's a funny coincidence, indeed, says Thomas.

— There are no coincidences, Thomas, Marie says, especially when you work in the field of karma and reincarnation. Everything has a meaning, I can tell you.

— What does all of this mean, then? Thomas asks worried.

— I don't know, I say, calmer.

— That surely means that Yogananda, who founded the Lake Shrine, was also there at the time of Marie-Antoinette, Marie says softly.

— Really? And do you have an idea of who he was? I ask, surprised.

— You have to discover it, Marie answers with half a smile. You've got all the skills, you know that.

— Since I have been meditating there, I feel at home... As I do here... I say thoughtfully. This is exactly the same feeling, it's very weird.

— Kiera, what is the story of this hamlet? Thomas suddenly asks. Maybe the answer is there. You have to admit that this place is very different from the château of Versailles.

— Marie-Antoinette built the farm in order to withdraw from the court, whose constraints she despised. She always tried to have a simpler life; one more in tune with herself.

— So what?

— The people of the Court did not accept it.

— Would someone have betrayed her, then? asks Thomas.

— Of course, the nobles have contributed to her loss and some were behind the French Revolution. But I feel that there is something else. Why are you asking? Do you have any idea?

— Two different psychics coming to you with the same information around a similar place, but thousands of miles from each other.

— Do you think Yogananda would have betrayed me in another life?

— I don't know. You're the expert on past lives. Not me!

We remain silent for a moment. I am very emotional and start crying without understanding why. This is the first time I witness Marie leaving me in my distress like that.

— That's it, I finally say. I think I betrayed myself, by building the hamlet, in fact. I wanted it to look like a real farm, even though I was queen; I wanted to have a life like everyone else while I should have had assumed my role as a queen, I say, soothing myself.

— And what's the connection with your present life?

— Today, I have to take my role regarding reincarnation and to prove the truth about everything around the subject. I'm afraid to do so because I'm afraid to expose myself. I'm afraid to assume my role, once again.

— And Yogan ... I cannot remember his name.

— Yogananda ...

— Right. Don't you think that this guy could have betrayed you in the past and is now trying to make amends in this life with this meditation center?

— He's dead, you know!

— Oh, I thought he was still alive! Sorry ...

— I have the impression that he is helping me and protecting me instead. Why else would I feel so well since I have been going to meditate there. Let's walk to see what will come to me.

We walk around the lake as I do at the Lake Shrine. When we pass one of the houses, which is the home of the Queen, I suddenly stop. The decor dissolves and I found myself at the time of Marie-Antoinette. I am with my little boy, Louis Joseph, in my arms and we walk into the building which served as the dairy. I make him drink pure milk and eat fresh fruits. We then come out and walk into the house that was mine at the time. A man, rather short and round, is waiting by the fireplace, beside Antoine d'Allonville, my son's tutor. I put my son on a chair and the man kneels in front of him in silence. He listens his chest and gives him energetic treatments, then makes him swallow a potion. My son, whose suffering disfigured his face and mouth, completely relaxes and falls asleep in an instant. The setting dissolves.

— He was Cagliostro! I say, coming back to myself.

— Who are you talking about? Thomas asks, surprised.

— Yogananda was Cagliostro!

— How do you know?

— I just saw him treating my son, I mean, Marie-Antoinette's son. I often had the vision of a woman who was taking a child with breathing problems to Yogananda since I have been meditating, knowing that he would die, but I never made the connection, because I thought that the child was me. But in fact, I was his mother ... That reminds me that I've read that Louis Joseph died, among other things, from tuberculosis.

— What does all this that mean? That Marie-Antoinette believed in this kind of nonsense, is that it? Thomas asks, skeptical

— It wasn't nonsense, I assure you.

— Cagliostro was known to be a charlatan.

— But he wasn't, Thomas. I just saw him heal Louis Joseph, without any question. And you know as well as I do that someone's reputation has sometimes nothing to do with the truth.

You just have to see what has been said about Marie-Antoinette at the time and subsequently.

— I don't believe in this stuff ...

— I know! I say suddenly, resigned and shot down.

— What do you mean, you know?

— Louis XVI stopped Mesmer's research work, because he did not believe in the magnetism that Mesmer sought to demonstrate. Marie-Antoinette was protecting Mesmer for years so he could complete his research, I guess she was also relying on his services... This is probably why she said that if her son had been the son of an individual, he would have been better taken care of. She would have had the choice to seek treatment and she would certainly have chosen Mesmer and Cagliostro to treat him. She had begun to do so, but was prevented by someone, I am sure. I will have to do more research on the subject, that's for sure.

— What about going back to the château. Otherwise, it will be too late for us to visit it, says Thomas to change the subject.

We enter the château, Thomas and I, Marie still a bit away. Her silent presence reassures me and calms me, although I would love her to be more involved in my journey. We arrive in the king's bed-chamber. I do not recognize it, I do not understand why. I read a sign that says that the room has been decorated in the Louis XIV style. I am relieved to see that my intuitions are correct.

When we arrive in the Queen's bed-chamber, I recognize it immediately, because it is decorated in my favorite colors, blue-green and pink, and I have the same ones in my home in California: blue-green and pink. I am amazed to see that the colors and patterns of this room are about the colors and patterns of carpet Tania, my friend gave me, some time ago.

While lost in my reverie, we arrive in the Hall of Mirrors, without me being aware of it. This gallery is a work of art with its gilding, chandeliers and mirrors. As soon as I put my feet on the floor, I immediately want to let them glide at their ease, as I used to do in the past and I do it discreetly. I hear the music, the sound of shoes and the rustle of dresses. I feel the characteristic cold of Versailles on my skin when I see myself going through the gallery from one place to another. Everything is ecstasy. I let myself go. From far away, I hear the guide say that the château will soon be closing. I come out of my reverie and we move quickly toward the château bookstore.

Once in the bookstore, I rush to a salesman and ask to smell Marie-Antoinette's fragrance. Thomas and I are transported, when the perfume reaches our nostrils. A feeling of intense déjà-vu overwhelms us and we look at each other with a smile.

— I can't deny that this scent is really familiar to me, says Thomas, surprised.

— Me too, I say, trying to stay connected to the reality of the moment, even though I feel more or less in a constant alternated state of consciousness since my experience at the 'Petit Trianon'.

— You know, Kiera, you must be right about Louis XVI. How do I know these scents if I hadn't smelled them before?

— I'm glad to hear you say so. Take time. It will make its way, you know. I took me thirteen years to accept I could be the reincarnation of Marie-Antoinette!

— I imagine. Anyway, I hope the publisher will publish your book, because your story is really exciting, Kiera.

Chapter 2

Fears

Thomas drops us off, Marie and I, in front of the publisher's. We enter, but I stand petrified in front of the grand staircase, that looks so much like the one at the 'Petit Trianon'. The images of the crowd that wants to kill me come to me. An old wheel on the cobblestone. Nothing seems to stop it.

— What is happening? Marie asks me anxiously.

— I can't. I'm too scared, I say overwhelmed by my nightmare.

— Breathe, Kiera, Marie says very gently.

I take a few breaths.

— Come back in the present moment. You are no longer in Marie-Antoinette's life. You are here today in Paris.

— It's precisely here where I don't want to be, I say as I walked toward the door.

— What are you afraid of? Marie asks, while following me.

— I don't know. Although, I don't want to publish my book, I'm sorry.

— I understand, but you can stay for the interview, at least. Maybe your fears will disappear.

— I can't. I don't want to be accused again of all those things that are not true. I would never have the strength to face the gazes and the insults again. I would rather die, I say on my way out, Marie on my heels.

Thomas sees us and comes toward us.

— What happened?

— I can't go in, I say.

— Too bad, says Thomas. You're here. You just have to put one foot after another and everything will be fine.

— I'm telling you I can't.

— Marie, why don't you take Kiera's place and I will take care of her, Thomas says, taking me into his arms.

I think back to what Kevin Ryerson told me and that I kept to myself hoping that Kiera would not be influenced; I hoped I could change destiny. I take a deep breath and enter the building again. I look at the staircase that has driven Kiera away; I feel part of another reality, the reality of synchronicities where everything overlaps and exposes itself to work smoothly and perfectly.

The literary editor, comes to meet me as I am admiring the beauty of the place.

— I'm Dominique, he says, holding out his hand. I must tell you that you are radiant, Kiera.

— I am Marie, actually. Kiera couldn't come because she didn't feel well.

— I'm sorry. Follow me, he says, pointing to the staircase. It's nice to see someone like you when you always live in the gray light of Paris, says Dominique as we enter his office. What is your secret?

— Reincarnation, perhaps! I answer with a smile.

— If it is, I am ready to believe in it.

— Does that mean you don't believe in it, then?

— Actually, I don't really know. I've never asked myself that question before reading Kiera's manuscript. Speaking of that, I read most of it. I must say that her writing is good and her story is very interesting. Although, I will have to edit some sections and rewrite others.

— No problem, I'll help Kiera.

— I made some corrections and I will send them by e-mail. Do you live in California too?

— Yes, that's where we met, Kiera and I.

— What is your role in all this?

— I was Kiera's therapist and I became her friend in the meantime. I'm helping her with her research.

— Wonderful. It is valuable to have someone like you. When are you going back to California?

— I don't know. Kiera and I have to figure when we will be able to see the child of a friend who is very ill and whose illness could well be explained by reincarnation.

— Really?

I tell Dominique Baptiste's story. He is fascinated.

— Is it Kiera's story, this story of Marie-Antoinette? Dominique asks me suddenly.

— Yes, but we have changed many things because she doesn't want anyone to recognize her or her entourage.

Thomas and I are waiting for Marie in the little square in front of the publisher's. We are both silent, watching the entrance anxiously. Marie finally appears at the door. We wave at her and she advances toward us with a big smile on her face.

— So, Thomas asks when Marie joins us.

— It's a yes. Kiera just needs to remove some passages and rewrite others and the editor will send the contract after that.

— Wow! Congratulations, Kiera, says Thomas.

— I won't write anything, Marie, I say. I am exhausted and I don't want to accept the consequences of the publication of this book. I am not strong enough for that.

— I understand, Marie replies, hugging me gently.

— Well, I don't understand, Thomas says, nervously lighting a cigarette. How can you do this to me, Kiera? I brought you here and paid for everything so that you could get your book published!

I remain silent. I would like to be far away. I wish I had never returned to France.

— That's all you have to say? You're really flaky... Thomas says.

— And what about you?! Weren't you flaky when you were supposed to pay the child support? Weren't you flaky during the revolution when you got us all killed?! I say angrily.

— We got there because you were spending all the money.

— That's not true and you know it. You spent the money on loans to finance the American Revolution...

— Thomas, Kiera, calm down. Kiera has her reasons and it's normal to respect them. It is a heavy responsibility to publish a book like this.

— That doesn't surprise me. You're on her side and let her do whatever she wants when she just needs a little push, instead.

— It suits you to tell her that. What about you. Everybody pushed you to escape. What did you do? Nothing.

— Stop it both of you! You're acting like children, says Marie by putting herself between us. Calm down. I have something important to say. Ahtun Re told me you wouldn't want to publish your book and I may have to do it. That is why I wanted to come to Paris with you.

— Oh. I remember now. That's what I felt when you finished your session with Kevin Ryerson. Why didn't you tell me back then?

— Because I didn't want to influence you, Kiera. I hoped that you would change your mind.

— Liar, it's because you wanted to get the recognition for my book, I say angrily.

— You know that's not true. At no time, have you seen me take your place. I've always been there for you and you know that.

— Come on, Thomas, we are leaving. I don't want to see her anymore, I say, taking Thomas' arm.

Thomas resists, then he lets me propel him to the car. His cell phone rings as we enter the car. Thomas answers.

— It's Bastien, he says, handing me the phone.

— So how did it go with the publisher? Bastien wonders at the other end of the phone.

— I don't want to publish it!

— What happened?

— Marie told me that a psychic told her that she had to write it.

— That's why you don't want to write it anymore? Come on! No psychic should be able to tell you what to do or decide your future!

I then realize the absurdity of my words and my misunderstanding of the situation. I open the door and run over to Marie who remains seated on a bench in the square.

— I'm sorry, Marie. I don't know what I am doing anymore. It's too much for me.

Marie gets up and wraps me in her arms, without saying anything. I suddenly hear Bastien in the handset repeating 'Hello' several times.

— Excuse me, Bastien, I forgot about you! Thank you for your help.

— You're welcome.

— How is Baptiste?

— He's ok, but we cannot travel with him. He is too weak.

— I'm sorry.

— My wife still doesn't want you to see him. She doesn't believe in this story of reincarnation.

— Okay, I say disappointed.

After hanging up, I realize that I've put myself in the same position as Marie-Antoinette who would have hoped every day, not only that Louis Joseph would heal, but also that Louis Charles would be returned to her. I relive my distress of that time and manage to detach myself from the situation.

I am aware that Baptiste does not belong to me, as the son of Marie-Antoinette did not belong to her. The key for me is to have found my children again and to have discovered that Baptiste is loved and well cared for by his parents, as Emily, Sophie's half-sister, is by hers. I think of Sophie. I miss her. I remember when I held her in my arms in my previous life and I told her 'Pauvre petite, you were not desired, but you will not be less desired for me. A son would have especially belonged to the State. You will be mine; you will have all my care; you will share my happiness and you will soften my sorrows.'

Chapter 3

Links

I am glad to be back home. As I walk through the door, Sophie rushes up to me.

— Mom, Mom, I missed you so much. How was it? She wonders while hugging me.

— It was great, honey. Hey, you look so tan, I say, while stepping back to take a better look at her. You're really beautiful.

— Surfing!

— That makes me want to go!

— Want to go now?

— No, I'd rather walk on the beach? I need some fresh air after this long trip.

— Okay. I can't wait to hear everything.

We walk to the beach. I tell Sophie in detail everything that happened to me. I avoid telling her that I do not want to write the book and Marie will take over.

Sophie is fascinated by the visit to Trianon and my meeting with Baptiste's father. Although, she is not surprised at Thomas' attitude when I told her what happened at the airport: he left me when I got my boarding pass, telling me he would come back. He never returned.

— You see, Mom, I told you so. Thomas is not really reliable and that's why I've never liked him. He always says he will do things and he never does them.

— I know! As in his past life!

— What do you mean?

— Louis XVI had promised to come back to us before his execution the next morning and he did not.

— And the child support he is supposed to pay? He promised before you left that he would pay.

— He hasn't kept his promise, either: he said he had no money and accused me of all sorts of things. I was very disappointed.

— I wonder why I chose him for a father, as I would have loved to have Philippe as my papa. There must be a reason.

— I brought books from France so we can do the research. What about looking for that answer together?

— Let's go back home now. I want to start right away.

Excited, we open my luggage and take out every book about Marie-Antoinette that I have. Sophie grabs the book about Marie-Antoinette's exhibition and I take the one written by Antonia Fraser. Sophie is amazed by the pictures in the book about the exhibition.

— I look a lot like you when you were a child, it's crazy. Look, she says, handing me the book.

— I noticed it at the show, it's true. See if you can find anything about Marie-Antoinette's relationship with her children.

— I can't find anything, says Sophie disappointed.

— I have nothing here, either. Although, it says that Louis XVI adored his daughter, even though she was not a boy and an heir to the throne.

— He doesn't really show that in this life. You know mom, speaking of Thomas, I must tell you something, says Sophie suddenly very serious.

— I'm listening, I say, putting my book aside.

— I think he touched me when I was little.

— What do you mean?

— I don't know... but you know when I saw him, I couldn't stand to have him touch me.

— That's normal, Sophie. You didn't really know him and you met him when you were a teenager. Remember, you didn't want to hug me either, at the time.

— Do you remember when we went to the pool with the whale and the diamonds, when I was a child? That's where I believe it happened.

I immediately dial Thomas' phone number.

— How was your trip?

— Good apparently because I'm back. It was a bit cavalier the way you left me anyway. Although, that's not the reason for my call, I say, while going on the balcony to have a private talk with him. Sophie just told me you touched her when she was a child.

— I never did that. You know me.

— You know, in this kind of thing, no one really knows anyone.

— I swear I've never done that. I have many faults, but not that one. Remember, I called you because I was disgusted that a man of my age would go out with a girl of Sophie's age. I just wanted to be sure she didn't have to endure the same kind of thing.

— You're right, I say, sighing. Well I have to go, hanging up when I see my daughter approaching.

— So? Sophie wonders.

— He said no. The other day, when he called me and invited me to go to France, his first intention was to know how you were doing, after he met with a man in his thirties that was going out with a girl your age. And honestly, I think that's true. Look, I believed you for Samuel and I did what was needed. But now, I have the intuition that it might be something else, Sophie.

Sophie remains silent and looks down. That reminds me the episode during Marie-Antoinette's trial, when she was falsely accused of incest by her son. Now, I remember now being at the trial. When a juror demanded an answer to this accusation, I say totally outraged that 'if I did not answer it is that nature refuses to answer such a charge against a mother and I call on any mother that may be here'.

— For Samuel…, says Sophie.

— What did you say? I interrupt her, suddenly returning to the present when I hear Samuel's name.

— It wasn't true about Samuel, Sophie says.

— What do you mean? I ask in shock.

— I lied. Samuel has never abused me!

— Why did you say that? I ask completely stunned by what I just heard.

— I wanted to destroy you as you had destroyed me by doing me with someone else. I wanted to destroy you as you destroyed dad.

— My God, how horrible! That's why I can't forget him.

— Mom, I tried to tell you several times...

— When did you try to tell me?

— Just after you asked Samuel to leave. But you were too stuck in your depression.

— My God. What a mess! I say, falling to the floor, completely overcome.

— I'm sorry, Mom. I didn't want to. I assure you. It was as if there was something forcing me to do it.

I look at her, surprised: I remember suddenly that was what happened to me when I wanted to have a baby with Thomas: it was as if something had forced me to do it too. I cannot blame Sophie for doing the same thing, especially after all she suffered because of me. I reach out my arms and we cry in each others' arms.

— How did you know about his birthmark on his penis, then?

— I didn't know! I just said it! I never thought that this would go that far!

— This entire thing is so stupid! I really loved Samuel, you know.

— It may be not too late, Mom! What about calling him?

— No, I can't. He would never want to talk to me.

— I can call him if you want to.

— I'll think about it, Sophie, I say with a faint smile. I'm so sorry, darling. I realize how I have hurt you, I say, holding her in my arms again.

— Mom, I'm sorry too. I didn't know what I was doing.

— Don't worry. I understand, I say, letting my tears flow.

— Do you think that the explanation for everything that happened would be in our past lives?

— It's possible, I say, surprised to hear my daughter talking about that possibility.

— We will continue to do our research and then we will call Samuel. Okay?

— Okay.

We spend the day and subsequent days in reading the books about Marie-Antoinette and doing research on the internet.

— Mom, I think I found it, Sophie finally says. She then reads me a paragraph from the book by Antonia Fraser. 'The Queen was not present at her daughter's baptism. Thus Marie-Antoinette was spared the incident when the malicious Comte de Provence protested to the officiating Archbishop that 'the name and quality' of the parents had not been formally given, according to the usual rite of christening. Under the mask of concern about correct procedure, the Comte was making an impertinent allusion to the allegations about the baby's paternity made in the *libelles* (scandalous satires about the Queen). The allusion was certainly not lost on the courtiers present.' What does this mean? asks Sophie.

— This means that the Comte de Provence spread the rumor that you were not your father's child.

— Is it as simple as that, then? Says Sophie surprised.

— It must be! His previous action turned against him in his present life. As we were affected by his gossip, during the revolution, he felt the effects in this life: so he had to live what we were accused of. How perfect!

— That's why he had an illegitimate child in this life, then?

— Yes! Because he said that my children were illegitimate.

— I do not understand the logic.

— He must accept the consequences of his actions. This is called the law of karma. Everything we do to others, we have to experience it in return, at one time or another! This is what allows us to better understand others and improve ourselves.

Sophie remains silent for a long time.

— What about his wife in this life? Why does she hate us so much? Sophie finally asks, curious.

— She was Jeanne de la Motte . She was of royal descent. One of her ancestors was the illegitimate son of Henry II. Her family fell out of favor and lost their entire fortune. She never stopped trying to regain her status and prior wealth. Helped by circumstances, Jeanne de La Motte was in contact with the Cardinal de Rohan, who dreamed only of returning to Marie-Antoinette's good graces. The jeweler, Boehmer, who wanted at any price to get rid of some diamonds which cost a fortune, contacted Jeanne de La Motte so that she could influence the Queen to buy them. Jeanne convinced them that she knew Marie-Antoinette intimately and could therefore fulfill the hopes of both Boehmer and the Cardinal. She made Cardinal de Rohan believe that he would gain the Queen's esteem if he would buy Boehmer's necklace, what was false of course. She made the jeweler Boehmer believe that Marie-Antoinette was finally interested in acquiring the precious jewel, what was false once again. When Jeanne de La Motte finally got the necklace, she disappeared and the diamonds were sold separately. The jeweler Boehmer, after weeks of waiting, seeing no future payment from Marie-Antoinette, ran to her and admitted the truth. The culprits were arrested.

— And what happened then?

— The Cardinal de Rohan was acquitted. Jeanne de La Motte was beaten in public and marked by the 'V' iron for 'voleuse' (thief). She was locked at the Salpêtrière, a women's prison, from which she later escaped — we do not know how. She wrote her memoirs, which totally defamed Marie-Antoinette. Jeanne de La Motte died some time later, after being pushed or jumping out of a window.

— Did she commit suicide?

— She wanted to escape her creditors, because she owed money to many people, but it is unclear, in fact, if she committed suicide or if she was pushed.

— And what about the Cardinal de Rohan in this life?

— I don't know. In fact, if reincarnation is as logical as I think, because the Cardinal de Rohan was Cagliostro's close friend, Rajarsi would be Yogananda's best friend. But I must check everything.

— What a story! And what happened to Marie-Antoinette, in all this?

— Innocent, she was a lot discredited, to her dismay. This really affected her standing with the people during the French Revolution.— And why is Dad with Jeanne today?

— They were apparently in contact, I don't know how. I wonder if he was the one who helped her escape from the Salpêtrière, so she could write her book!

— That's why they are married now?

— I think it's because they had the same objectives back then: they were ready at any point to regain their rights around the monarchy: he allowed us to be guillotined and she participated to the greatest scam of all time. They found themselves together in this life and are the parents of your step-sister, who was Louis Charles, the heir to the throne at the time and who died, partly because of their actions. I guess they had to give him back his life, and Louis Charles restores a meaning to their own lives as well.

— But why do they hate you so much today? You had nothing to do with this affair in the past and she got what she wanted today: Dad and my little sister ... the legacy of royalty in a way.

— It looks like you understand how it happened. You know, Jeanne de la Motte tried to get Marie-Antoinette's attention several times without success. She even pretended to faint in front of her.

— And why didn't Marie-Antoinette pay attention to her, then?

— Marie-Antoinette was in great demand, as you must imagine, and apparently she did not receive any information of the attempts that Jeanne de La Motte made to get her attention. Maybe if she had, she would have helped, who knows. Marie-Antoinette really helped many people around her. And that might have changed the course of history.

— It's amazing how everything fits perfectly, finally says Sophie. I don't believe in God, but there must be a force that governs everything, for sure, Sophie says while flipping through the book by Antonia Fraser, as if she was still seeking an answer.

— Of course!

— Oh mama, says Sophie surprised. You were right, Jeanne de La Motte and dad already knew each other. Look what it says in the book: the Comte de Provence's wife gave an allocated pension to Jeanne de La Motte, when she heard of her situation.

— Unbelievable, I say in shock. I always knew they had met previously since they are now husband and wife, but I've never had confirmation. And today, Dad continues to give her a pension in a way, because she doesn't need to work. I wonder if the Comte de Provence wasn't much more involved in the necklace affair than history tells us?!

— What do you mean?

— The diamond necklace plot was the biggest scam of all time and only someone endowed with great intelligence could have instigated it. Your father is so brilliant in this life, he could have devised a scheme like that back then. I don't really have evidence and I would not speculate too much on this story, but in my opinion we are far from knowing everything.

— I still don't understand why Thomas is my biological father in this life?

— To prove that his children were his own, while there was a rumor at the time they were not.

— Hey Mom, how does it help me to know all this? I would rather have a normal life like everyone else, you know.

— It helps you to understand things that you would not understand otherwise. Like the fact that you were born with two dads ... drugs too.

— You told me the other day, I took drugs during the same years when Charlotte was in prison. What does that mean?

— That you probably remembered deep in yourself that you were in prison, but that you could not understand it because you were not in prison in this life. You had to choose to build a sort of virtual prison with drugs.

— Mom, I'm sorry for not having believed in you. I feel much better now, since I know all this. What happened to me after that?

— You went to Austria to marry your cousin, the Duc d'Angoulème, the Comte d'Artois' son. You were at the Comte de Provence's, who was to later become Louis XVIII. That is why you are so close to him in this life.

— What happened to Marie-Antoinette's son who accused her of incest?

— He died in prison as a result of neglect and malnutrition.

— Are you sure?

— Yes. I saw him in a past life regression in 1995, because I couldn't escape from the prison where he was dying. I checked later on the internet. There was a controversy over whether the child had died in prison or not. In 2000, DNA tests were carried out by the team of Jean-Jacques Cassiman, a well-known researcher in genetics, and proved that the child that died in the prison of the temple was indeed the son of Marie-Antoinette.

— What would be the link with Samuel, Mom, I don't understand?

— He did not help us during the revolution. He was a very strong monarchist and would not concede anything. The Comte de Provence and the Comte d'Artois even disassociated themselves from us, when Louis XVI had to sign the agreement, that took away from us all our rights. All these disagreements divided us, while we should have been sticked together. All this story lost us. And the charge of incest happened during Marie-Antoinette's trial just before her execution. Maybe, the whole story happened to Samuel to help him remember the consequences of his actions and help him burn his karma.

— What about me, mom? Why did I accuse Samuel of incest if that was not true?

— Maybe because you wanted him to pay for what he did to your parents in your previous life and you had the unconscious memory of the accusation of false incest in yourself because of what happened to us during that time .

— I am calling Samuel, Mom. I want to apologize for all the harm I've done to him.

Sophie has to wait many rings before someone answers.

— Samuel, it's me, Sophie.

— Oh, Samuel answers, while drawing himself up painfully in his armchair.

He puts his book down gently on his knees and press the receiver closer to his ear.

— I want to apologize for what I told Mom about you, Sophie says, bursting into tears.

— It's in the past, Sophie, Samuel says weakly. I guess you had your reasons.

— I wanted Mom to pay for what she had done, Sophie shamefully admits. It had nothing to do with you, actually.

Samuel does not respond.

— I feel so bad. I want you to know that Mom really loves you, Samuel.

— I know and I love her too. All these stories with your father and my break-up with your mom completely broke my heart.

Samuel and Sophie remain silent for a moment.

— I feel that you have changed Sophie, Samuel suddenly says. I am pleased to hear that.

Sophie remains silent so as not to show her emotions.

— Will you ever forgive me, Samuel? Sophie says unable to restrain her tears anymore.

— It was all done a long time ago. Although, I'd love to know how you knew about my birthmark. This question has been bugging me.

— I just said it without knowing it, admits Sophie. It's something that came into my head by accident and I just said it. I never thought it was true and it would cause so much damage, Sophie says sadly, while twisting her hair nervously with her index finger.

— My God, Samuel says while holding his head in his hands. I thought of all the possible scenarios except this one. I tortured myself all those years for nothing. I even asked myself if I could have done it without even remembering it later.

— I'm sorry, Samuel, Sophie says, looking down again. Really!

— Does your mother know, at least? asks Samuel with a voice full of hope.

— I just told her and she wants to talk to you, says Sophie.

— I'd be happy to talk to her too. Before, I just want to tell you that I'm really glad that you called me, Samuel says to return to a more positive note. I've been waiting for your call for so long! Thank you Sophie.

— Thank you, Samuel.

Sophie hands me the telephone and leaves the room.

— Samuel I wanted to apologize, too, for everything I've done to you.

— It's forgotten. I am so happy to talk to you today, you have no idea!

— Me too.

— I missed you, Kiera says Samuel very moved.

— I missed you too, Samuel, I say, suddenly aware of the weak voice of Samuel. How are you doing? I ask worried.

— Very well! How could I not be well, when I am so pleased to hear your voice.

— What is happening with you, Samuel? The truth! I ask softly.

— Nothing, I'm just sad to have wasted all those years without you and to have lost you, Samuel says, crying. Had I known, I would have come back earlier.

— But it's not too late, Samuel. We could try again, don't you think?

— I would love to, Kiera. But I think it's too late.

— Ah? I say, without being able to hold back my tears anymore.

— It's not what you think Kiera. I have never replaced you.

— What then? If you want, I can come back to France in a heartbeat.

— It's more complicated than that, Kiera!

— Don't you love me anymore?

— I've always loved you more than anything, darling.

— Then what? Can't you forgive me?

— Of course, I can. I already have. I understand you wanted to protect your daughter! I guess I would have done the same thing.

— There is something you're not telling me. I can tell since I've been talking to you. I've never heard you like this.

There is a long silence.

— I need to know, Samuel. It's a real torture of not knowing what is happening.

— I'll be leaving soon ... says Samuel, sighing.

— What do you mean? I ask suddenly panicked.

— I have a brain tumor. The doctors don't even understand why I'm still alive. They told me that a month ago and gave me a maximum of six months to live.

— It is not possible, I say, crying. Not you. It's not fair.

I remain silent for a moment.

— Come and live with us, Samuel, I say.

Samuel is silent.

— Samuel, I want to take care of you, I continue. And I'm sure you'll make it.

— I can't. I have no strength to fight and I don't want you to see me the way I am right now. You wouldn't recognize me.

— I don't care, Samuel. I love you.

— I'm so tired, you have no idea, says Samuel, looking into space.

— Look, Samuel. I'll come and get you. With the air, the sea and the sun, we'll make you healthy again.

— I don't think it's a good idea for Sophie to see me like this, Samuel says, crossing his arms over his chest.

— It's the least that I can do and I'm sure Sophie will agree, don't worry. We've already wasted enough time.

— It'll be hard, you know, Samuel says, well aware of his situation.

— I know, Samuel. But this can't be harder than the fact I've missed you so much all these years.

Samuel weeps in silence.

— I love you, Samuel, and I never stopped loving you since the first day I met you, I say with tears in my eyes.

— I love you too, Samuel says, crying.

— So, will you agree to come and live with us?

— Yes. Give me some time to organize my departure here. I'll call you tomorrow to tell you how I will manage it.

I hang up, happy to have found Samuel again and yet sad to have to lose him again soon. I do not understand destiny. I find life unfair. I go online to learn more about the life of the Comte d'Artois. Why must we be separated again? I do research until I find something interesting: Samuel and I separated when we were about the age we were when Marie-Antoinette died. When we left Montreal, Samuel returned to France and Sophie and I went to California. When he fled the revolution abroad the Comte d'Artois aspired only to return to France. When Marie-Antoinette had to stay in France because of the revolution, she aspired to go abroad. When Marie-Antoinette died, the Comte d'Artois survived — today it is the opposite, he is dying and I am alive. The roles are reversed, but we live today exactly what we wanted to live at that time.

In both lifetimes, Samuel did not recover from losing me. He has always loved me and that is what he is showing me today. Contrary to what Marie-Antoinette thought when Artois was abroad and scheming against her. Contrary to what I thought when Sophie told me what he had done to her.

All this discovery heals the past as well as the present: this allows me to accept what would seem unfair to anyone else, because I know that everything has its purpose and that death does not exist.

Samuel calls me every day and we resume our former closeness. We laugh and joke about everything. I feel his voice becoming stronger in our conversations. I restrain myself from going to France because he wants to see me under the best possible conditions. A week passes. A second. A third. I do not understand the time he imposes on us. I insist to come to him. He finally tells me that he must have a surgery that might save him and he will not be reachable for a few days. He promises to come two weeks after me and surprise me with his visit.

I am tired of waiting. I'm afraid of something, but I do not know what. Not having heard from Samuel makes me very anxious and at the same time, I feel him close to me, I do not understand why. I live only for our reunion.

Chapter 4

Reconstruction

Next Wednesday morning, while I am meditating, the doorbell rings. I ask who it is. "Delivery" someone answers. "I am not expecting anything", I reply. "It is a flower delivery" and then, my heart jumps in my chest. I know it's Samuel! I open the door, all excited as I am, and grab the flowers, expecting Samuel to be behind them. But it's only the flower delivery guy, who hands me a letter with the bouquet. I give him a tip and take the vase and the flowers. I put the vase on the table and open the envelope hastily.

My dear love,

I love you so much I could not resolve myself to let you see me as diminished as I am. You allowed me to live my last moments in the most wonderful way in the world. I know life exists after death and that we will find each other again, you proved it to me, thanks to our conversations, and I never want you to doubt this. Thanks to you, I could die in peace.

I would like you to keep the same memory of me as the day I came to meet you in Montreal. You remember the flowers. They are the same as the ones you are holding now. Time and space does not exist. I am in these flowers, as I am in you and around you.

Continue to spread hope, even when people think there is not any left, like you did for me. Take that book you were writing and finish it, my love. Prove reincarnation to others, like you proved it to me.

Death does not exist, you are convinced of that and this is your strength. You will be even more convinced when you dispose of my ashes, which are at the bottom of the vase you just received. Please, if you can, spread them in the ocean, but do this only when you are ready.

When you do, you will see a dolphin coming to you and jumping three times out of the water, just for you. Then, you will never ever have any more doubts about reincarnation and you will know that I will always be there for you. You will be able to recognize the signs that will lead you little by little to the accomplishment of your projects. Go toward science, honey, and do not forget that what we went through with the DNA test for your daughter was there to prepare you for an even bigger research: the research of eternal life.

Do not regret anything for either of us. You know that it was what was best for us, to make us grow, because everything is perfect on the divine plan when we are dealing with karma. These are your own words, aren't they? I can see you smile, it makes my heart melt.

Smile at life as much as you can. Be happy because I am happy thanks to you. Continue to live with all that I love about you and all that you know about me. Meditate, do yoga, continue to run on the beach, enjoy life. Connect to your soul, my love, the only way you have the secret for, because it is that vibration that will bring you toward your destiny.

You will meet another man soon, my love. You will recognize him: he is me, as I am him, as I am you, as you are me, because we are all one.

I love you forever and ever.

Samuel

I reread this letter a hundred times. I feel Samuel close to me. I hear him and I speak to him, as if he were still alive. I miss his touch but I am fulfilled by his soul that lives entirely through me. Time and space do not exist anymore, he is right. I am with him every moment that goes by and nothing else matters anymore.

I read all the books on Marie-Antoinette I can to be closer to Samuel and better understand my relationship with him. This helps me to accept that we are no longer on the same plan at the moment, although I feel that at the level of the heart we are still together.

While reading a book about Elisabeth, Louis XVI's sister, I find confirmation that I never hoped to find: two simple lines say that women were inappropriately touched and sometimes raped at the Conciergerie. I am in shock. This shock is so violent that I have to lay down: I feel a huge weight lifting off my shoulders. I see my past life rising slowly. I feel lighter and lighter and more serene. Suddenly, I see Samuel in front of me. He gives me a big smile and rises too. I remember my dream where I saw the senator Samuel dying in a tsunami while I was resuscitating. I feel liberated.

I am at the beach with Sophie. We light the candles around Samuel's urn. The moon is at its zenith and illuminates the sea with a delicate, silvery light. After lighting the last candle, we sit and meditate in front of the urn. I get up, take the urn in my arms and hold it against me, crying. I head toward the sea and Sophie follows me silently. I open the box, take a handful of Samuel's ashes, bring them to my lips and whisper 'I love you forever, honey'. I wade into the ocean mid-thigh. The waves are strong. I would go down with them and join Samuel, but Sophie, right next to me, keeps me in touch with life. I release the ashes into the ocean. Meanwhile, a group of dolphins begins to jump a little further ahead of us and one of them comes towards us. He stops and jumps into the water three times before swimming away.

— This is the proof Samuel told you about, mama. Do you remember? If the dolphin comes to us and jumps three times, it is proof that reincarnation exists and that he will help you in your projects.

— Yes, I say, smiling sadly.

— Mom, it's great, Sophie says enthusiastically.

— Yes, I say, handing the urn to Sophie who slowly takes it and turns it upside down to let the ashes escape with the wind in the ocean.

We remain there a long time in silence, watching the dolphins, and go back home.

I return to my computer, after several weeks of absence. I have hundreds of emails to read. I stop on one of them, that Marie has forwarded me. This one particularly catches my attention because it says: 'Science and Reincarnation'.

Dear Friends and Colleagues,

After four years of research and writing, I understand that my new book The Soul Genome: Science and Reincarnation is now available on Amazon.com.

The focus of the book is the testing of a scientific model of how a past-life legacy might be an integral part of human reproduction. It treats reincarnation as an central aspect of nature's process of physical and conscious evolution. For this reason, the experiment's focus is on the areas of empirical evidence that suggest tangible and verifiable links between specific lifetimes.

The book's primary goal is to expand interest in the phenomenon we call "reincarnation" among those with secular worldviews, and to encourage increasing scientific investigation. The model cannot yet be considered as the ultimate proof, but it does offer a powerful challenge to those skeptical of any form of reincarnation.

I hope that over the coming months I can exchange views with those of you who have reactions to the book and suggestions for the ongoing Reincarnation Experiment Project. Perhaps some of you will offer up your own life data in the interest of scientific exploration?

Best regards to all,

Paul

I see in this message the signs Samuel told me about. This instantly gives me back the taste for life. I immediately order the book that Paul refers to in his e-mail. I then call Marie and ask her to immediately send Paul a message to tell him my story. She says that she was only waiting for my green light to do so.

Subject: Re: Science and Reincarnation

Dear Paul,

Congratulations on your book. I've just ordered it and I'm in a hurry to read it.

I am a psychotherapist specializing in past life regressions and I am working on a case that might interest you. My client wishes to do things anonymously and that's why she asked me to contact you to make all of her information available to keep your research on reincarnation moving forward. Her pseudonym is Kiera Hermine. After being told by a psychic that she was Marie-Antoinette in her previous life, she has been confirmed by Walter Semkiw and Kevin Ryerson.

Kiera had nightmares in her childhood: she was guillotined every night. She has many memories of this pas life in her present life. When we researched about Marie-Antoinette, it's amazing how many facts, traits, people, dates, anniversaries, that confirm the fact that she could have been Marie-Antoinette.

So you know, I am actually correcting the book Kiera wrote about her past life (she asked me to publish it under my name, when she realized the implications of the publication of this book). Later, we want to work on another book where we would recount the past lives of everyone she has met again in this life (about a hundred people). The soul cohort of Kiera corresponds a lot to the 'robust set of individual cases' you talk about on your website and that may interest science because of their interconnection and the group's current dynamics which reflect the historical records.

On your website, you also talk about the DNA as a possibility to prove reincarnation. For your information, I contacted Jean-Jacques Cassiman in Belgium, to ask him questions about Marie-Antoinette's DNA. I did some research to confirm a regression Kiera had made in 1995. She saw Marie-Antoinette's child dying at the Temple prison. At this time, there was still a controversy as to whether or not Marie-Antoinette's child who died in the prison was indeed Marie-Antoinette's son or an impostor. Jean-Jacques Cassiman confirmed that the child in the Temple was indeed Marie-Antoinette's son and he compared the child's DNA to that of Marie-Antoinette's. It could be an avenue for proving reincarnation as Kiera has also done DNA testing that she is willing to make available for research.

Feel free to contact me, if you're interested in learning more.

Sincerely,

Marie

The next day I begin to run, do yoga and meditate on the beach again. I finally find my life's meaning without Samuel. I know he is called to follow his own path as I am ready to stand on my own, following the signs that life puts on my path. As soon as I get home, I find Paul's answer in my e-mail, that Marie has forwarded to me.

Subject: Possible case of Kiera Hermine

Dear Marie,

Thank you very much for taking an interest in my book and ordering a copy. After you have seen my approach, I would love to have further discussions with you about possible documentation of Kiera Hermine's case according to my evaluation protocol.

It takes clues from channels and extra-dimensional sources as hints for further empirical evidence, but the ultimate confidence-level for scientific purposes is based on data that can be verified and replicated by third-parties.

I believe this approach is necessary if we are to make inroads into the scientific community - which is my goal.

Have you identified a possible lifetime in between the present life of Kiera and her psychoplasm/soul's posited incarnation as Marie-Antoinette? Since it appears that each incarnation has an effect on both the genotype and personality, the last one is likely to be more reflected in her current life. However, there is enough historical and biographical data on Marie-Antoinette, that we should be able to get good measures of correspondences between that life and that of Kiera. That would be the focus of my assessment.

I am not hopeful about any immediate value of DNA from Marie-Antoinette. On the question of DNA samples from hypothesized past-life matches, we do not yet know what to do with them. In reincarnation we are not dealing with the biological family tree. Most cases have no family-tree connections between the biological parents and the newly reincarnated being, and those that do will obviously have family genetic markers.

If Jean-Jacques Cassiman agrees though, we may be able to use the MtDNA test of Marie-Antoinette to compare it to Kiera's, but I am quite sure they would not be of any help. But that could be a first step in the DNA research in an attempt to prove reincarnation.

We have to have a pool of well-documented cases with my model and then begin the search for genetic correspondences in other parts of the genome. They might turn out to be specific markers for certain body features in the first stages. When we get to that point, Kiera's case would be a good example.

Let's please communicate again after you've had a chance to get a clear picture of my methodology. If Kiera and you are still interested after that to work with me, I would be happy to collaborate on that project with you.

Waiting for the pleasure to know each other better,

Paul

Paul's answer gives me the energy to get back to painting and finally fulfill the gallery order. Meanwhile, I receive Paul's book and read it in two days. I then call Marie, who also just read Paul's. Marie comes to my place and we write a letter to Paul together.

Subject: The interest of Kiera Hermine for research

Dear Paul,

Kiera and I just finished your book, we loved it. Congratulations!

We are now starting to work on your forms to compare Kiera's data to Marie-Antoinette's. It will be interesting to gather all our research into something more concise.

We have not identified past lives between Marie-Antoinette's and Kiera's lives. I will send you Kiera's DNA test tomorrow.

Take care,

Marie

Marie and I spend a lot of time together comparing my data with that of Marie-Antoinette's thanks to Paul's forms. When I am not with Marie, my painting allows me to regain stability and strengthen myself emotionally.

After finishing the work on my previous life, Marie sends Paul a message with all the comparisons we have made.

Subject: Datas on the case of Kiera Hermine

Dear Paul,

Kiera and I have finished filling out the forms and comparing pictures together. It is rather similar in many aspects. The confidence level is 3, which is a very good score.

Yesterday we gathered all the links we made with Marie-Antoinette over the past two years and we added those that Kiera made thanks Simone Bertière's book on Marie-Antoinette (the best book we've read so far along Antonia Fraser's). You will have a lot of material to read! I must add that Kiera has found her father of her past life and they have written some beautiful things that can help you in your research. The exercise of putting everything together and comparing the data was really interesting.

Talk to you soon,

Marie

Subject: MA/Kiera biometrical similarities

Marie,

Thank you for this very detailed information. All the correspondence you sent me is truly amazing. As I read Marie-Antoinette and Kiera's notes, I have to confess that I see many correspondences between those two women. It is also very interesting in that I see evidence of the progression of consciousness in both of them.

All that to say that 'we have a very interesting process which is now manifesting!'. Because of this, I wish that we remain very cautious in how we collect evidence and correspondence, before being totally convinced that Kiera was Marie-Antoinette.

I have found that people who come to a point when they accept the possibility that they are the present incarnation of a particular past-life, they subtly, even overtly, change behavior to coincide with what they consciously know about the past life. Even I have noticed the tendency in myself (and I'm supposed to be a serious and objective person).

For this reason we need to have evidence of behaviors before the individual reaches that point, so we avoid the scientific trap of a self-fulfilling prophecy (where we create who we believe we are). This does not always happen, but we must consider the possibility.

Sincerely,

Paul

While Marie is correcting my book 'Marie-Antoinette's Present' and continuing her exchange of e-mails with Paul, I feel the urge to paint something else, something that comes from the depth of my soul.

This access to my soul takes me to a distant past, as far as the period of the pyramids: a love scene that depicts a departure that neither of the two protagonists seem to suspect. A man I deeply loved a long time ago left without telling me. I was married then and could not leave my husband, given the circumstances of the time and saw my social status. I never understood why he left me without saying 'goodbye'. He was tall with brown hair and dark eyes. His gaze was so intense that it took me an infinite time to reproduce it the right way on my canvas.

After several days of hard work, I look at the result, satisfied: the man's eyes pierce my canvas to the point where I feel them constantly staring after that. I call my new painting 'Reunion'.

Subject: MA/Kiera biometrical similarities

Marie,

I just finished measuring the geometry of the portrait of Marie-Antoinette with a photo of Kiera.

We must keep in mind that this process to-date is not very precise. It would not meet the standards of a professional biometrician. One reason is that unless all the team members making the measurements have been trained in a similar fashion, they are apt to vary in their approaches a bit. Second, our use of copies of portraits makes any measurement less exact than modern photo comparisons.

Nevertheless, I believe our work offers a reasonable credible set of data. You did two different measures and averaged them I also did to measures, before having studied yours. I used the Photoshop grid one time and a millimeter ruler the second time against points on the printouts of the computer images you sent. I averaged my two sets of ratios, and them averaged mine with yours. This means we got the best collective result of our four efforts.

It is rather amazing that with that hand/eye process, the overall variance between the facial geometry of Marie-Antoinette and Kiera is less than 1% (or the standard used by professional to declare a security-photo match). This means Marie-Antoinette's and Kiera's facial architecture is more alike than any two live people likely alive today.

This is a very good news and that would allow us to put that case on the website of 'Reincarnation Experiment', if Kiera agrees.

My best,

Paul

Subject: RE: MA/Kiera biometrical similarities

Dear Paul,

We are so relieved that your measurements confirm our intuitions and all the work that Kiera and I have done so far.

Kiera agrees that you may use her example on your website, if she remains anonymous. For her, all this research gives real meaning to her life and that makes her feel that Marie-Antoinette did not die in vain and everything has a purpose. And who knows, maybe her case will help prove reincarnation later, with the research on DNA!

Have a good day and see you soon,

Marie

Chapter 5

Exhibition

This is the big day. I arrive at the gallery, rather anxious. Sophie and Marie are by my side and try to reassure me. I introduce my daughter to Georges, who is troubled by our likeness. It is spontaneous collusion between them. Georges takes Sophie by the arm and shows her my paintings one by one, as if she has never seen them before. Sophie, to my surprise, plays along with the game.

The guests gradually arrive. Georges introduces me to some of them. Others come to me directly. Sophie is excited to recognize some celebrities and whispers their names discreetly to me. I am very busy with everyone and don't stop one second. I try to stay focused not to be invaded by my deep fear of the crowd, which grows gradually as people arrive, and I am surprised to be able to do it relatively easily.

At one point, I see a photographer and a journalist arrive at the gallery. I question Georges with my eyes because I do not know what to do. Georges gives me a wink and let me welcome them. While walking in the gallery, the photographer takes pictures of my paintings and the guests; the journalist asks me some questions, before leaving to mingle with other people. I take this opportunity to go toward the entrance and get some fresh air. I find myself in front of my painting 'Reunion'. I look at it thoughtfully. I asked Georges not to sell it, regardless of the price offered, and I am reassured to see the absence of a red circle on the label. I do not know why, but it is the only painting that I cannot separate myself from. I step back to have a better look. Sophie comes to join me:

— It's really great what's happening to you, Mom.

— I have to admit that it hasn't quite sunk in yet...

A man walks into the gallery at the same time and stumbles, interrupting our conversation, without realizing it. He stops in front of 'Reunion'. I look at him, puzzled. I would love to see what he looks like, but I can only see his back. Sophie gives me a nudge, without a word and walks away smiling. I dare not move in order not to interrupt the meditation in which the painting seems to have plunged the man in. He finally turns toward me, but I did not even have time to see him as George comes up to me and takes me back inside the gallery.

— I've been looking for you everywhere. A rich heiress insists on buying 'Reunion' and there is nothing I can do to convince her that this painting is not for sale. She is ready to pay whatever the price.

— You didn't try to sell her another painting, did you? I say, while turning around to try to find the man that I saw in front of 'Reunion', but he has disappeared.

— I tried, but first, she is not interested, and secondly, your other paintings have all been sold!

— Are you joking?!

— No, I assure you... Well, I'll let you convince her, he says as Lise approaches. Lise, this is Kiera. Kiera, this is Lise, says Georges while leaving.

— Hello, Kiera. Georges told me that you did not want to sell your painting 'Reunion', but I have to tell you that I would pay anything to have it.

— It's not a question of price, I say while looking around for the man.

— What is it then?

— I cannot part with it I do not know why... I'm sorry.

— This painting touches something in me that I need to discover. It's like a previous life being revealed when I'm in contact with this painting and I feel that it has answers for me. I look at her suddenly with surprise.

— What do you mean?

— I feel as though I know the man in the painting.

— Really?! I say taken aback.

— I feel that he was my husband in a previous life and he disappeared, I don't know why. I have often dreamed of this man and when I first saw your painting, I immediately recognized him.

I remain silent, overcome by emotion.

— Do you know at which period of time it was by chance? I finally ask, still in shock.

— Yes, it was in Egypt, at the period of the pharaohs. The colors of your painting bring to mind this period of time.

— I have to tell you something. I painted this canvas from a previous life that I had. It was a lifetime in Egypt and I understood that the man in this painting disappeared under mysterious circumstances, I say, without mentioning that I loved that man deeply.

— It's an incredible story that you're telling me, says Lise, very emotional, too.

— What if I make a copy of the original? I offer spontaneously.

— I would rather buy the original, Kiera, because you put an energy into it that won't be in your copy.

— I see we speak the same language, I say, smiling. It's yours for the price that you will pay for it.

— You have no idea how happy that makes me, says Lise, taking my hands.

— On the other hand, I would like to ask you one thing in return: I'd like to stay in touch so we can discuss this past life again.

— I promise... Do you think it's the same man? At the same time, I recognize the back of the man who appears and disappears in the crowd.

— I beg your pardon? I say absently.

— Do you think the man you painted and the man I told you about are one and the same?

— I suspect so, but I need more evidence to be convinced.

You know, it's strange… There's this man who seemed fascinated by this painting too. He is in the crowd, but I cannot find him, I say, scanning people. There he is, I say, pointing toward the exit. Do you know him by chance?

— I don't think so...

— I'll try to catch him. Excuse me.

I run toward the exit, but he has disappeared again. I re-enter the gallery, disappointed. I am looking for Marie and cannot find her. People and their conversations now seem futile to me. My head is somewhere else. I cannot wait to get home and be alone.

In the car, Sophie tells me about the people she has met. I listen half-heartedly. When she tells me of a boy she met and who she likes, I pay more attention.

— Are you expecting to see him again?

— He invited me to go surfing with him. He'll call me.

— I am happy for you, honey.

— The man in the lobby seemed to please you, mom.

— I really liked his fascination with my painting actually. I didn't manage to see what his face looked like. Did you?

— I have no idea. Sorry, Mom.

At home, I read my e-mails and find out Paul's e-mail Marie forwarded to me.

Subject: Marie-Antoinette / Kiera's case on the website

Hello Marie,

I started a section on "cases in progress" on my website. Please check it out -— realizing that it's only a start -— and let me know what you think.

I add all the information I found pertinent on Marie-Antoinette and Kiera to assert reincarnation. You will find it below.

Sincerely,

Paul

Here is the information:

Marie-Antoinette (1755-1793) was born in Austria, was married to the future King Louis XVI of France, gave birth to four children and was executed, as well as her husband — during the French Revolution. Kiera H. was born in France, near Paris, was married and divorced and now lives with her daughter in California. The lives of these two women have many more connections between them than the space we have to describe it. The assumption of such similarities between these two women is that Kiera H. inherited in the 1960's psychoplasm who also led the life of Marie-Antoinette in the 1750's. Extensive data related to five factors (physical, cognitive, emotional, interpersonal, and vocational) that constitute the psychophysical model that we use to compare these incarnations, as well as memories that we can check and meaningful coincidences have been evaluated.

NOTE 1: Conscious clues of connections between the life of Kiera H. and that of Marie-Antoinette began when a psychic told to Kiera about her previous life as Marie-Antoinette when she was 26 years. This reminded Kiera H. of her childhood nightmare in which she saw a wheel on the cobblestone, some wooden steps and then she had a horrible metallic taste in the mouth. Then she woke up horrified, anxious and very scared of death. The psychic then suggested to her that the dream could be the memory of the guillotine. It took thirteen years to Kiera to collect evidence of her past life. That allowed Kiera to develop herself consciously in a new direction. Kiera participates in this project to increase understanding of the implications of the fact that she had been born with the legacy of the soul of Marie-Antoinette.

PSYCHO-PHYSICAL CORRESPONDENCES BETWEEN MARIE-ANTOINETTE AND KIERA H.

Genotype/Phenotype. A comparison of Kiera Hermine's photograph and Marie-Antoinette's portrait reveals a very strong physical similarity. Application of the biometric technique described in The Soul Genome reveals that the underlying bone structure differs by a very small percentage. This correspondence of facial geometry suggests that these two women, separated by two centuries, are more genotypically like one another than any other person in their respective lifetimes.

They appear to have the same body types, hair patterns, ear forms, and hand-finger proportions. Problems in one of Marie-Antoinette's legs are mirrored in Kiera.'s left leg. Kiera H.'s nightmares described above began about age two after a fall that left a scar on her forehead. Interestingly, it is in the same area where Marie-Antoinette bumped her head descending stairs going from the Temple prison to the Conciergerie, journey that resulted later in her execution. In many cases it has been confirmed that physical events in the present lifetime mimic scars or other marks from the alleged previous life. Biometric similarities and these unique features suggest the likelihood of a psychoplasmic carry-over (embedded in the inherited genotype) of energetic patterns from one life to another.

In addition to this genotype summary of matches between Marie-Antoinette and Kiera H. (referred to subsequently as M-I and Kiera H. respectively), confirmed matching personality factors will be added below as they become available.

Cognitive Cerebrotype. Based on historical descriptions and more recent biographical studies of M-I's personality and life and Kiera H.'s written documents and professional assessments through interviews, we can compare the cognitive or mental profiles of the two women.

Both women have a similar mode of thinking: much more Emotional than Rational. They favor an intuitive approach to looking at life and their experience. While grounded in Traditional worldviews of their respective religious cultures (Catholicism and New Age spiritualism) each possesses an Experimental nature receptive to unconventional ideas of the age. In M-I's case, she was interested in Mesmerism and research in the subtle energies. Kiera H. is interested in past-life regressions.

Both are artists - M-I loved interior design, fashion, classical music (she played both the harp and the harpsichord and supported several musicians like Saint-George and Glück), and art (she helped establish Elisabeth Vigee-LeBrun's career as a portrait painter of the court) — and Kiera H. is a contemporary artist/painter in her own right.

Regarding the Reactive/Disciplined scale, both thrive on the stimulation and reinforcement of others. Their intellectual openness makes them receptive to new ideas; they avoid the discipline necessary to create from scratch. Both focus on the Particular, especially on their own personal circumstances and the pursuit of their own agendas. Neither devotes much attention to a Global perspective in either political or social terms. Their mental life strongly tends more in the direction of Impulsive than Reflective. They are credulous, immediately responding to external stimuli (people and circumstances). They accept new ideas quickly, open to those who present different and intriguing ideas.

<u>Emotional Egotype</u>. While both can be Cool, detached, and diffident about their immediate environment, they can also become quite passionate about their interests, emotionally and seductively Warm. Each has a self-Confident streak that borders on stubbornness. They are strong-willed, determined to follow their own inclinations. Each is individualistic and non-conformist. While they can be Depressed, the prevailing mode is

towards continuous activity, almost at the level of Manic. Easily bored, they must be active, needing immediate satisfaction.

Their innate predisposition is impatience, coupled with an Anxious trepidation that leads to delay in making bold moves (as in M-I's hesitancy to escape during the French Revolution and Kiera H.'s plan to publish her reincarnation story). A stranger to others, each has difficulty defining themselves or knowing just how they fit into their environment. A Pessimist streak results in a fear of both the future and having nothing to do in the present. This is overcome by filling the present with activities of immediate interest and possible distraction. Aware of this possible legacy Kiera H. works to mitigate this immobilizing trait.

Interpersonal Personatype. In their interpersonal style, neither is very Timid. They are more Uninhibited, willing to follow their own priorities and inclinations. Energized by spontaneity, they cannot abide the imposition of routines or rituals imposed by society. Their pride will not let them easily bend to the wishes of others. They balance this pride and even disdain for others with a fresh, fragile appearing intimacy to gain their own way. Both energetically serve their own agenda, aggressive in defense of their own priorities.

Independent, they are capable of scorn or contempt for those close to them, husbands and others. Defiance of the expectations of others is almost an absolute trademark. Not easily pliable; the more they are pushed the more they resist. While some see them as Extroverted, both are basically mistresses-of-self and very private, distrusting of those outside their intimate circle. M-I is skeptical of others, very secretive. Kiera H. exhibited the same tendency early, but now tries to mitigate being too Skeptical.

NOTE2: In terms of inter-rater reliability, the scores of two independent raters varied from the same or adjacent blocks on the rating scales only twice among the 15 items rated. This suggests a high degree of reliability for the biographical material assessed.

I call Marie to tell her how happy I am to have been confirmed as the possible reincarnation of Marie-Antoinette in a more scientific way. Excited also by what happened at the gallery, I ask Marie her opinion about the mysterious man. She advises me not to worry about him and says our paths will cross again. She offers to go to the 'Egyptian Museum' of the Rosicrucians in San Jose in ten days. In the meantime, she advises me to do research on Egypt and Rosicrucianism. Reassured, I begin my research.

Sujet: RE: Marie-Antoinette / Kiera's case

Dear Paul,

The work you have produced on the comparison of the lives of Marie-Antoinette and Kiera is truly admirable!

We want to thank you from the depth of our souls, for our work, past, present and future together. You have allowed us to find confirmation of years and even centuries of research.

Just to let you know, Kiera finds herself very much involved in all of this and it provides us good clues so we may continue along the path.

The coherence of life despite its rambling appearance, and faith in a transcendental force that brings what needs to happen, allows us to accept the evolution of our souls whatever the price.

I can see how Kiera's perceptions have improved and become more balanced since her past-life, through meditation and yoga.

My best,

Marie

Sujet: RE: Marie-Antoinette / Kiera's case

Dear Marie,

It is very natural that we change and that we do not see the same patterns from one lifetime to another. There are of course people who do not really change in their life.

From my point of view, the psychoplasm recognizes and continues to evolve, but it has more time now to move in Kiera because she becomes more aware of the legacy of her soul and makes changes with meditation and yoga. What she transmitted when she died is the same spirit as that of Marie-Antoinette and Kiera's, but it will have evolved at the same time, thanks to the experience of these two lives.

Some people call it karma, but it is only the result of the actions you take to get better and reach more potential.

We should see many developments in this psychoplasm during this incarnation in Kiera's body through her practice, her choices and her gifts. That is why I am interested in working with you, as she progresses on her psychoplasm.

Sincerely,

Paul

Subject: Re: Marie-Antoinette / Kiera's case

Dear Paul,

Talking about evolution, Kiera recently discovered that Marie-Antoinette had a much closer relationship with Cagliostro, then the one we found in books written about it: Marie-Antoinette asked for his services to cure her son and certainly for his clairvoyance, also.

We did some research on him and found that he really was a healer and had received thousands of patients. He healed the most hopeless cases. He was a Rosicrucian, Freemason and Master of the Maltese cross. Antoine d'Allonville, who was the tutor of Marie-Antoinette's son, was awarded the Maltese cross, the year in which Cagliostro was in Paris. Everything leads us to believe that Marie-Antoinette had asked Cagliostro to treat her son whom traditional doctors had condemned. Kiera had an altered state of consciousness in Versailles where she clearly saw the scene. Yogananda may have been Cagliostro's reincarnation and we both feel very close to this spiritual master.

Meanwhile, Kiera found out that many of Marie-Antoinette's favorites (Vermond, De Guigne, De Besenval, among other ones) become disciples of Yogananda in their lives today. They must have been in contact with Cagliostro, in Marie-Antoinette's time.

Kiera and I have been researching Yogananda and Cagliostro to compare their lives and their portraits: the portraits of these two people correspond and that of the Cardinal de Rohan, Cagliostro's friend, with that of Rajarsi, Yogananda's best friend, too. We compared Cagliostro and Yogananda's lives, and the similarities are, there again, very striking. They both have helped many people and gave lectures in many countries.

The objective of Cagliostro was then to unite all the masonries together in two major axes: the belief in a creator and the belief in the immortality of the soul. Cagliostro failed, but it seems that he came back as Yogananda to continue on with the mission he had not completed in his past life, but in which he succeeded, in this life.

Marie-Antoinette may have organized secret parties so that she and her favorites were able to learn from Cagliostro's teachings. This had to happen at Marie-Antoinette's home around the hamlet, since that is where Marie-Antoinette received Cagliostro, and the Lake Shrine, one of Yogananda's temples, is so similar to Marie-Antoinette's hamlet. If not, how is it that Marie-Antoinette's favorites are disciples of Yogananda in this life?

We have realized, through all this research, that Cagliostro / Yogananda protects us both, and that Marie-Antoinette was really a mystic, as Kevin Ryerson told me!

What do you think of all of this?

Marie

Subject: Re: Marie-Antoinette / Kiera's case

Marie,

Your message is really interesting. You go quickly and efficiently in your way of connecting things together. My scientific side asks me more time to do things in perspective!

We have to be careful about the question of contamination. It is difficult to get away of that question.

Paul

Subject: Re: Marie-Antoinette / Kiera's case

Paul,

Is there contamination when everything is so well synchronized? I find, however, that with everything we are discovering, reincarnation should be even easier to prove. We can see that Yogananda has already done considerable work on this issue!

Marie

Sujet: Request for astrological points

Dear Marie,

Would you mind if I give Kiera's details requested by an astrologer that would be willing to compare Marie-Antoinette's and Kiera's charts?

She said that she was interested in Marie-Antoinette's story because her visit to the chateau of Versailles was her first trip outside of her own country. Over the years, as she continued to learn more about Marie-Antoinette's life, as well as Karmic astrology, she prayed, 'God, if reincarnation really does exist may I one day meet the reincarnation of Marie-Antoinette?'

Let's see what she will find. That will be very interesting.

Just to let you know, I have started to get in touch with an important laboratory for the DNA testing to start the research about reincarnation. I'll keep you posted.

Sincerely,

Paul

Subject: Re: Request for astrological points

Dear Paul,

You are welcome to do it. Thank you.

So excited to know the conclusions of the astrologer.

My best,

Marie

Subject: FW: MA/KH Past-Life Astrological Comparisons

Dear Caroline,

Thanks you for your comments. They are interesting. I will copy this to Kiera.

Best wishes in your studies and work,

Paul

Caroline wrote:

Paul,

According to Karmic Astrology there are great chances of Marie-Antoinette and Kiera Hermine being the same soul.

Kiera has the North Node in Taurus and the South Node in Scorpio, which means in her past life she was born under the sign of Scorpio.

Marie-Antoinette was born on 2 November, therefore she was a Scorpio too. Kiera has the Rising sign in Leo, which makes her 12th house be ruled by the sign of Cancer.

The 12th house corresponds to the Rising sign of the person's past life, so Kiera's Rising sign in her past life was Cancer exactly the same Rising sign of Marie-Antoinette (who was born at 7:30 PM).

Kiera has the Moon in the 12th house under the sign of Leo, which means she was probably someone with lots of power, to be more precise, a Queen.

Her Saturn is in Aries, which means she was very criticized as person, she had to fight and argue in order to protect herself from gossip and offensive words. And that's exactly what happened to Marie-Antoinette when she was being judged by the revolutionaries.

Kiera has Neptune retrograde in the 4th house (the house of family) and that means she probably saw herself being separated from her family and couldn't do anything about it, exactly what happened to Marie-Antoinette during the French Revolution. Since retrograde planets show our karma, this aspect means that

Kiera still might have trouble regarding family in this present life because of past mistakes.

According to what I saw in her chart, Kiera didn't have a life as someone else between this one she has now, and the one she was Marie-Antoinette.

By now this is all I could see, if you want any further information about her birth chart, both of you can contact me. Sorry if I wrote something wrong or if I wasn't clear enough, English is not my first language.

Thank you for trusting me. I have to tell you that Kiera is actually the only person I've seen that really is Marie-Antoinette. Many people claim they were famous people in past lives specially Napoleon, Cleopatra, among others... and I feel relieved that I've found the real Marie-Antoinette.

I really hope that Kiera has a beautiful and happy life.

Best wishes for you and her,

Caroline

Subject: Re: FW: MA/KH Past-Life Astrological Comparisons

Dear Paul,

Kiera and I are really blown away by those comparisons and the confirmation that astrology has given us. Could you thank Caroline on our behalf?

Feel free to give Caroline my information so we can exchange with her about the matter if she wants to.

Through this confirmation, that came to us without asking, I can tell that the power of Marie-Antoinette / Kiera comes from a higher source, as Cagliosto / Yogananda keeps on showing us.

Continuing my research in that direction, I just read about Cagliostro, in different books. It seems he had the secret of the 'the Royal Art' or 'Great Work', and was able to heal anybody without asking for any money. He also founded his own Egyptian lodge. Although he was respected at the court of Versailles, the Medicine Body tried to stop him, in vain. Cagliostro may have then been a victim of a manipulated cabal to destabilize the monarchy with the famous Necklace Affair.

At that time, the 'Royal Art' was in every conversation, in lodges and in salons. Everybody was a philosopher, a Freemason or a revolutionary. Regarding Free-Masonry, we found in different sources, that Marie-Antoinette said at Versailles: 'Everybody is in it.'

Knowing that Kiera is the most probable case of reincarnation of Marie-Antoinette so far and that she is currently a disciple of the spiritual master, Yogananda, who is the most probable case of reincarnation of Cagliostro, it would not be surprising to learn that Marie-Antoinette had been influenced by all those esoteric movements around her. I am wondering, why history still continues to hide how mystical Marie-Antoinette really was.

Knowing, too, that Cagliostro was a Rosicrucian and that Marie-Antoinette might have been too, Kiera and I have decided to go to the Rosicrucian Order in San Jose to see the Egyptian museum and check some data that could facilitate our research and help us on our spiritual journey. I will keep you posted.

Take care.

Marie

Chapter 6

Reunion

When we arrive at the Rosicrucian center, Marie parks the car in front of the Egyptian temple that is the most visible from the street. Even if the temple calls me very strongly, Marie offers me to visit the gardens first, so we can breathe some fresh air, after this long trip. The place is very relaxing, despite the overwhelming heat.

I cannot wait to enter the Egyptian temple. I feel that something important is about to happen in my life. Intrigued, I look around for clues in the garden. Marie feels my impatience. Finally one allows us to enter the temple.

We pass a fountain and arrive in front of large statues of Gods shaped as Rams. At their feet are small Egyptian statues. We climb the steps of the temple, Columns with lotus-shaped motifs, invite us to enter.

— It's really beautiful, Marie. Thank you for bringing me here.

— You're welcome, Kiera. You know, it's been a while since I came and I have to admit that it looks much better today. Come on, let's go to the daily-life gallery, because I feel you will never want to leave the after-life gallery, once we get there.

— Why?

— You'll see soon enough!

We go down some steps on the left. I recognize the Rosetta Stone that was discovered by a soldier in Napoleon's time in 1798. Jean-François Champollion was then able to translate it in the early 20th century, after years of research. I studied this period of Egypt as a child and it has always fascinated me.

As we move through the gallery, I feel very attracted by the jewelry of the time which was worn as magical protection to the wearer. Seeing these jewels, I cannot help but think of the diamond necklace affair at the time of Marie-Antoinette. I suspect a link between those two eras, even though I have no idea of the link that would be.

When I arrive at the section that talks about Egypt after the pharaohs, I see that Egypt fell into the hands of Alexander the Great in 332 BC. Comes back to my mind the information that I heard from some people of the Lake Shrine: Yogananda used to say that he was the reincarnation of Alexander the Great. I feel my spine beginning to vibrate intensely: I feel that links are slowly beginning to connect, even if they are at the beginning stages. I need to exit the section. I climb the stairs, followed by Marie, to return to the entrance. We descend further steps down to the famous section which Marie told me about: the after-Life gallery.

We are now surrounded by glass cases housing sarcophagi and mummies of all kinds. The mummies were then regarded as an eternal home for the spirit after death. It was therefore vital for the Egyptians to preserve their bodies as much as possible. The steles and images of the family were the gates between the worlds of the living and the dead, magical portals through which the mind could pass offerings.

The Egyptians left nothing to chance: everything from the decoration of the tomb in the mummification was done in order to ensure eternal life. At the end of that process of mummification that lasted seventy days, a celebration was given in the grave. The funeral ceremony included the Opening of the Mouth, where the body 'was brought back to life' in a magical manner: the soul was liberated in order to travel in space of life after death and be judged. 'You are still young, you will live again, you're still young and forever ...' was the mantra that was recited during the ceremony.

— You look hypnotized, Marie says softly. Come back to earth!

— Everything reminds me of the work I have done for years on reincarnation.

— And you haven't seen everything. You know that survival of the soul after death was very important at the time of the Egyptians. It looks like you're ready for the surprise!

— I forgot about it! What is it?

— Go into the tomb and you'll see, Marie says, pointing to a door of the tomb in front of me. It's quite an experience, I guarantee it. I'll wait for you outside.

— You are not coming?!

— I never particularly liked this place, ironically.

— But it is only a reproduction!

— I know, but as it is based on the actual graves, it must surely have some influence! Anyway, I feel that you have to do this experience by yourself. Take your time, says Marie as she goes away. See you later.

To the right of the tomb, are the four jars that enclosed the bodies of the deceased. I take the explanatory note of the grave, then I go in the hallway that is very dark. I arrive in the first chamber. I've barely entered, and I begin to feel bad. I take several deep breaths and focus on the place not to let myself be overwhelmed by the discomfort. I see on the walls that the sculptures are the offerings symbolically given to the dead to accompany them on their journey after death.

I read the document that I took at the entry that says 'the first chamber of the tomb is the House of Offerings, a chamber for receiving the members of the family or the priest, KA, hired by the family to make donations to the ancestors. Often the mummies were buried in a pit that was dug in the ground of this room.'

I see at the right of the entrance of the room, the 'false door', that was the door of the spirit and allowed the soul of the deceased to enter the room.

I continue to move forward and go down some stairs. I have more difficulty breathing. I stop to take deep breaths again. I feel better. I look around and see, despite the darkness of the room, brightly colored frescoes. In the midst of the room is the grave with the coffin moved from its resting place by grave robbers. Then I am more attracted to one of the walls. I read on my paper that it is the judgment wall. The heart of the deceased is placed on the balance of Ma'at, goddess of order and justice. If the heart is heavier than the feather of truth, the dead will be eaten by the vile devour that is waiting at the foot of the balance. Anubis, protector of cemeteries, holds the hands of the deceased while Thoth, the scribe of the gods, asks his questions:

'Did you steal the milk of children?'

'No', replies the deceased.

Forty-two questions will be asked and they all should receive a negative response. If the deceased passes the test and his heart is not weighed down by guilt, he will receive all the good things of the daily life that are represented on the walls of the tomb. It will then be considered 'Akh', which can be translated by 'justified mind', and remain 'young, forever young', as the ancient funeral mantra says.

With all this information, I look more specifically at the fresco. I suddenly feel that it is growing up before my eyes, whereas it has not moved. I close my eyes to adjust my vision.

When I open them again, I am dazzled by a great light. I do not see anything for a few seconds and I suddenly got a strong headache. I have to close my eyes and lean against the wall to avoid falling. My head is spinning. I try to open my eyes and I see a shadowy figure in the dazzling light. I close my eyes again, because the intensity is too high.

— How are you? someone asks me, touching my shoulder gently.

I jump with fright while having a strong sense of déjà-vu. I think back of my first meeting with Samuel, in the Luxembourg Gardens, in his words in his last letter: '... an even bigger search: the search of eternal life. No regrets for both of us ... You will meet another man soon, darling. You will recognize him because he is me, as I am him, as I am you, as you are me, because we are all one. I love you forever and ever.' I feel like crying. I miss

Samuel so much and I would love so much to have him by my side now.

— I'm sorry, the man continues. I didn't know there was someone here. I didn't see you from the corridor, otherwise I would have waited to take my photos.

Still emotional, I cannot answer him.

— Are you ok?

— Yes! I say, holding my head, overcome with grief.

I try to open my eyes and I realize that my vision is blurred and that this increases my headache. I close my eyes again and take deep breaths, then I open and close them more quickly to return my normal vision. The tears flow before I can do anything about it. I don't know if it is because of the light, the headache or Samuel.

— I have to get out of here, I say, trying to move forward somehow.

— Let me help you, the man says, taking my arm gently.

I let him guide me, because I still can't see enough to advance by myself and the man leads me to the exit. I'm surprised and relieved to feel much better once outside: my vision comes back in an instant and the headache disappears right away.

— It's ok, now, thank you, I say, letting go off his arm.

— Are you French? Wonders the man surprised.

— Oui.

— Are you on vacation? He asks with a beautiful smile.

— No, I live in Santa Monica.

— And I live in Marina Del Rey. We're neighbors then! How long have you lived there?

— Almost three years and you?

— Twenty-two years! Do you like California?

— I wouldn't live anywhere else.

— Me, too. My name is Charles, he says, holding out his hand.

— My name is Kiera.

— Delighted!

— Are you a photographer? I say, looking at the big camera around his neck.

— Yes. I volunteer for the museum.

— It must be interesting!

— Yes, I have always been attracted to Egyptology, and it allows me to link business with pleasure.

— I had forgotten how, as a child, I loved Egypt.

— Really? Charles asks. I would love to show you the Aten's gallery if you haven't seen it yet.

— I would love to.

In the Aten's gallery, a magnificent statue of Akhenaten is waiting for us, highlighted by a golden disk on the back of his head.

— I never noticed that the Egyptians were making solar disks with rays like hands. It's special!

— Only Akhenaten did it. He was the first pharaoh to adhere to a monotheistic religion, the religion of the God Aten, the Sun God.

— It's special, this statue. It's amazing how it is different from what we usually see. His elongated face is kind of weird. His large hips and his hanging belly are strange too. It's not really fancy!

— At that time, they used to make more structured bodies, that's true, but Akhenaten decided to allow artists the freedom to represent him. We see that very well with his wife, Nefertiti, also. He wanted to show the world that she was his equal.

— And why do you think he wanted to be represented like this?

— He believed in the balance of feminine and masculine. That's the message he was trying to give in the way he represented himself with more feminine forms.

— He was ahead of his time, it seems!

— He was different and he wanted to break the thought patterns of the time.

— Did he succeed?

— He succeeded during his reign. When Akhenaten passed away, his son, Tutankhamun, left the capital and the religious center his father had created and erased all traces of his father's work. He did not believe in monotheism. There are theories that say that Moses may have continued the work of Akhenaten by spreading monotheism.

— You know a lot of things!

— I am a Rosicrucian myself, actually.

— What synchronicity! I say, smiling.

— People do not realize the importance of Akhenaten's work in our present life, Charles continues with passion.

— What do you mean?

— If Akhenaten had not recognized the existence of one god at the time, religion would not be what it is today.

— True, but at the same time, religion is being challenged because people are looking for deeper answers than religion can give them.

— That is why if we find strong elements around Akhenaten and a potential relationship with Moses, it will certainly bring a spiritual revolution, at one time or another.

When I hear the word 'revolution' I stop and look at Charles, surprised. I look at him more closely, trying to access something, in vain.

— Speaking of revolution, continues Charles, without noticing my confusion, did you know that Egyptology began just after the French Revolution?

— I didn't realize that actually, I say even more troubled.

— Yes, one of Napoleon's soldiers discovered the Rosetta Stone in 1798 and it was Champollion who managed to decipher it in the early 19th century. I've always wondered if there was a link between the two.

— Between the two what? I ask, becoming more and more troubled.

— Between the French Revolution and Egyptology. The revolution was orchestrated by the Masons...

— I didn't know that, I say, shocked by all these revelations.

— The emblem of the Freemasonry is on the top of the chart of the Human Rights. At first, the French Revolution was a spiritual movement but the terrorists took advantage of it.

— The terrorists?

— The revolutionaries, in fact.

We remain silent a moment and go down the stairs to get to the gallery of the kingship and religion. At the entrance, I am particularly attracted by a statue of Ramses II.

— After Tutankhamun, Ramses II also continued to remove all traces of monotheism that Akhenaten had attempted to set up.

— Ah? I say absently.

— What about you? What do you do? Charles asks me suddenly.

— I paint. Sometimes this leads me to spontaneous past-life regressions, I say coming out of my reverie.

— I have always been fascinated by the subject! Charles says enthusiastically.

— In fact, I wrote a book about reincarnation and one of my friends is making corrections, because I feel unable to bear the consequences once it is published.

— Why?

— It's a long story!

— Can I at least know what it's about?

— You won't believe it: the French Revolution, I say with a smile.

— There are no accidents! Charles replies with the same smile.

— I believe it, I say intrigued, while looking at Charles more closely.

— You know, I've had a lot of dreams that seemed to be past lives. I don't know if it was real or if it was just my imagination, or the resurgence of things I had read in books at school.

— What time these dreams refer to? Egypt?

— Yes! Charles says, surprised. Egypt has been my passion since I was a little boy.

— When one is very interested in a period of history in particular, as you seem to be, it can be considered as a serious evidence of past life. Even if the information you found has its origin in school books, your subconscious uses this information as a starting point to access the memory of your past lives.

— You're telling me that my dreams are past lives?!

— It is possible! We should study them more carefully and do research to be sure though. But this can be a first track to pursue.

— I have to show you something, Charles says, suddenly pulling me gently by the arm.

We leave the main temple. Charles precedes me in silence. I suddenly realize that his back tells me something. I'm digging in my memory; I cannot remember where I have seen it. I am following Charles. We head to a cute little temple surrounded by columns and plants. I suddenly remember where I saw him: at the gallery in front of my painting 'Homecoming'. Trembling with emotion, I look for Marie and I see her on a bench in the shade of palm trees, meditating. This immediately calms me.

— It's the temple of Akhenaten, explains Charles. It's open and has no roof because it is dedicated to the god Aten.

— It's really lovely.

— It's my favorite place to meditate and I love coming here, says Charles, sitting cross-legged on a bench and asking me to do the same.

I sit in the posture of lotus like him. When I close my eyes I see the eyes of my canvas before me. Surprised, I open my eyes immediately. I look at Charles. He feels it, turns his head toward me and opens his eyes slowly, still lost in his meditation. I startle: Charles is the man in my painting!

Bibliography

In English

James Bonnet, *Stealing Fire From The Gods, The Complete Guide To Story Productions For Writers and Filmmakers*, Michael Wiese, 2006.

Antonia Fraser, *Marie-Antoinette, The Journey*, Anchor Books, 2001.

Munro Price, *The Road From Versailles*, St Martin's Press, 2003.

Stanley Looms, *The Fatal Friendship*, Doubleday, 1972.

Susan Nagel, *Marie Therese: The Fate of Marie-Antoinette's Daughter*, Bloomsbury, 2008.

Parahamsa Yogananda, *Autobiography of a Yogi*, Self-Realization Fellowship, 2005.

Paul Von Ward, *The Soul Genome: Science And Reincarnation*, Fenestra, 2008.

Walter Semkiw, *Return Of The Revolutionaries*, Hampton Roads, 2003.

Walter Semkiw, *Born Again*, Ritana Books, 2006.

Walter Semkiw, *Origin Of The Soul*, Ritana Books, 2008.

Kevin Ryerson and Stephanie Harolde, *Spirit Communication: The Soul'sPath*, Bantam Books, 1989.

Brian L.Weiss M.D., *Many Lives, Many Masters*, A Fireside Book, 1988.

In French

Simone Bertière, *Marie-Antoinette l'insoumise*, Le Livre de Poche, 2002.

Jean Chalon, *Chère Marie-Antoinette*, Pocket, 1987.

Philippe Delorme, *Marie-Antoinette*, Pygmalion, G. Watelet, 1999.

Gérard Messadié, *Marie-Antoinette, la rose écrasée*, l'Archipel, 2006.

Chantal Thomas, *Les adieux à la reine*, Points, 2002.

Évelyne Lever, *Marie-Antoinette, Correspondance (1770-1793)*, Tallandier, 2005.

Hortense Dufour, *Marie-Antoinette, la mal-aimée*, Flammarion, 2001.

Stéphan Zweig, *Marie-Antoinette*, Grasset, 1933.

Carolly Erickson, *Les carnets secrets de Marie-Antoinette*, City, 2006.

Xavier Salmon et Pierre Arrioli-Clementel, *Marie-Antoinette*, album de l'exposition, Broché, 2008.

Ludovic Miserole, *Rosalie Lamorlière, Dernière servante de Marie-Antoinette*, Les Éditions du Préau, 2010.

Georges Bordonove, *Louis XVII et l'énigme du temple*, Pygmalion, G. Watelet, 1995.

André Castelot, *Madame Royale*, Perrin, 2002.

Élisabeth Reynaud, *Madame Élisabeth, soeur de Louis XVI*, Broché, 2007.

Patrick Drouot, *Nous sommes tous immortels*, Poche, 1998.

Patrick Drouot, *Guérison et immortalité*, Âge du Verseau, 1994.

Patrick Drouot, *Des vies antérieures aux vies futures*, Âge du Verseau, Le Rocher, 1993.

Baird T. Spalding, *La Vie des Maîtres*, Poche, 1984.

www.ingramcontent.com/pod-product-compliance
Lightning Source LLC
Chambersburg PA
CBHW030243030726
47493CB00023B/573